BRIAN JAFFE

SQUEAKING BY

WWW.SQUEAKINGBYTHENOVEL.COM

Cover Design by Frank Dain

www.squeakingbythenovel.com

For Nuch and Cooper

With Special Thanks to Juliette

SQUEAKING BY

PART ONE

THE WIGGLE, 1957

My parents didn't notice my wiggling nose until dinner, when they could get a good long look at me.

"What are you doing, Barry?" my father asked.

"What?" I replied as if I didn't know exactly what he was talking about. I loved my father and was sorry that he noticed. He hadn't shaved that day and I could see his beard growing. It was a mixture of white hair and black hair like he had on his head. He called it salt and pepper as a joke. My father had a small dark spot on his cheek from when he was born.

"What are you doing with your nose?" he asked.

"Nothing. I'm not doing anything."

"You're wiggling it."

"Oh," I replied as if I didn't realize it until he pointed it out. "Maybe it happens when I smell the food."

"Well, you shouldn't smell your food, you should be eating it."

"Yeah," my brother said, sticking his two cents in. He always sat directly across the table from me. My sister sat to his left near my mother.

"I see you smell your food all the time!" I told him right back. "You always smell your vegetables."

"At least I know how to smell. I don't have to move my nose," he answered.

"I don't have to move my nose either."

"Eat your food. Both of you," my father added. That was his way of telling us to shut up. I flared my nostrils trying to keep my nose still while I ate.

"So how was *your* special day, Barry? What was your first day like as a brand new third-grader?" my mother asked changing the subject. I knew that I couldn't tell her how much I hated being skipped. She would start explaining over and over again how lucky I was to be skipped, even though I knew it wasn't true.

I hated my first day of school. I had started the day all alone with Mr. Casey. Mr. Casey was the principal of the school and had a very deep and very strict voice. His hair was dark black and he was as big as a giant so the top of my head only reached Mr. Casey's fly which made looking up into his eyes practically impossible. Maybe he didn't even know his own strength because his huge hand was holding onto my shoulder much too tightly as he pushed me slowly through the door and into the back of Mrs. Curtis' classroom. He was standing so close behind me I couldn't even back up. I was lonely and felt like crying as he squeezed my shoulders, now one in each hand, in front of everyone in my new classroom.

"It was good," I replied to my mother. "It was really good."

"What does good mean?" my father asked me. "You can tell us more than good. It was a whole day of school."

My parents told me that I already knew everything that was taught in the second grade so I could skip the second grade and go from the first grade directly to the third. I didn't really understand why I had to go into the third grade except that my parents wanted me to skip the second grade. I think it was because my mother grew up in Brooklyn and they let kids skip in Brooklyn a lot. I was only born in Brooklyn so my mother should have known that they had different rules on Long Island.

My older brother, David, was promoted from the fourth grade to the sixth grade but he was really, really smart and when my parents told the story about him skipping the fifth grade they always laughed at the part when David was asked to tell the teachers how he would feel about being the smallest kid in the sixth grade. My parents said he answered the question by saying,

"What's the difference? I'm the smallest kid in the fourth grade already." And then my parents would laugh and their friends would laugh too. They told this story about a million times so they must have thought it was very funny but I thought they told it too often and the thought of my own skipping a grade, frightening. I already missed my friends.

"It was good. I sit by the window," I said.

"They're not asking you where you sit, stupid," David said quickly.

"Shut up!" I told him. I couldn't hold my nose still any longer and it wiggled all over the place. I knew that David noticed it.

"Knock it off," my father said very seriously. He turned to David. "And I want you to mind your own business."

I was glad that my father told David to mind his own business but when I sneaked a look up at David I could tell that he didn't care. He was smiling because he was glad that he started in with me. He wiggled his nose at me making fun of what I was doing. I decided that I would hate him forever.

I believe that my parents made the school skip me so that now they could boast about both of their sons. If anyone had asked me I would have told them that I wanted to stay with my friends. I knew that I wasn't really smart enough to skip. It wasn't like my brother's skipping, which I think was really the school's idea. My parents made me skip.

From the little bit I overheard I knew that sometime during the summer my parents went down to the school and made them skip me. They knew everybody. They weren't even afraid of Mr. Casey and could look him right in the eyes and even smile because my parents owned a school in town themselves. They were important people and could just make me go into the third grade.

I didn't understand what funny things my parents would be able to add to their story about my skipping. There was nothing funny about it that I could think of. I would just be like an extra part of the David story; Barry, an extra son who skipped the second grade. There was nothing funny about it. That was all my parents accomplished as far as I was concerned. My parents took me away from my friends and now I was standing in the rear of Mrs. Curtis' third grade class.

"Mrs. Curtis, this is Barry Golden, the little boy I spoke with you about." He spoke with his deep, low voice and now every single kid in the class was turned around and staring at me. They weren't friendly stares. The kids in the class looked much older than me. They were probably wondering if Mr. Casey told Mrs. Curtis that I was a discipline problem.

Sometimes I did get into trouble like once for telling a dirty joke in the boys' room. The same kid who asked me to tell the joke told the teacher on me; talk about mean. I hated him too. His name was John and the reason I didn't act angry at him was because he said his father was a detective. It didn't matter anymore anyway because I was just skipped so I'd never see him or any of my friends again.

I looked around Mrs. Curtis' room but tried to pretend that I was just looking at the floor. Her class was staring at me to let me know that their class was already filled up and that I wasn't welcome. They could tell how frightened I felt. I was terrified.

All my friends were on the first floor in the second grade but I was upstairs far away from them. Right then and there, out of nowhere, my nose began to wiggle out of control. It was like I was a baby rabbit.

This one kid in the back row was really staring at me hard. He had freckles and must have just gone to the barbershop because he had a perfect flattop with the front waxed up the way I had always wanted mine to be. But his hair was blonde, mine was plain old brown and I still had to train my hair to stay in position. That was something you had a lot of time to do in the second grade. I would be the only one trying to train his hair in the third grade and that was exactly the kind of thing kids make fun of you for.

I could tell without looking that my wiggling nose wouldn't stop so I lowered my head even further hoping that no one would notice. I grabbed it to hold it still but it was like trying to hold on to a minnow. If I grabbed the head, the tail would wiggle around anyway. I squeezed it so hard that some mucus got on my hand.

"Well you come right in, Barry. As you probably already know, I am Mrs. Curtis and I will be your third grade teacher."

"Let me know if you need me," said Mr. Casey.

"I'm sure I won't," was her quick reply, but Mr. Casey was already gone. I wiped the mucus off my hand onto my pants when I thought that the class was watching Mr. Casey leave and I could get away with it. As he walked away I could hear the hard leather soles on his shoes smacking the tiles in the hallway with each step.

I was given the second seat in the row closest to the windows. I still stared at the floor as I moved to my seat feeling blind as I walked across the room. I felt nothing but stares of resentment and hostility with every step I took. I did hear some laughter that I knew must have had something to do with me. As I took my seat I was still trying to stop my nose from wiggling around but quickly discovered that this was one part of my anatomy I no longer controlled. I kept my face hidden by looking out the window with my hand rubbing my nose as if it itched.

Mrs. Curtis walked to the front of the room. "Now, let's all settle down," she said. "Thank you. This is Barry Golden. He's been promoted to the third grade and will be joining our class this year. I would like to go around the room starting with Michael and I'd like each of you to stand and introduce yourself to Barry and to the rest of the class."

What was she crazy pointing me out like that with my nose still jumping all around my face! It just made more people stare. My parents had made a big mistake but I could never tell them how I felt about it. It wouldn't do any good anyway. They would just tell me that I didn't understand, but I really did. And besides, they would never put me back with my friends.

As I sat in my new seat, I put all my concentration into getting my nose to stop wiggling. I could barely see my nose and it made me cross-eyed when I looked down. Mrs. Curtis was in the front of the classroom and the clock was on the wall right over the blackboard behind her.

Mrs. Curtis had her blonde hair all puffed up. She was wearing a sleeveless blouse and I had to look away quickly so that she wouldn't catch me staring at the gigantic vaccination scar she had on her arm. I looked down at my feet. They were too big for my age but that was no reason to skip the second grade.

Because my seat was next to the window I could always see what was going on outside. I liked that. I would be one of the first kids in the class to know when it was snowing badly enough for them to call for an early dismissal. I would always be able to look out the window and see what was going on outside. It was the first time ever that I actually wished I had a dentist's appointment and my mother would pull up to the curb in our red station wagon to pick me up early from school.

"What else did you do at school today?" my mother continued.

I felt like saying that I learned how to wiggle my nose. And I felt like saying it angry, like David would, through my teeth. "We did columns in arithmetic," I said instead.

"Stop that with your nose. What is that? Something that you just picked up?" she asked.

"It must be something that he learned in the third grade," David added unafraid of anyone.

"Well, we want you to stop it," my father said.

"I'm trying," I replied.

"Then try harder," he said. My nose was still wiggling and it seemed the more I tried to stop it the more it wiggled. Something else was controlling my nose.

I saw some of my real friends at lunchtime but the second graders had their lunch and their recess before the third graders so I only got to pass them in the hall. It looked like they were mad at me for skipping second grade, but they didn't know the whole story and I hoped I could tell some of my best friends the truth after school.

I wasn't ever as smart as my brother but I still got almost all straight A's. One big difference was that he seemed to like his schoolwork. He'd lie down on his bed almost every day and read science fiction and had to be called to dinner every night. I don't think he wanted to be with us really. He didn't even look like the rest of the family. He was great with his erector set and could hook up motors to it and make the parts move. He even bought a kit through the mail and built his own short-wave radio! I didn't know what a short-wave radio was and I couldn't ask because I didn't want to look even more stupid because everyone was making such a big deal about him building it. I peeked into his room sometimes while he was working on it and I saw that he even had to use a soldering gun to make it, which I was afraid of anyway.

I think that I purposely didn't work as hard as he did so everyone would think that that was the reason I seemed dumb about some things. I made it my work to watch television, the Late Show, the Late, Late Show, and if I could stay awake I would even watch the Late, Late, Late Show. I loved to see all the lights go out, one by one, in the make believe city on television. All except for one light and I would pretend that that one was mine.

My television was small so I would pull the little table it sat on very close to my bed. That way, no one would hear me watching and I wouldn't get into trouble for staying up so late. My favorite movie of all time was *Mighty Joe Young*. I loved the sad music in the beginning and the way Mighty Joe almost got killed saving the kids in the burning orphanage. It was hard to stay awake until the end and the music would make me fall asleep.

Later that night, before I went to bed, I was washing my hands and brushing my teeth. It was the third time I was washing because I couldn't get out the specks of ivory soap that got caught deep down underneath my fingernails. I scrubbed and scrubbed those little white dots near the bottom of my nails but it was no help at all. I never felt the soap get down in there but it always got in no matter how careful I was.

I washed my hands the way my father taught me, one hand over the other making lots of suds and counting up to fifteen. Then I rinsed my hands and dried them off with the towel that had my initials on it. I think my mother had our towels made for us so we wouldn't get confused and use each other's towel. Mine had a big "G" in the middle with a small capital "B" on each side even though there was only one in my name. My mother said that that was to make it fancy.

I climbed up on the small stool to look at myself in the mirror. I watched my nose wiggle and tried to make it stop but I still couldn't and now it had been wiggling almost all day and it was tired. I wiggled it slowly, on purpose, and watched it carefully. Not only did my nose wiggle but parts of my face had to move with it in order for the wiggling to work. My nose moved in every possible direction and during one of the wiggles my top lip had to tuck itself under my top teeth. It looked ugly. I thought that maybe I could just hold my face still so that my nose would have to stop but that didn't work either. My face was tired and it hurt all around my nose.

"Barry, it's bedtime." my mother was calling out to me from downstairs in the kitchen. Our steps to upstairs were divided into three sections. There was the first landing with the bookcase that had most of my father's books. My father said that he read them all.

There were really a lot of books and one of them was Pinocchio so he must have started reading them when he was a little boy. I planned on reading Pinocchio in a year or two. Right now it had too many pages and very few pictures. My brother could probably read it in a second if he wanted to.

My mother opened the bathroom door. "It's bedtime. I came upstairs to say goodnight."

"I'm almost done," I replied, quickly jumping down off my stool.

"What is taking you so long?"

"I don't know," I didn't want to tell her about looking at myself so carefully in the mirror.

"You're not even in your pajamas yet."

"I'm doing everything backwards tonight," I told her.

"Well do things backwards tomorrow. Did you brush your teeth yet?"

"Yup."

My mother felt my toothbrush. "Then why is it dry?"

"Is Ellen's dry? I might have used her toothbrush by mistake."

"I want you to brush your teeth. And I don't want to have to remind you every night.

"O.K.," I replied with my nose still wiggling. "Will you wait by my bed and tuck me in?"

"Of course. But hurry up because you have school again tomorrow."

"What if I get sick?" I asked.

"No one gets sick on the second day of school."

"Why not?"

"I'll wait in your room."

This was the very first night that I brushed my teeth with a wiggling nose.

My mother was holding my pajamas in her hand when I got to my room. I think she thought that that would speed me up. I was already moving pretty fast because I didn't want to get her mad.

"Do you want help?"

"No," I told her politely.

My pajamas had small green ducks all over them. Some of the ducks were cut in half on the front where I buttoned them.

Sometimes I wore my underpants underneath my pajamas and sometimes I didn't. It was up to me. They said Jockey, Jockey, Jockey across the elastic band around my waist. My mother called them briefs but my father called them shorts.

"Mom?"

"What is it?"

"Would you get me pajamas like Daddy's yellow ones?"

"Yours have ducks on them. I thought that you liked ducks," she replied.

"I do. But Daddy's bottoms have a string to tie them up and I like that more than elastic, even more than ducks."

"I don't know if they make that style for little boys."

"I'm not that little anymore. Why don't you sew them?"

"I don't really sew, Barry."

"You have a sewing machine."

"That's Grandma Rose's sewing machine. In the meantime, it's time to go to sleep, not to ask so many questions."

I knew that my mother didn't want to talk anymore. "O.K. But do you know when Grandma's coming here next?"

"Very soon. Goodnight, Barry." My mother pulled my blanket and sheet up around my neck and tucked me in tightly for the night. "Do you want your puppy?" she asked.

"Maybe I'm too old for that?" I didn't want her to think I thought I was a baby.

She turned out my light and kissed me gently on the forehead. "Goodnight sweetheart."

As soon as she left, I reached over my head and pulled my stuffed red puppy under the covers with me where no one could see it. I smelled it and hugged it tightly against my cheek. Then I kissed it goodnight, put its chewed up ear in my mouth and rolled over with it tucked in my arms to go to sleep.

THE BLINK

My next-door neighbor was named George Kierse. We used to go down to Mill Pond together to catch frogs and newts and other cool stuff. He was better at it than I was because he wasn't afraid of falling into the water. I was. And I never really knew whether or not something would bite, like snakes. It's very hard to catch a snake but George would just pounce on it. It was so amazing. They were mostly garter snakes except for the big ones. We looked up snakes in the Book of Knowledge and thought that they were called black snakes.

George was taller and stronger than I was and his hair was jet black just like his father's. He was skinny but he had a lot of muscles. Instead of freckles George had pimples on each side of his nose. My mother said they were because he was an older boy. She also told me secretly that George must have been left back before his family moved here because she figured that, at his age, he should have already been finished with one more grade in school. I liked George, especially because he was one of the few people who never asked me about my wiggling nose.

"C'mon. I found something really great," George told me one day after I got home from school.

"What is it?" I asked.

"Come with me and you'll see."

"Where are we going?"

"I found something in the woods," he answered leading the way. A block away from our houses was a corner lot that must have once been weeds. Now it was woods but I knew that it wasn't an old woods because the trees weren't that big. I could tell how old a tree was by counting how many rings it had inside. My father told me that trees get one ring a year but that sometimes my mother gets two. He liked to say that. He used to buy her jewelry as a special gift for when she lost weight. I think that she purposely gained a little weight and then lost it just so that he would buy her something.

When we got to the woods we took the path. It was just wide enough to go through it on a bicycle. I had a Schwinn. It was my brother's old three speed and I got it because he got a new one.

"So what is it?" I asked.

"Let's cut through here." George took us off the path and into the woods. "Look," he said pointing to an old mattress.

"It's just an old mattress," I told him sounding disappointed.

"I know," he replied. "But the stuffing is coming out and look what I brought." He took out some pages from the newspaper and some matches.

"If we light it on fire we could get in a lot of trouble."

"We're not going to light it on fire," he replied pulling out some of the stuffing. "I'm going to show you what people could do if they were stuck in the woods with nothing but an old mattress, some matches and some newspaper."

I watched him take some of the stuffing and roll it up in a newspaper.

"What are you doing?"

"I tried this the other day." George took out his matches, put one end of the rolled up newspaper in his mouth and lit the other end as if it was a real cigarette.

"See. You can smoke it." He took a puff and then handed me the burning newspaper. "Here."

"I'm not allowed to smoke," I told him.

"Don't be a little kid," he replied. I didn't want to be called a little kid so I took a puff on his make believe cigarette and started to choke. He laughed.

"It isn't so funny."

"Yes it is."

The newspaper began to burn much more quickly up one side than the other. "Oh, look what's happening!" I felt the heat from the flame and threw the cigarette down on the ground. It started to burn some of the dead grass but George quickly stomped it out. "We're lucky that we didn't start a fire."

"I'll make another one," he said grabbing a little more stuffing out of the mattress.

"Don't, George. If you do I'm not sharing it. I'm not smoking anymore. I'm not allowed to and I'm going to go home."

"O.K., O.K.," he said throwing the stuffing away. He plopped himself down on the old mattress as if it were his bed at home. He put his hands behind his head, squeezed his eyes shut and smiled at the sun that flashed through the trees making patterns on his face.

"Aren't you going to sit down?" he asked opening his eyes and squinting up at me.

"Not on that thing," I replied. "It's probably got bugs in it."

"There's bugs in everything in the world," he said. "Didn't you know that?"

"Of course I know that. But that doesn't mean that I have to sit on a buggy mattress. I'll sit on the ground," I replied wiggling my nose and squeezing my eyes shut just like he did. I held them shut as hard as I could until it hurt a little and then I opened them once and closed them tightly again.

"What are you doing?" he asked.

"Nothing," I lied. "I think I got something in my eyes," I continued.

"But you're scrunching up your whole face," he said.

"You would too if you had something in both of your eyes."

"You do that all the time," he added.

So much for George not mentioning my wiggling nose.

THE SQUEAK

When I first met Sharon her hair was all sweaty and stuck to her forehead. Her two-wheeler looked brand new and was made for girls because it didn't have a bar between the seat and the handlebars, which, as everyone knew, was because girls didn't have penises. It seemed to me that it should be the opposite because we could crush our balls so I didn't get it at all. I kept forgetting to ask David. He'd know for sure.

Even though I hated freckles, they looked O.K. on Sharon. I didn't think I'd have any friends this year but she became my second best friend. Not my best friend because my best friend was already Thomas who lived two doors down in the yellow house with the swings in the back yard. But Sharon and I were such good friends that everybody teased us and called Sharon my girlfriend. But Sharon didn't pay any attention to the teasing at all. The teasing bothered me but not enough to hate Sharon. Once I even kissed Sharon on the lips when everyone was saying that I was chicken to do it, so I guess I wasn't a chicken after all.

"I have cough drops," I said. "I've had them in my pocket all day. Pine Bros. Medicated Cough Drops! But they're candy flavored so that you can take them even if you don't have a cough."

"Then why do they call them cough drops? They could just call them drops. Like Dots are Dots. Or they could call them cough dots," Sharon replied.

"I know that you can eat these all the time because my

brother David had five of them yesterday and he doesn't have a cough and my mother would have told him not to if it was dangerous."

"Oh," she told me back, giving right in. I hoped that they weren't dangerous. I had stolen them from David's room in the morning before I went to school and I was planning to put them back, but now they were almost gone.

"They're really good," I said popping one into my mouth.

"I'll try one," she said as she held out her hand. I gave her the very last one.

"If we see David at my house, don't look like you ate one of his cough drops."

"I won't."

"Good." We sucked on our cough drops as we walked.

We had just finished our last day of the third grade. I had already decided to call myself a fourth grader during the summer and just let people wonder if that meant that I had finished the fourth grade and was starting the fifth grade next year or if it meant that I had just finished the third.

"You missed a crack," I told her.

"What?" Sharon asked.

"You have to step on every crack in the sidewalk," I said. "I've been doing it the whole way."

"Why?" she asked.

"That's the way I walk," I told her. "It's a game," I lied. It had started as a game about three months ago but now, whenever I thought about it, I found that I had to do it. Once in the morning I was even late for school because I thought that I missed a crack near home and I had to run all the way back just to get it.

"So I'll do it from now on when I remember to. We'll do the same thing. O.K.?"

"Sure," I replied. We leaped from crack to crack. I missed a crooked one and had to jump backwards to get it. "If you miss one you can take an extra step back as long as you get it on two," I yelled out."O.K.," she said without looking. Sharon was already three cracks ahead of me. When we got to my house, everybody was busy as usual, getting the kids from my parents' nursery school lined up for their bus rides home. My parents owned over fifteen school buses but they were green instead of yellow and they were smaller than the regular buses that we used at our school. Sharon and I were walkers but we went on school buses for field trips.

We decided to play in the attic above the garage. The attic was always dark, even on bright sunny days. The only light that came in from outside was from the air vents on the pointy side of the attic and the big square hole cut in the floor which allowed a wooden ladder to lean on it. We could climb up from the garage below. There was an old carpet on the floor, and an old open army cot, but mostly there were old paper cartons filled with letters and other stuff. Some things just couldn't be thrown out.

Sharon and I had been up here before but never as fourth graders. We sat on the cot peeking out through the air vent.

"Wouldn't it be great if we lived up here?" I asked.

"How would we eat?"

"Our parents could bring us food," I answered.

"That's true," Sharon replied. I don't think that Sharon always thought things out completely but I liked her because she was so pretty and always so clean.

"Let's lay down on the army cot and pretend that we're resting," I said knowing that we had done this before.

"O.K.," Sharon replied.

"I'll take this side," I told her pointing to my favorite side of the cot. We lay down so close that we touched from our shoulders all the way down to our knees. Sharon's hair always smelled like shampoo and this way I could smell it for a long time. "Do you want me to tickle you?" I asked her.

"I don't like to be tickled," she told me.

"I don't mean like tickled tickle?"

"Then what do you mean?" she asked.

"I could just sort of wiggle my fingers up and down on

your skin, just very lightly, and it gives you the goose bumps."

"Why are they goose bumps?"

"I don't know exactly why. But I'll show you." I said. I crouched down alongside the cot. "Pull your skirt up a little so I can see your knees?" She accidently pulled up her skirt more than I said and I could see too far but I didn't tell her.

Her panties were all white with tiny purple flowers and it look like they were soft like cotton and they had a thin strip of lace on the edge. She had tiny blonde hairs on her legs and her arms and I saw tiny little drops of sweat on her head near her hair because it was so hot in the attic.

"O.K.," I said.

"What?"

"I'm going to start tickling."

"I'm ready."

I felt like she was really my very best friend, not Tommy.

"What are you doing?" My mother was at the top of the ladder watching us! "What are you doing?!"

I tried to jump up quickly, but I wasn't up in time. My mother grabbed me and jerked me into the air. She slapped me hard on my backside.

"This is disgusting. You are eight years old! What is the matter with you? And you too, young lady! This is such a terrible thing I wouldn't even tell your mother." It wasn't Sharon's fault. I asked her to do it.

My mother wouldn't let me go. I was stuck in my mother's strong hand. "This is just disgusting, Barry. I wouldn't even tell your father about this. This will never happen again!"

"I was just giving her goose bumps, Mommy," I said.

"I'm not interested in what you were doing or anything that you have to say. There is nothing you can do to ever make this better."

I knew that my mother was right. I made a high-pitched squeaking sound, loud and hard. This was the worst thing I could do. I was with Sharon and we got caught being bad. I looked at Sharon and tried to hide the tears in my eyes knowing that I would never be able to look her in the eyes again.

"Sharon," my mother pointed her finger at my prettiest and my best friend. "You get down from this attic and go home. You two won't be playing together this summer. I closed my eyes tightly and started to cry as Sharon did as she was told and disappeared down the ladder.

Later that night, my mother came in to kiss me goodnight.

"Are you angry at me, Mom?" I asked.

"No," she replied. She looked away from me like she was lying. "I came upstairs to kiss you goodnight."

I blinked my eyes tightly, again, and again and again.

"Please try and stop that, Barry."

I didn't answer her. Instead I wiggled my nose and I squeaked and I squeaked, just like I squeaked when she spanked me in the attic. She leaned over to kiss me goodnight.

"I hope those noises aren't a new bad habit you picked up."

"They're not," I said hoping that I was telling her the truth.

"Goodnight, sweetheart," she said kissing me on the forehead. She usually kissed me on the lips and I didn't think that she meant it this time when she called me sweetheart.

"Goodnight, Mom." I pressed my pillow against my mouth so that my mother wouldn't hear me squeaking. I squeezed my eyes tightly shut once again. I wiggled my nose and squeaked and squeaked trying to get it all out of my system by morning.

THE SNIFF

"For God's sake Sam, it's his tenth birthday. You never take him out alone, just you and him, not once."

"I took him to the movies," he answered.

"Once," she replied.

I was sitting at my desk in my room and overheard them. My mother's voice was louder than my father's.

"He's your son, too," she said. I couldn't hear my father very well so I just imagined what he was saying and it wasn't very nice. "The fact is that Barry is a lot more like you than David is." I don't think that that was what my father wanted to hear. I figured he was embarrassed and angry when she said that. "I don't really care, Sam. *I* think it's a good idea."

My father had tickets to the Metropolitan Opera. They were tickets to see *Don Giovanni*. I think one of the reasons that my mother thought that my father should take me and that it was such a good idea was because she hated the opera but still felt she had to go once a month because of their season tickets.

My father had a book about all the different operas. It was like a book of short stories but they were the stories behind each of the operas. They were called synopses. My father told me that I had to read the synopsis for *Don Giovanni* or we wouldn't go.

The opera was in Italian and I wouldn't understand anything if I didn't read it before we went. It wasn't too much to read so I didn't mind. I didn't like listening to his opera records and wasn't even sure if he even did since he only listened to them the night before he'd go. He used to close his eyes, sway with the music and wave his arms around as if he were conducting. I don't think that it meant much because I also once saw him swaying to an album called "Easy Listening Favorites." But whatever his relationship was to the music, I know that my father loved *going* to the opera and I was prepared to love going there with him as well.

"What time are we leaving, Dad?" I asked him.

"That's about the fifteenth time you've asked me that over the past two days. We have dinner reservations for six o'clock. We'll leave around four-thirty. Is that good for you?" He asked.

"Of course it is," I replied. My father was being sarcastic but he thought he was being funny.

"Did you read the synopsis?" he asked.

"You told me to, didn't you?'

"I tell you to do a lot of things."

"Ask me some questions," I suggested.

"I don't have to ask you any questions," he replied. "Just be sure that you read it so that I don't have to explain the entire opera to you."

I wiggled my nose, scrunched up my face and blinked a few times. I squeaked once and then again, turning it into a scale and then into a little song as if that had been my intention all along. My father turned away.

The restaurant at the Met was special. I think that you had to be a season ticket holder to even make a reservation.

"Golden, for two," my Dad told the maître d´.

"Golden. Sam Golden." My father repeated himself like that a lot. He even practiced saying his name sometimes when he was all alone. I was spying when I saw him doing that..

I squeaked more loudly than I'd expected. My father and the maître d´ ignored me but when I turned half way around I could see that the people behind me were staring. I ignored them.

My father acknowledged a few people as we passed their

tables but I couldn't tell whether he was saying good evening to them because he knew them or because they had just caught his eye.

Our table was really sharp. The tablecloth was a fairy-tale white as was the china. The only color on it was a pale green design around the table's edge and a small green plant in the center of the table. I touched one of the leaves and stuck my thumbnail into it to see if it was alive. It was.

One of the waiters poured some water from the side of his pitcher. The ice-cubes that fell looked like they were made of the same crystal as the glass. I took a sip from the water and wondered why water never tasted this good at home.

When I opened my menu I half expected to see sandwiches named after great composers like The Puccini or The Ludwig Von Beethoven as if we were in a sophisticated version of the Carnegie Deli. My Grandmother took me there for my ninth birthday the year before. But instead I saw a list of foods I barely recognized. I pretended to be reading the menu carefully.

"Hmmm," my father said to himself.

"Hmmm," I said in repetition.

"What would you like to have?" he asked.

"Can I pick anything on the menu?" I was thinking about my nightmarish trip out West with my cousins when my Uncle suggested that I try something different besides cheeseburgers. When I then ordered the filet mignon he screamed at me in front of the whole world because I ordered filet mignon, *the most expensive thing on the menu*! What a prick.

"Of course you can. It's your birthday, Barry."

I remembered that he didn't really want to bring me. "Can I have an entrée and a main course?" I asked.

"An entrée is the main course." He smiled.

"Then why do they call it an entrée?".

"If you want, you can have an appetizer and an entrée," he replied. I stuck my nose back in the menu and squeaked quietly.

"Can I have a shrimp cocktail?"

"Of course." I had seen one on someone else's table as we

walked in. The shrimp were gigantic. When we ate shrimp cocktail at home it looked like they were baby shrimp. We had it once at school and they barely looked like shrimp at all. They looked like shrimp embryos.

"I'd like lamb chops, or something like that. But all they have is whole rack of lamb."

"That is lamb chops. And a lot of them," my father replied. He looked like he was going to laugh at me.

"Then they should just call them lamb chops."

So that was my birthday dinner, shrimp cocktail and rack of lamb. My father had a whiskey sour, a salad and a half a chicken. He even pulled the skin off it because he didn't want to eat the cholesterol. I think the skin is the best part. After dinner, we each had some key lime pie. But my father was wrong; it was not at all like lemon meringue pie, which was both of our favorite.

"And what I like about the key lime pie is it is also very low in cholesterol," he told me.

A few years ago my father had gone to the Lahey Clinic in Boston and they had told him to watch his cholesterol. Ever since then, my father had the same lunch every day, a scoop of fat free cottage cheese, one small tomato and a single stalk of celery. And every night before going to bed, he had a glass of Alba and a fresh pear. He said he needed the roughage. He took the milk and the fruit into his bedroom and watched TV. I always wondered if he came out again after he ate the fruit to brush his teeth.

"At the end of Don Giovanni, how do they make all the smoke and fire to show that he's going to hell?" I asked. I wanted to show my father that I really did read the synopsis.

"Probably with lights. They probably flash orange and red lights everywhere," he replied.

"They only have to flash them behind the doorway, right?"

"I suppose," he said.

"But what about the smoke?"

"Why not wait and be surprised?" he said. I think he didn't

know the answer and that's why he said that. I leaned down and smelled the pie. Then I sniffed three times quickly. I didn't really sniff. It was more like a *huff, huff, huff* as I tightened my stomach muscles and puffed out through my nose.

"What are you doing, now?" my father asked.

"Nothing. Not a thing," I told him quickly. He thought I was lying and I knew it for sure. I sat up straight in my chair, scrunched my nose and huffed three times again, and then three times again right after that. My father looked around at the tables near us. I guess that he was trying to see if they saw me huff. I felt miserable and knew that my father was even more embarrassed about me than usual.

"No one heard me, Dad," I said quietly, trying to reassure him.

"What are you talking about?"

"I see you looking. Nobody heard me." I huffed once quickly like I didn't want to get caught.

"Is that something new?" he asked.

"I hope not," was all that I could say back.

We finished eating in silence, me trying to stop my new bad habit and my father trying to pretend that my disgusting behavior didn't bother him.

My father's seats were not on the aisle like I had hoped but were instead smack in the middle of the row between the stiffest people I had ever seen. There were no pleasantries exchanged as we sat down and I assumed that this was because of their general displeasure at having a ten year old in their midst. Ten year olds do not belong at the opera and this was clear to me as I scanned the audience for other kids.

I loved to listen to the orchestra warming up. I liked the discordant sounds and my ability to single out each of the different instruments. I listened to the flute and then the oboe. I heard the violins and tried to distinguish them from the violas.

My favorite instrument was the trumpet, well, that isn't really true; the trumpet was *my* instrument. I played the trumpet since the fifth grade. It was my first instrument after the tonette. I had convinced my parents to buy me an expensive Bach trumpet for my last birthday so now it had better be my favorite instrument. I could never tell them that about two months after they bought it for me that I got sick of private lessons and didn't want to practice anymore. I was content knowing how to read music and being able to play the melody line of sheet music. I didn't care that the song "Fascination" wasn't written for the trumpet. I enjoyed playing it. And didn't everyone say that that was all that mattered. You had to enjoy what you were doing.

The trumpet players in the orchestra liked to play scales and I liked to listen to them play them. I just hated learning scales and playing them myself.

Most of the women at the opera were dressed as if they were going to a fancy bar mitzvah and most of the men wore tuxedoes like my Dad.

"The overture should start soon, right Dad," I asked trying to make conversation and desperately show that I belonged.

"Hmmm," was all he said. He looked at me over his left shoulder and nodded quickly before turning back to look at his Playbill and pretend that I wasn't his kid at all. My head jerked side to side, I squeaked and then huffed twice quickly. My father seemed to lean more deeply into his seat and his head leaned forward into his Playbill. The fat, sweet-smelling, ugly woman to my left peered down at me and then whispered something to her husband. I tried hard to control myself but huffed and squeaked again anyway confirming her worst suspicions. I couldn't see her but imagined that she was rolling her eyes as she turned back toward the stage. As I thought about rolling eyes I tried to roll mine up into the back of my head. It hurt.

My eyes blinked, my nose wiggled and my face grimaced as the overture to *Don Giovanni* began to play. I was surprised at how much I really loved listening to the live orchestra playing the music from my father's record.

I would hold everything back until the music got loud and then let loose with a squeak or my sniffs assuming that the people seated around me wouldn't be able hear me that way. As the curtain came up and the opera began I recognized Don Giovanni and his servant Leporello from the synopsis I had read. And there was the Commander who I knew was going to get killed. Their voices were powerful and the sound filled the theatre. I suddenly realized why we were taught that vocal chords were considered musical instruments. The costumes were the most colourful and expensive looking I had ever seen and I was amazed at the detail on the elaborate sets. I was proud that I now understood what was meant when people referred to the spectacle that was the opera.

I felt a tap on my shoulder from behind and turned to see an older man with a bald head and a long white moustache.

"Could you please stop making those noises?" he asked. "I'm trying to watch the opera." My father heard him too.

I tried to stop. I could manage to stop for a few minutes but then I'd squeak or sniff or something and I'd hear the people around me rustling their Playbills or moving around in their seats angrily. The angriest were the couple seated directly in front of me. They kept turning and staring at me, not once but almost every time I moved. It reached the point that I didn't even have to twitch or squeak or anything, they'd just turn around and glare at me whenever they felt like it.

I wished my father had told them to watch the opera themselves and to mind their own business. But he didn't. Instead, it seemed as though he were on their side, and that I was disturbing him as well. I lost all track of the opera and kept looking in the program hoping we were near intermission.

My father didn't say a word to me as the curtain came down at the conclusion of Act One. We got up along with everyone around us to go to the lobby for intermission. Now everyone could stare at me and whisper to one another without the fear of missing any of the opera. I felt surrounded by enemies as we exited our row. I heard someone behind me say, "it was him" and thought I heard someone say, "What kind of noises are those?"

Once in the huge red lobby we moved away from our unfriendly neighbors into large pockets of people who hadn't yet heard of the "Crazy Squeaker in Row F."

"Would you like a soda, Barry? Or some candy?"

"What kind of soda do they have?"

"Soda, Barry. Regular soda. It's not a fountain. They don't have lots of kinds. Just Coca-Cola and I think they may have ginger ale," my father replied. He sounded irritated and I didn't want to ask any more questions.

"Coke is fine," I said. "Can I go to the boy's room?" I asked.

"Call it the men's room, Barry."

"Sorry." I felt silly that I didn't say the men's room in the first place.

"Do you want a candy bar too?"

"Sure," I replied sniffing in and out again, this time harder and a small piece of snot blew onto my sleeve. "Oh, Jesus," I thought as my father turned and walked away. I wiped off my sleeve.

The men's room was big, one of the biggest men's rooms I had ever seen. There must have been around twenty-five or thirty urinals alone. I stood on line and waited for my turn to piss. The men in the bathroom were farting, clearing their throats and spitting into the urinals as they each took their turn, so no one cared much if I made a little squeak or a sniff or two as I waited in line. The older men seemed to stand at the urinals much longer than the younger men and they fussed a whole lot more shaking off their dicks as well.

When I finished peeing there was still a long line waiting to go. I saw a television near the ceiling that showed the curtain on the stage from inside the Met. I supposed that it was there so that you wouldn't miss a word of the opera, even if you had to use the bathroom during the performance.

When I left the bathroom I saw my father and thought he

looked a little foolish standing in the lobby in his tuxedo holding my drink and my candy bar.

"It took you long enough," he said handing me my stuff.

"There's a big line in the men's room," I told him.

"There usually is. I don't know why they don't just put in extra toilets."

"It wasn't because of the toilets," I said. "It was because they don't have enough urinals."

"Same difference," he replied. And I knew that he was right because what was stopping anyone from just peeing in one of the toilets? Absolutely nothing. Who would even know?

"The intermission will be over soon. You'll have to hurry with your soda, Barry. They don't allow food and drink in the theatre."

"I was thinking that maybe instead of rushing I could watch part of the opera from the men's room. Did you know that they have a television in there that shows the opera from inside the theatre?"

"No," he replied. "I didn't know that." I was surprised my father didn't know about the television because I always thought of him as a man who had peed in almost every bathroom.

"That way I won't have to rush with my soda. It's a pretty big drink," I said. I didn't want to tell him that I preferred to watch the opera from the bathroom television than to have to sit in the audience again and interfere with everyone else's enjoyment of *Don Giovanni*.

"And then you'll join me back in your seat?"

"I might like watching the opera in the men's room."

"Where would you sit?" he asked. It was then that I realized he liked the idea and actually preferred me not returning to the seat next to him inside the theatre.

"There's a lot of room on top of the heater and it looks pretty comfortable."

"What will we tell your mother?"

"We don't have to tell her anything, Dad. She wouldn't understand anyway about how cool it would be for a ten year old to be able to watch an opera from a television in the men's room!" I was trying to sound excited about the idea but I really only thought that it would be fun for a few minutes. The lights in the lobby were flashing and the intermission was ending.

"And if you don't like sitting in the men's room, you'll come inside?" he asked.

"Of course I will, Dad. What do you think?"

"But if you don't come back inside, I'll meet you right here, in this exact spot, immediately following the opera."

"O.K."

"Do you want some more candy or anything?" He asked me before going back to his seat.

"I'll be fine." I said, squeaking twice quickly. The lights flashed again and the bright red lobby was almost deserted. "I better hurry," I told him. "I don't want to miss anything."

"You know that you can come in to the theatre anytime if you want to, Barry."

"Of course I do. You better hurry. I'll meet you later, Dad." He hurried off into the theatre and I went into the men's room.

There were still a few people in the men's room. I could hear toilets flushing and the sound of zippers and buckles. I hopped up onto the heater that I had told my Dad about. It wasn't very comfortable after all. It was much hotter than I had expected it to be so I could only sit for a minute or two at a time and then when it got too hot I'd have to jump down and let my pants and rear end cool off before I could hop back up again. But at least I didn't bother anyone in the men's room and I watched the rest of *Don Giovanni* on TV.

When we got into the car at the Lincoln Center Parking Garage my father asked me again to promise not to mention the men's room to my mother because she wouldn't understand. I was glad to make the promise. I wouldn't have told her anyway because I knew it would just have started a big fight between them. I could tell the kids at school about it because I could

always pretend that watching the opera from the men's room
was   really   fun.

WOODSHOP

I was wandering around the kitchen foraging for sweets and listening to the loud whirring blade of the table saw in the basement. My father's woodshop was down there. He built things; large picnic tables and benches, little tables for the little classrooms for the little kids in the school. And he was proud of his work.

He wasn't a craftsman. Everything he built was rough-hewn. Even the steps to the basement remained unfinished pine and were dangerously steep.

He tried to save money everywhere, even at the expense of his work. He painted the kitchen cabinets a pale orange. He used the paint left over from one of the nursery school rooms he'd painted two years before.

My Mom complained to him many times that we only had one bathroom in our large five bedroom home so, one rainy day, my father magnanimously surprised her by adding a toilet downstairs; not a bathroom, just a toilet. A toilet installed in the pantry! It was so close to the canned goods that I had to lift my knees close to my chest in order to take a shit and still suffer the embarrassment of everyone hearing my farts and splashing through the thin door.

But, like the basement stairs, he managed to squeeze things into the space he had available. It was installed Sam Golden style. And idiot *me* was secretly proud, proud that he even knew how to do it; proud that he stuck with his projects at least until they were functional; jealous that he learned these skills from his father. Again, the work wasn't complete and always had some silliness about it but everything worked. In that sense my father could do it all.

I knew all along that my father was mimicking his own Dad, Julius Golden, who could *really* do it all. Sam was my grandfather's legacy; that and a mortgage free house on East 17th Street and King's Highway in Flatbush. That's what he left the world; my Dad, a house, and so many stories about his cheap, belittling, mean, nasty spirit. My grandfather had once existed but he never lived.

I grabbed a box of Mallomars and leaned back to keep my balance as I walked down the stairs to see what my father was building.

There he was, leaning low at the edge of the table saw like a pool shark lining up a shot. He slowly pushed a plank forward into the saw blade. As the wood hit the blade, it's whirring took on a painfully loud warning of its power to rip. I couldn't think of anything but the noise and closed my eyes in an instinctive act of protection. The screeching only lasted seconds and but sounded much longer because of its strain on my senses. The plank was cut.

"What are you doing?" I shouted to my Dad.

"I'm building something for the school."

"Mind if I watch?"

"Of course not," he replied. "But stay back from the saw because it's very dangerous."

I was almost fifteen and this might have been the thousandth time he'd warned me. I walked behind him but not too close. He shut off the table saw and reached for a two-by-four.

"What are you making?" The noise from the saw faded as I spoke.

"A new picnic table for the lunch area. We stain them every year but the legs still rot."

"They're probably fourteen years old. Anything would rot."

"We should get a few more years out of them," he replied and I realized that was why he still had shirts from his honeymoon hanging in his closet. They had to be thirty years old and he still added stains to them every year. I rolled my head, sniffed and squeaked. He looked away as if I'd suddenly disappeared. I squeezed my eyes tightly shut in an ostrich style disappearance of my own. I picked up one of the large bolts he used to hold the legs in a criss-cross to support the table.

"Please leave them on the bench."

They had been counted out and aligned parallel to one another spaced equally apart. I was disturbing the obsessiveness we shared. I put the bolt back down and he gave it a compulsive, irrelevant, fraction of an inch adjustment. I rolled my head again and twisted my wrist.

He laid the two-by-four on its side, picked up a pencil and readied his straight edge to mark the miter line.

"Want some help with that?" I asked.

"No. Not right now. This part is a one man job." There never was a two man job in his workshop, just warnings about the dangers of inanimate tools. I'd heard so many "be carefuls" that one would assume a hammer could suddenly leap into the air and knock a nail through my head. There would never be the fun of woodworking with my Dad that I so secretly wanted.

My grandfather was a prick but at least he'd toss my Dad a screwdriver and expect him to know what to do with it. He worked beside his father in angry silence. I stood beside my Dad, did nothing and strained to make small talk. Both situations sucked but I'd have chosen his over mine. Mine sucked worse.

"How much more do you have to do until it's finished?"

"This is the final cut. Then, of course, I have to knock it together."

"That's a two man job."

"I usually do it during the day. I use saw horses to hold the wood up. It's the way I'm used to doing it."

"Why don't you let me stain it?"

"That would be fine." He looked at me. "Except for the fact that I need it done this year." He smiled at what to me was a sarcastic and dismissive remark. "You always seem busy with your friends when I'm doing that work. And, besides that, it needs to be done carefully, not fast and just slopped on."

"How do you know I'd slop it on? You never let me do it." My face scrunched up and its features jumped about.

"Well, we'll see. If you're around when I do it, we'll see."

That meant no. He'd wait until I was doing something, something away from the house and I'd come home to the stained tables.

"Did you finish all your school work for today?"

"Sure," I replied thinking about Earth Science. I had a chapter to read but had a friend in my class who was a compulsive and meticulous outliner. I copied his notes instead of doing my own reading. I imagined that he'd get a job with Cliff Notes when he finished school. Everyone seemed obsessed or compulsive to me, just some in more constructive ways.

My biggest obsession was about getting laid.

ESCAPE FROM VIRGINITY

"Bullshit," I told her leaning over the back of my desk. "You never got laid. You never fucked anyone."

"Oh, yes I did," Christine Ashton answered me sharply. She sat at the desk directly behind me and was clearly annoyed by my accusation. She was the only girl in the tenth grade who wanted to make it clear that she wasn't a virgin.

"Then who did you fuck?" I pushed on.

"Why should I tell you?"

"That answer alone proves you're full of shit. Otherwise, what would you care about saying who he is? He's not your boyfriend because you don't have a boyfriend. Not that that's a big deal, I mean, I don't have a girlfriend and I don't care. I don't even want a girlfriend." I was tap dancing around, being careful not to insult her.

Christine lived down the block from me and, frankly, I already believed that she wasn't a virgin based on previous conversations. But I was waggling to lose my own virginity now and a part of me was just showing off in front of Eric Westphall who was one of the most popular kids in the tenth grade.

Although a sophomore like the rest of us, Eric was already a star on our high school wrestling team; a team that was headed to the State Championships.

I was secretly humiliated by my constant urge to please Eric. I always wanted to be one of Eric's friends, one of his best friends, and was willing to swallow my pride to win his praise. At present, however, the time we spent together consisted primarily of crinking in the woods next to the parkway, and that seemed to be only when I was buying. I hated this willingness I had to subordinate myself in an effort to try to make friends.

Sometimes my cheeks would cramp from the stiff pathetic grin I wore when in his presence. He would ask me to run errands and do favors for him and I found it impossible to deny him. The worst favor of all was stealing a copy of our third quarter biology exam from Mr. Porter's closet. But it didn't matter to me. It was the price I had to pay for him to pretend he was my friend.

Eric was seated in the row next to us. He would have to move back to his own desk when the rest of the class returned from lunch. We were five minutes early and the first three there.

Christine Ashton was built in squares and overweight. First her head was square with hair cut like a helmet for emphasis. Her eyes were perpendicular to the sides of her head and her nose had no other purpose than to direct you to her lips which were small, thin, straight and, a perfectly parallel to her eyes. Her sharp angular jaw fed into her perfectly square neck which then fed into her squat upper torso with its huge tits. Her torso seemed to plunge deeply into her square hips. Her wide rectangular thighs and calves supported her, balanced on her tiny, almost dainty ankles and feet. She was not good-looking and was most certainly not a virgin.

Eric and I, on the other hand, were virgins.

All my thoughts about losing my virginity were desperate. I was in a race against time convinced that I was late; a latecomer to the world of sexual intercourse. Love and romance never crossed my mind. I remembered overhearing Dick Grochowski talking to another one of the guys on the football team in the locker room.

"Man, oh, man. I don't know how the fuck I'm going to get through practice today. I got laid last night," he continued. "I can barely walk, my legs are so weak." Apparently that's one of the things that happened to him after getting laid. For him, it seems, his legs might be weak for a couple of days after.

"You don't have to tell me," replied his buddy, Kenny Imhoff. "You saw how much slower I ran my wind sprints last week? Same thing."

"I thought it was 'cause you're so fucking fat," Grochowski answered.

"Fuck you, Grouch. Help me with my pads."

I considered most of these tales I heard idiotic. I assumed that getting laid, as mysterious as it remained to me, had to be like jerking off and I could jerk off sometimes as many as three or four times in a row and it didn't make me weak. It just made me feel good.

I must have practiced putting on a Trojan two hundred times. I even jerked off in one a few times, but I much preferred jerking off without a Trojan. However, like everyone else, I always carried a trusty Trojan in the far outside pocket of my wallet which I then tucked away in the back pocket of my pants. It caused a permanent circular imprint on the wallet's inexpensive leather.

"So who did you fuck?" I repeated my question to Christine.

"Just one person so far. But I'm going to fuck his younger brother Michael sometime next week."

"Who has a brother named Michael?" Eric asked. I squeaked and shook my head side to side.

"Come on, Christine. Who was it? You've practically told us already. Not that I necessarily believe you ever got laid, anyhow."

"All right. It was Ray Higgins. Are you happy now?" she asked me.

"Get lost," I told her. "What bullshit, Christine. He's not even in school anymore. He graduated two years ago. He was almost in my brother's class. You would pick someone who graduated, so there's no way for us to check."

"So, don't believe it."

"It could be true," Eric chimed in. Christine rolled her eyes when he spoke and even if she was homely I knew that she liked me more than Eric.

"You could prove it if you wanted to. There's a way that you could make us believe it," I continued. "I'm no virgin," I lied to both of them. "And, I've gotten it more than just a few times." Eric was watching me carefully. I realized that he couldn't tell where I was going with this. "If we had sex, Christine, between you and me, I could really tell whether or not you're a virgin. I could tell in a second and then it wouldn't matter who you said you laid. I'd know for sure."

Eric finally understood.

"How would you know?" she asked.

"Because I could tell if you still had your cherry. You know what I'm talking about, your hymen."

"Ray got that a long time ago."

"Maybe he did, maybe he didn't," I replied wiggling my nose and tapping my dick. "That's the point of what I'm saying, Christine. You could prove it once and for all," I told her.

Christine thought for a moment. "I'd do that," she said. "I'm willing to do that. I can prove it. When?" she asked.

"Why wait. How about today after school?"

"Where?" Christine was proud and seemed pleased with the challenge. She was fully prepared to prove it because she knew she wasn't a virgin and I think that she might have even wanted to have sex with me. One thing for sure, there was no way that I was going to squander this unbelievable opportunity. I quickly turned to Eric who was mesmerized by the conversation.

"Are your parents going to be home today after school," he didn't react. "Eric, I'm talking to you. Are your parents going to be home after school or will they still be at work? Snap out of it. Will your parents be home after school today?" I couldn't believe how many times I had to ask him the same question.

"Uh, no, no," he finally answered.

"No, what?" I asked.

"They both work until five-thirty," Eric replied. He seemed to suddenly realize that he was committing his house for me to fuck Christine. "Will it make a mess?" he asked. He was starting to sound stupid. I turned back to Christine.

"But you have to fuck both of us. One at a time, of course," Eric's mouth fell open. He no longer cared about his parent's possible reaction if the house was a mess when they got home. He couldn't believe that I was letting him in on this great opportunity. He was suddenly in tune with everything that was going on and, for the moment, my new best friend.

I think I had convinced both of them that I wasn't a virgin and hoped I could bluff my way through this whole thing. I looked at Eric and could see how excited he was with this prospect of losing his virginity. We wouldn't just be drinking in the woods this afternoon.

"Do you have some kind of protection?" Christine asked.

Finally, after two and a half long years, I had an opportunity to whip out my wallet with purpose and show someone the ring in the leather that evolved over time. "I always have it with me. Just in case. What about you, Eric? You have a Trojan?"

"No," he replied half-embarrassed. "But my father uses Ramses and I know where he keeps them in his bedroom. I could use one of his."

"So, we'll go to Eric's house after school and we'll see whether or not you're telling the truth," I was trying to sum up the conversation quickly as many of the other students from the class began returning from lunch. I put my wallet back in the rear pocket of my corduroys. I liked having the ring in the leather but would be embarrassed if some of the nice girls in the class saw it. It was more of a guy thing.

"Where do you want to meet?" asked Christine.

"Do you have anything after school?"

"No," Christine replied.

"Good," I said happily. "Then look for us across the street as you come out of the school. Use the front door of the building and we'll be on the right side across the street near the Bide-a-Wee Home. Then follow us and we'll meet you at the light at the top of the hill. Eric only lives about five blocks from there."

"It's eight blocks," said Eric.

"Wouldn't it be easier if you both just met me in front of the school?" asked Christine. My dick tapping was getting a little out of hand. I blinked tightly and sniffed in and out.

Christine wasn't stupid. She knew that she was neither pretty nor popular at school. I think that she was secretly hoping that her willingness to go all the way would help her along, at the least she'd get to hang out with a couple of guys.

"You'll see us across the street. I may want to grab a cigarette." I couldn't tell her that I would feel sadly embarrassed to meet her so publicly. I wiggled my nose, scrunched up my face and squeaked quietly. I felt mean that Christine was willing to fuck me but that I didn't want people to think that Christine and I were together. I didn't want people to link us, even as friends. It wasn't nice and I knew it. It was mean. I squeaked again.

"Hey, we better sit down. Mrs. Rios just walked in."

Eric went back to his own seat and I turned around in mine to face forward. I was a little concerned with my boasting about not being a virgin. I wasn't so much worried about Eric because Eric was really a virgin but Christine was not and the last thing I wanted was to give myself away and look like a jerk. After all, I had presented myself as an expert on the subject of virginity. I tensed my shoulders one at a time, tapped my dick three times and pretended to be fixing its position in my pants. I emitted a loud, shrill shriek followed by two short little blasts, jerked my head back as far as I could and then quickly snapped it down chin extended into my chest. I felt a sharp pain in the muscles behind my neck as if someone was trying to yank off my head and I could feel the looks at me from around the room.

I ignored them and instead thought about how I would handle things at Eric's if he looked to me for expertise. I knew that I would just play it by ear. I had certainly done that before.

My first clear memory of my being manipulative was in the fourth grade. The victim was Anthony Lomangino, the only Italian kid in the class. He was an only child and the tallest kid in the class, always at the rear of line when the class lined up by height, which was practically all the time. Anthony always wore dungarees to school and was the first kid I ever knew who was allowed to drink beer by his parents.

Anthony brought an injured pigeon in a shoebox for *Show and Tell*. I loved *Show and Tell*. You could show something unique to everyone and tell them about it, or, you could tell a good story about something interesting that happened during the week. If I had nothing to show I would just make up a story, often bizarre but always entertaining for the class and disturbing to my teacher, Mrs. Brautigan. I used to always see my father making up stories to the little kids at the nursery school and telling big lies to grownups.

So, Anthony had a pigeon that was hurt and couldn't fly in a shoebox. I figured that the pigeon probably had a broken wing. Why else couldn't a bird fly? I looked into the shoebox. The pigeon's feathers looked soft and I wanted the pigeon. I watched *Show and Tell* impatiently and caught up with Anthony quickly after school.

"Hey, let me see the pigeon again," I asked.

"I have to get home."

"I just want to look at it again for a second."

"O.K."

I looked into the box, reached in and touched the pigeon. It's claws scratched on the brown cardboard bottom of the empty shoebox as it tried to get away.

"What are you going to do to make the pigeon get better?" I asked.

"What do you mean?" asked Anthony in reply.

"Well, first of all, you can't keep the pigeon in a plain old shoebox like that."

"What should I keep it in?"

He was hooked, but not knowing any more about pigeons than Anthony, I had to make things up. "Straw," I told him confidently. "They live on straw and a special kind of grass that my father has. And is this pigeon a city pigeon or a Long Island pigeon?"

"How could you tell?" asked Anthony eager for the information.

"Let me look at it again," I said. I looked at the pigeon closely. "It's a Long Island pigeon."

"How do you know that?"

"I just do. My father used to have pigeons. And he had parakeets, millions of them. We're sort of a bird family."

"Oh."

"You know what I could do?" I asked.

"What?"

"You don't know how to make the pigeon better, right? But I could make it get better at my house."

"How?" asked Anthony innocently.

"My father has all the stuff and knows exactly what to do. I'll take it home and just keep it until its better. It's your pigeon, Anthony. As soon as it's better, I'll bring it back to school. It will die if I don't help it. You didn't even know what kind of pigeon it was." I looked Anthony in the eyes. "How will you feel if it dies?" I asked.

When I brought the pigeon home that day my parents really didn't like it and made me keep it on our screened in porch. But they were nice about it and my father gave me a huge carton to keep it in. That way it would have plenty of room. The carton was so deep that I could barely reach the bottom and that was with my arm all the way over the edge, jammed into my armpit. I gave the pigeon some old birdseed that I found in the basement, some stale bread, and a little dish with some water.

For over a week I watched the pigeon scratch around in his box and then one morning the pigeon was gone.

"It probably flew away," my mother told me. "Did you check that the screen door was latched?"

Well, I hadn't. And my older brother, who was in the sixth grade, told me that he thought that the wild black cat that lived around in our neighborhood ate the pigeon. He reminded me that cats love to eat birds, referring to Sylvester and Tweety as a good example. Either way, I no longer had the pigeon.

In the meantime, Anthony Lomangino wanted his pigeon back. He began to ask me about it and I continued to tell him that all was well and that he would have his pigeon back very soon. I didn't know what he was going to do. I was so nervous. I had no idea what Anthony would do when he found out that I had lost his pigeon.

"It's been a very long time, Barry. How long will it be until I get my pigeon back?" Anthony asked. "How long?" he asked. He asked me every single day.

Finally I blurted out, "I let it go," shocking both Anthony and myself simultaneously.

"What do you mean?" asked Anthony clearly upset and annoyed.

This is where I really had to wing it. "They're not supposed to be pets. My father made me let it fly away. I told you that he knew all about pigeons. Well, he wouldn't let me bring it back to school. He said they're supposed to be free."

Even Anthony couldn't argue against nature and it seemed like I was quickly off the hook. But I figured that my brother, Danny, was right and the pigeon was probably dead.

After school we joined Christine at the traffic light about three blocks away from school on the way to Eric's. The school buses already left so we weren't worried about being seen. We walked together the rest of the way but in silence.

"You want to check to see if your parents are home before we go in?" I asked Eric standing outside his front door.

"If either of them were home, there'd be a car in the driveway," he replied.

"What if their car broke down?"

"I'll go inside first," he said putting his key in the front door. Eric's house wasn't near as big as mine. It was in a development called Forest Park. He was lucky because the houses were so close to one another that all the kids in Forest Park could play in their yards right out in front of their homes. They could even play in the streets and the cars had to watch out for them. I lived on a big fenced in block. Sure we had playgrounds and basketball and a big swimming pool but it was on a busy avenue with no other kids around and my brother, my sister and I stayed away from the street.

All the homes in Forest Park were ranch houses unlike the split-level homes in "Little Israel." I was Jewish but most of my friends were Irish, German and Italian. My parents made me have a Bar Mitzvah but I thought of that as just a big party for their friends.

I think we thought that other Jews were watching so we had to do some Jewish things like go to Temple on Yom Kippur. We also lit candles and gave out gifts on Hanukah. But they were always the crappy gifts. They reminded me of the kind of shit I used to steal from Woolworth's so that I would always have surprise presents for my little sister, Ellen. The good gifts were always withheld and given out on Christmas. We couldn't get a tree to put the gifts under because that would have been way too Christian, so they just sat in a pile waiting for my cousins to arrive on Christmas Day. One big Jewish thing we did was eating gefilte fish and horseradish even if it wasn't a Jewish holiday. My father was a huge fan of gefilte fish partly because gefilte fish was also a low cholesterol food.

Eric opened the door and looked inside. "No one is home."

"You can tell that easily?" I asked.

"Come on in," he said almost in a whisper.

"Why are you whispering if no one is home?" I asked. Eric ignored my question and we walked inside. We were standing in the small foyer of his parents' living room. From where I stood, given the layout of Eric's house, I could see almost everywhere. I was in the living room, just outside the dining room and I could see into his kitchen through a pass through. There was a door to my left that seemed to lead to an office or a guest room. The house had several identical flat hollow wooden doors leading into each of the rooms.

With the exception of those wooden doors everything in the house was green, gray, or red; a decorator's work. I could never have imagined so many different shades of the same color. I saw a gray Formica kitchen with gray Formica cabinets, mottled gray counter tops, and linoleum floor tiles so gray that they were really black. The curtains in the family room were gray as well and hanging in the center of the wall, a print of huge green tropical leaves on a light gray background. In this tropical paradise they had splashes of red everywhere. A red-antiqued frame wrapped around a mirror over the fireplace and bright red oriental figurines stood stiffly on the mantle and on every table. It looked like Christmas decorations.

"How are we going to do this?" Eric asked.

"I'll go first and give you directions and a map when I'm finished," I answered trying to maintain an air of confidence, in this case, at Eric's expense. There was also no way I was going to take sloppy seconds. "Where can we go?" I asked wondering what Christine was thinking.

"How about the guest room?" Eric suggested. "It's right here."

"Let's take a look," I said to Christine. She was the first one to look in. I peered in over her broad shoulders. The room had a couch tucked underneath a built-in bookcase with large floral patterned cushions stacked against the wall to make it seem like a couch. "We can pull that couch out, right?" I asked.

"Yeah," Eric replied. "But don't take off any slip-covers. My Mom would have a conniption."

"But we have to pull it out from the wall. There's no room on it for two people."

"Well, that'll be all right."

"Is that OK for you?" I asked Christine.

"Sure," she replied walking into the room and rolling the bed out from against the wall without hesitation. She was ready to go.

I looked at Eric. "You get ready out here and I'll come and get you when I'm done."

"What do you mean?" he asked.

Christine was inside the guest room.

"I mean take off your fucking clothes and I'll be right out."

"Just sit out here naked?" he asked, a smile crossing his lips. I smiled back wide-eyed.

"What are you going to do? Just pull your dick out of your pants when it's your turn?"

"I don't know," he said laughing now. "I didn't really think about it."

"And don't forget a bag," I reminded him. We were both laughing now and I wished I could have had that moment forever frozen in time. We were buddies at last, best friends, if only for a few seconds. "I'm going inside," I said, laughing quietly. "I'm really going inside; deep inside if you know what I mean?" I joined Christine in the guest room closing the door behind me.

Christine was sitting on the edge of the couch, feet on the floor. She had tossed all the cushions on the floor except for the one she had set at the head of the bed as a pillow. She began unbuttoning her white oxford blouse and I pulled off my tight purple muscle shirt. It's not that I had big muscles or anything it was just a very popular shirt. A bunch of us wore them and said we had formed a fraternity. I felt silly in it.

"You know, Barry. I don't really believe that this is a test for you to see whether or not I'm a virgin. I don't even believe that you could tell one way or the other. I came here 'cause I like you. I'm willing to have sex with Eric too. I don't believe sex is that big of a deal anyway, but I came here because I like you." I felt flattered and embarrassed and I didn't know what to say in response. So I just silently looked from her bra to her knee length black pleated skirt. I tried to imagine her naked but never considered helping her undress.

When I saw her large white bra I realized just how big her

tits were going to be. There was a lot of elastic holding that brassiere in place. "Who do you have for Math this year?" I finally said feeling stupid, helpless and intimidated. I was embarrassed by my loud squeal. My nose wiggled wildly and I snapped my head down, chin to chest.

"What?" she asked incredulously at my question. I felt that I had to continue this conversation. For a moment I thought she was asking me about my tics.

"For math? Who do you have this year?" I asked again.

"Mr. Townsend," she replied. "What difference?"

"I was just curious."

"Oh," she replied finally unhooking her bra.

I reached out, touched her breast and then cupped it in my hand. It was soft. I stroked and squeezed it gently. I liked the way it felt and immediately got hard.

Last year, in the ninth grade, my English class went to the city to see the movie *Becket*. Kenny Levitt and I snuck into an adult book store while everyone was waiting outside the theatre for it to open. We were really nervous because we figured that you had to be at least twenty-one to be in the store and we were only fourteen. Anyway, we must have passed for twenty-one because the owner let us by two books. They were titled *Puta* and *Cum on Me*. *Puta* was far and away my favorite. I remembered what it said on the book cover. It said, "Rosa was very, very good, but when she was bad she was better!"

I loved this book. I remembered from the book that Rosa, needing money desperately, naturally had to turn to a life of strip tease and prostitution. But it didn't take her long to use her newfound talents to get even with everyone who had ever done her wrong. I think the book should be considered a classic. There was no question that I enjoyed it more than *Becket*.

So there is this fantastic scene in the book, the first time Rosa is made to disrobe and wouldn't you know that making this demand is this fat cigar smoking grease ball who owns the first strip joint she has to work in. It's the first scene where Rosa is forced to expose her delicate "love triangle."

Christine's "love triangle" was not so delicate. Instead of a soft mossy "V" I saw a chubby mound covered with hairs spaced equally like holes on a pegboard. There was nothing wrong with it, but there was nothing particularly right with it either.

I thought of fat Ramon chomping his cigar and watching Rosa with his hungry eyes before he tweaked Rosa's nipple causing her a sharp pain. I secretly quoted Ramon when I told Christine "leave your stockings on." She was kind enough to oblige me removing only her garter belt. I tweaked Christine's nipple.

"Oww," she said. "What are you doing?"

"Nothing," I replied, hoping she had never read *Puta* and wouldn't recognize the source of my performance. We were both naked now in Eric's guest room. Christine was certainly not Rosa.

She was lying on the bed, up on her elbows, big soft tits, round rippling belly, heavy thighs and calves made smooth by her stockings. I was standing next to the bed with an erection and my wrapped Trojan in hand. I had a sudden a rush of anxiety and worried that I would somehow screw up and seem amateurish putting on my Trojan so I tossed it on the bed next to Christine.

"I want you to put this on me," I said with mock confidence.

"OK," she replied as nonchalantly as I had been bold. She unrolled the lubricated bag sliding it onto my penis and now, fearful that I would miss the hole that was her vagina and look like a complete fool, I told her to put me inside her as if it was part of my test of her virginity. She mechanically obliged.

As my dick slid inside her effortlessly I felt it pulse and I wanted to ejaculate. I grit my teeth and thought of Willy Mays sliding into second like it said in the book that I read about how to prevent premature ejaculation. I didn't know anyone who used the word ejaculation and wondered what Willy Mays thought about as he was sliding into second; probably not premature ejaculation. I arched my back and pumped my hips maybe three of four times. I came almost immediately. Christine didn't really seem to care and I figured, now that I fucked her I could hopefully fuck her once in a while just for practice if she was available. I guess I was expecting more noise from her, you know, words and sounds like Rosa would say, "Oh my God, yes, oh, yes. Fuck me, fuck me Ramon, fuck me." I suppose that Christine just liked to keep her joy all to herself.

"Well, I guess you were right," I said, sliding myself out and throwing out my Trojan. "You weren't a virgin." Christine seemed to smirk a little but remained silent, not angry at all, maybe even bored.

"I'll get Eric," I told her. She lay back on the bed sliding her legs together and crossing them at the ankle. I opened the guest room door and walked out naked to get Eric.

"Did you fuck her?" he asked with keen interest.

"No," I replied. "We decided to play *Chutes and Ladders* instead. Of course I fucked her."

"And?"

"And what?"

"And you know what," Eric said.

"She was telling the truth. I could have driven a truck inside her."

"Get out!" he said laughing.

"It's your turn."

Eric already had an erection and he quickly tore the foil wrapper open on his father's Ramses and unrolled it around his dick. As he did,

"Oh, shit," he said.

"What?" I asked.

"I just came," he replied. It was over for Eric just like that.

We all got dressed, said good-bye and ushered Christine out quickly, no kisses or fond farewells at the door. The room smelled of her inexpensive perfume. We hoped that no one saw her leaving Eric's house and stayed inside for over an hour before venturing out ourselves. The good news was that at least I had escaped my virginity.

THE BIRDS AND THE BEES

I lay on my bed mindlessly opening and closing my eyes trying to relax and not tic. I stared at the television. I'd imagine gentle hands, girls' hands, slowly gliding down my head trying to calm a restless popping face. So it was my hair first, then my scalp, my forehead, eyebrows, eyes... my eyes. I always struck out at the eyes.

My eyes would revolt, jamming tightly shut, erasing the gentle hands. The force of my eyelids, like clamping jaws, tightened all the muscles in my head from my neck below back up into my hair. The disappointment was excruciating. After too long I could crack my eyelids open getting some momentary relief and start with my hair once again. I glanced back to the television to see what I had missed. Not that much, I guessed.

My father didn't knock. He just walked into my room even though I didn't want to be disturbed. But fuck me, really! Over the years, since the opera debacle, it had become more and more difficult between us. We barely spoke in public, not that we were so close before that. The situation between us was most disconcerting for my mother and that made me sad. This wasn't the family relationship she had planned on. I could only imagine his reactions when she tried to push him.

"I ran into Mr. Ashton."

I ignored him hoping he'd get uncomfortable and leave.

" Barry…"

I still didn't acknowledge him. He didn't belong in my room and knew I heard him. Finally I said, "What?"

"I saw Mr. Ashton at the pharmacy," he repeated.

"The big, fat guy?" I replied. I knew where this conversation was headed. "Is he as dumb as his daughter?" I was sorry I insulted her. After all, she'd been nice enough to fuck me. I thought about Eric, his scumbag and his wasted ejaculation.

"Do you know his daughter well?"

I wished he'd just get to the point. I turned around to face my father squarely. "His daughter's Christine. She's in my class. What does he do, Mr. Ashton? I always wondered. He's a plumber or something, right?" I asked as if I cared. I just wanted to make it difficult for my Dad.

"He does some plumbing but I didn't come in to talk about him."

"You also didn't knock."

"The door was open."

"Was the welcome mat outside?" I squeaked, sniffed and snapped my head down chin to chest. I knew I embarrassed him.

"Is this yours?" He was holding a wrapped Trojan.

"I can't see what you're holding. Hold it up."

He held it up between his fingers so I could see it clearly.

"Where did you find that?" I asked him.

"Never mind where it was."

I sniffed in and out several times like an angry bull but without a bull's probable self-control.

"It was in my drawer, Daddy! Who gave you permission to go into my drawers? Oh wait…that's right. Let me guess. It was like my door, slightly open. Like an invitation. You take my money too? I know you take the change off the top of my desk."

"If you leave it out…"

"It's my desk! It's in my room!"

"If you leave it out…"

"Oh, God… This is a joke," I squeaked and blinked and shook my head but didn't really care. He was being such a jerk. "And that," I pointed to the Trojan, "was really in my drawer!"

"None of that matters," he was raising his voice. "After my conversation with Mr. Ashton I think I had the right."

"Really?" I pulled out my wallet with its outstanding condom ring in the leather and showed it to him. "Is this the Birds and the Bees? I'm sixteen, not six. What do you want from me?" He was struggling now. He seemed almost dizzy. "Could I finish watching my show?"

"Well, did you, I mean…you know what I mean. Did you *see* his daughter?"

"I see her every day."

"You know exactly what I'm asking you."

"Does it really matter, Dad?"

"I don't like people making innuendos to me in the pharmacy."

"Ahhhh, so that's the problem."

"And imagine if you got that girl into trouble. Could you imagine? Is that the kind of family you want to be involved with? You want us to have problems with them?"

I no longer knew what to say. I made some noise that sounded like a bark. I could only look at him. I knew I'd never get to know him. "Please don't take the change off my desk. It's not yours."

"You just better be careful that's all I can say."

"Can I go back to the TV now?"

He hesitated and seemed to realize that we weren't, even at this moment, speaking to each other. "I don't want problems," he added and after another awkward moment he left my room. I went back to my show, "Have Gun, Will Travel."

GUIDANCE

"You have to think about applying to a safe school."

"You don't think any of my choices are safe?" I asked.

"I'm speaking about a school where you can feel absolutely sure that you'll be accepted."

Mr. Bradford was my high school guidance counselor. His reddish brown hair was short and curly and its texture matched his tweed jacket with the elbow patches. It was a bit professorial for a guidance counselor. His hair was so dense and his hairline so clearly defined that it looked like he wore a toupee. His head was large and round and his skin so busy with dark red freckles; spoiled spots on an old pumpkin.

I originally thought I was lucky having been assigned to Mr. Bradford. I didn't get along very well with my first guidance counselor, Mrs. Beuhl, and requested to be reassigned to Mr. Bradford. My parents loved Mr. Bradford and felt he had been instrumental in guiding David to an early admission acceptance at Yale University. My family and Mr. Bradford had become pleasantly acquainted during the process. They were all so very proud of David.

Guidance counselors weren't teachers. Their job seemed fairly simple, to help you decide on a college. But I found George Bradford obstinate and felt that he was working against me from the start. Like Mrs. Beuhl, he seemed to enjoy reporting negative things about me to my parents more than he should have and at least as much as he enjoyed reporting positive things about my brother. I quickly lost any interest in what he had to say.

"My brother was third in his class, right?" I was reminding him. "I'm tenth with almost one-hundred more students in my class than his," I paused to squeak twice quickly, sniff loudly in and out three times in succession and snap my head from side to side. "My brother's verbal SAT score was six fifty and mine was six twenty. Both our math SAT's were over seven hundred. I was a foreign exchange student and can speak Spanish. My Spanish achievement test score was over seven-fifty."

"Your brother was a merit finalist and excelled in all his achievements. I think you know exactly what I'm talking about, Barry," Bradford chimed in.

A short 'hoop' sound burst out of me sounding like a cross between a loud hiccup and a monkey's shriek. Mr. Bradford ignored it but it made him fidget in his seat. I wondered how much my tics effected this conversation.

" Barry...It's my job to be straightforward. That's how I help guide students to schools that are right for them and I believe they'll get the most out of. Your brother was more of a real student than you are. He clearly wanted to learn. You're probably as smart as he is, but you don't apply yourself the way he did. Whether or not you'd be accepted, I don't feel that it's the school for you."

His words seemed rehearsed, not at all spontaneous. I looked out the window. It was a beautiful autumn day. The leaves were starting to turn. His eyes closed for a moment and I noticed that he even had those pumpkin colored spots under his eyes. I was disgusted.

"What you mean is that David never got into trouble. He was never sent to the office. Maybe that meant he was less well rounded," I said trying to mask my sadness and humiliation at Bradford's words. "You don't think I can get good letters of recommendation, do you?" Even I didn't think I could get recommended as highly as David had been.

"You'll get letters of recommendation."

"You don't think Haverford is a safe school for me? Or Cornell?" I said still hopeful.

"It's not a simple question of where will you surely be accepted. That's not the only criteria we want to look at here. I think you can find a wonderful school, a great school, if you will, that would be both great and an enjoyable school for you to attend," he replied, but all I wanted was Yale. My brother got into Yale and I wanted to go there too. I didn't want to be the second best to David, or third or worse maybe fourth or fifth (if I included my cousins). No matter how well I did I was running in mud to keep up.

I lowered my head toward my lap, pushing it down hard from my neck. I scrunched my face and held it tightly as I squeaked a short tune, three notes up and two down. When I lifted my head Bradford was looking away as if waiting for me to finish.

"What do you think of Hamilton or Tulane University in New Orleans?" he continued. "They're both great schools." Neither one appealed to me.

"Not very much," I replied trying to seem knowledgeable. But I didn't know anything about Hamilton and all that I knew about Tulane was that my Uncle Norman went there for both his undergraduate and medical school studies and I didn't like my uncle. That was why I hated Tulane, because Uncle Norman had gone there and, of course, the humiliation of going anywhere aside from Yale. One of the few things that my father and I ever agreed upon was how much we both disliked my Uncle Norman.

Uncle Norman was married to my Aunt Helen, my mother's only sister and her best friend; a very special enviable pair.

Throughout our lives my father and I shared at least one habit, interrupting people. We were impatient to speak, or perhaps more accurately, too impatient to be silent. While on a cruise in the Caribbean a few years ago, my uncle had the balls to ask my father, however *politely* he imagined it, to *shut up!* It took my mother almost two years to get my father to speak with him again. Uncle Norman had even attacked *me* for calling him at 8:45pm one mid-week evening to ask him a *medical question!*

This motherfucker! Evidently I was supposed to realize that he was on call; a tired, weary, dedicated prick? He was the only fucking doctor I knew! And the question related to my school work! It wasn't even a personal question!

There was little satisfaction being told by my mother that Aunt Helen chastised him for the incident. Worse still, Uncle Norman made it a point to apologize to me the following day. He made me cry the night of that phone call. I was fifteen years old and in tears. I had no strength of character. While he apologized I felt so terribly weak and sad with a lump in my throat so great that it blocked any sound from me. I would never forgive him. Instead I chose my vendetta and waited my whole life to show my fearless anger. For then and forever I wanted him to misstep and allow me to slap his anger back in his face. I *would* do that; for me *and* my father. I could show I loved my Dad that way.

But my prayers were never answered. He never gave me the opportunity to retaliate. He walked on eggshells around me forever after as if he felt me waiting to pounce. I never got to satisfy my urge for revenge, to scratch that itch. And I gradually saw him as he was; a sad, follow the leader man wearing blinders and being swindled constantly by his friends and partners. You learn a lot about people after they die. I missed him as an outlet for my trumped up strength. His death left me with an emptiness that caught me by surprise.

With regard to selecting a college there'd be no substantive discussions or guidance from my family. Or, if there was, I have blocked it from memory. The result was that I disregarded most of what Bradford said and applied to Yale, Williams, Cornell, Haverford, and secretly to Tulane, because Mr. Bradford had, in fact, scared the shit out of me.

COLLEGE INTERVIEWS

When David applied to college Dad proudly drove him to each of his interviews at Harvard, Yale, and Williams. David seemed to actually be embarrassed of *him* (there's a switch) but there was no stopping my father's triumphant march from school to school. David seemed to be accepted so quickly into Yale that he actually wrote letters to the other schools politely withdrawing his applications.

My case was different, my father explained.

"David didn't have a driver's license and neither did any of his friends. You have your Junior License, which makes me very proud, and I know you'd rather go with your friends than an old fart like me."

"I understand," I replied and gathered some buddies for the trip. I went with two friends, John Baker and Frankie LaRussa. Neither of them was even applying to college and they relished the fun we could have. Their futures were already set. One was going to work with his Dad and join the plumbers' union and the other was headed to Vietnam to die killing the "gooks." What they both lacked in class they more than made up for by not giving me a hard time about my tics. We were all outsiders in one way or another. One of them was tough, one crazy, and neither very wise. We were all lazy and liked to drink.

My trip lacked the glory of David's. Before we set out for my college interviews we picked up a couple of cases of Pabst Blue Ribbon (PBR), a quart of gin, and then hit the road. Neither of them brought a change of clothes. I had to. I knew I'd need a jacket and tie for my interviews.

I felt safe with them. John was a tough guy. As a freshman playing football at our high school, he was a tall skinny kid mercilessly bullied by the upperclassman on and off the field. But unlike me, his gritty personality let him stay the course regardless of whom or how many people picked on him.

He continued with his sports, lifted weights and studied martial arts, silently vowing revenge on the meanest of his enemies. He turned eighteen as a junior having been left back in the fifth grade. Now, a senior, he had grown to six-foot four and weighed nearly two hundred and twenty pounds. Aside from his sheer massive presence, his notoriety came from spending several weekends driving his custom '57 Chevy and hunting down the same upperclassman who had bullied him most. All he wanted to do was to beat the piss out of them. And he did.

LaRussa, on the other hand, was a funny guy who knew the rules of the road (drunk or sober) and had those set plans; life in the plumbers' union with his Dad. He dreamed about enforcing union rules, about chopping up garden hoses at non-union jobs.

So…there we were, the three of us, late one night heading to Haverford College in Philadelphia. We were on the New Jersey Turnpike. I was light-headed from the beer and was driving.

"This is how it works," LaRussa told me from the back seat. "The truckers have a system for passing safely."

"Yeah," Big John said. "They're bigger than everyone else and they'll squash your fuckin' car if you get in their way."

LaRussa ignored him and continued. "Watch and do what I say."

"I'm not sure about this," I replied.

"Listen to me. Do what I say and you'll see I'm right. See, all the trucks are in the right lane. Naturally, you pass on the left. Watch," he said. "Go a little faster."

"I'm going seventy-five."

"I want you to see how it works. There's no cops around.

C'mon, Golden, I'm tryin' to teach you something about the rules of the road."

"Better listen to him," John chimed in. "He's drunker than we are."

"If you shut the fuck up, Baker, you'll learn something too." Frank turned his attention back on me. "Now, do what I say. Pull up near this guy in the left lane and flash your brights."

I followed LaRussa's directions and thought it great fun to see the trucks' rear lights flash me back.

"See," LaRussa went on excitedly. "That means he saw your signal and knows you're gonna' pass him. He's tellin' you it's O.K.; no problems up ahead and he sees you. Now when you pass him and it's safe to pull back into the right lane in front of him he will flash his brights. That's to let you know you're at a safe distance to pull back in front of him. This is how you communicate on the road."

I sped up and passed the truck. I was about fifty feet ahead of him on his left before he flashed his brights exactly as Frankie had said.

"See. What did I tell you? Now you can pull back into his lane, 'cause remember, by law you are always supposed to drive in the right lane unless you're passing."

"I'm doing almost ninety fucking miles an hour," I said both hands frozen on the steering wheel leaning in toward the window trying to see clearly through my dirty windshield.

"You're doing fine. Just keep going straight. Then when you are safely back in lane in front of him you tap your brakes as a thank you and he flashes his lights to say you're welcome."

"I would just fly by him. Who gives two shits about all this," said John finishing his beer, crushing the can and throwing it on the floor in front of him. "When we stop for gas we should throw out all the empty cans in case we get stopped," he added. Big John was the kind of guy who would help a friend with shit like that.

"You're supposed to pull in front of him now," continued LaRussa.

"O.K., O.K.," I replied. Putting his theory to the test, I quickly pulled in front of the truck and tapped my brakes a few times. At least I thought I was tapping my brakes. Apparently at ninety miles an hour what I was doing was more like slamming on my brakes with this huge truck close behind me.

"No!" LaRussa started screaming from the back seat. "Tap them! You're hitting them too hard!"

"Oh, shit," I said terrified watching the truck rushing toward us in my rear view mirror.

His airbrakes shrieked and I could hear the truck vibrate in an effort to avoid a collision. Big John laughed.

"I think you're gonna' have to practice this a few more times."

The truck's bright lights switched on and stayed on half blinding me.

"He is pissed," LaRussa said.

"I would be too," laughed John. "I'd fuckin' kill you."

"Shut up," I said. The truck was closing in behind me. "Goddamn it!"

"Maybe you can take Driver's Ed. over again in college."

"Will you shut the fuck up?" I yelled at John, my car shaking more than I thought possible. My eyes were teary and I couldn't see.

"Go, go," said LaRussa. "He's trying to ram us." I floored the gas pedal and my '53 Plymouth struggled over a hundred. The car was begging me to slow down. The truck seemed to easily pick up speed and close in again.

"Hey, LaRussa. How do you say 'oops, sorry we fucked up in truck talk?" Big John asked.

"There's a rest stop up ahead," LaRussa told me. "Look! Right there!"

"Goddamn! Get off my ass," I said into my side view mirror. I pushed the Plymouth over a hundred again. "I never drove this fast!" The lines on the road looked like dots.

"Don't slow down. Keep up your speed and then quick, pull in fast to the rest stop up ahead!"

"I can't! I'm going too fast!" I replied.

"Yes you can, goddamn it. He'll fly right by," LaRussa added.

"Either of you guys want another beer?" John asked.

"Asshole." LaRussa shot back. John just laughed again.

"Get ready. It's coming up fast."

"I'm not ready!" I said.

"Go faster," LaRussa shouted. I could hardly hear anything over the wind as it blew in my window and shook the car.

"I can't go any faster!"

"Turn! Now, Golden! Turn the fucking wheel!"

I turned to the right trying to steer my car and watch the truck behind me simultaneously. The trucker seemed to speed up wanting to clip me as I turned but he missed and I saw him zoom by us on the Turnpike. We fishtailed left and I overcompensated causing us to quickly fishtail right into a spin.

"Ooh. Och," was all I could say trying to regain control of the car. We spun one hundred and eighty degrees sliding off the exit ramp rear end first and into a small ditch. We thud to a halt. My heart beat hard and I worked to catch my breath.

"All right!" said John unfazed by our death defying experience. "Way to go Golden. I think we finally found your sport, demolition derby."

My mouth was dry and I couldn't speak.

"Holy shit," said LaRussa. "Why'd you hit your brakes so hard? I said to tap them. You hit them too hard."

"I don't want any more lessons, Frankie," I managed to squeeze out.

"Well, that *is* the way truckers pass each other," he answered back defensively. My heart finally slowed a little and I drove my car out of the ditch. The exhaust system must have been damaged when I hit the ditch because the Plymouth sounded like a race car.

"Listen to that shit," I said driving around the long dark exit ramp to a parking space at the end of the lot far away from any other cars at the rest stop. "The car sounds really fucked up."

I looked over at John and he shrugged. We stared at each other for a minute as LaRussa continued defending his driving instructions. As John offered me a beer he had this big stupid shit-eating grin on his face and we both burst out laughing.

"What is so fuckin' funny?" LaRussa asked angrily.

"Nothing," I answered and then John and I started laughing again. John secretly offered me a beer again waving it back and forth out of Frankie's sight and we cracked up again, this time even harder. It had nothing to do with Frankie. We were on a jag and couldn't stop.

"Fuck both you guys," LaRussa said angrily. "It wasn't *my* fault."

"Have a beer," John said offering a warm one to Frankie. We laughed again harder still. My stomach muscles were starting to cramp.

"I have to take a leak," I said.

"It was your fault, Golden," Frankie snapped at me.

"It was not," John told him right back.

"Bullshit. You were probably twitching your leg and jerking it around. I've seen you do that, Golden. You were probably twitching. You know, like this," Frankie started to mimic my facial tics and then he let out a good long squeak and a few sniffs for good measure.

"Maybe," I answered back sharply as I opened the driver's door to let myself out. I wanted out quickly.

"What the fuck is wrong with you, LaRussa?" I heard Big John say as I got out of the car. The windows were open and I could hear them speaking.

"Fuck him," LaRussa replied. "That *is* what truckers do. I can't help it if he fucked it up. I didn't do anything wrong."

"We were just laughing. We weren't laughing at you."

"It was his fault," LaRussa repeated.

"Fuck you," John added just to get in the last word as he got out of the car to join me.

I was in front of my car and had already started to pee. Big

John stood alongside me, took out his namesake Big Dick which I pretended not to look at, and began to pee as well.

"I'll bet I can piss farther than you," he said.

"I'm sure you can," I replied in a monotone.

"He's an asshole, Barry. He didn't mean it."

"Right," I replied. We stood for a moment in silence. All I could hear were the cars and trucks traveling fast on the Turnpike and the sound of our urinating on the grass. We seemed to both be aiming at the same small maple sapling.

"Ahhh," Big John moaned. "Look," he said seeing our streams crisscross. "Dueling piss. C'mon, Golden. Let's duel."

"You're pissing right near my foot!"

"No I'm not."

"I can see it splashing!"

"Are those the shoes you're wearing to your interviews?" John asked as he turned toward me a little more and gave a grand smile as only Big John could.

"No they're not," I said stepping back to avoid John's spray and pushing my dick back inside my pants. "You're nuts"

"Yes, I am," he replied joyfully. I looked back at LaRussa sitting alone in the car. "He didn't mean it," John said.

"Yes, he did," I replied. "What a prick."

"Why do you have those twitches?"

I turned slightly away as he asked his question to wiggle my nose and blink my eyes tightly shut. "Don't know, John. But I've had them pretty much as long as I can remember. Maybe I am crazy. What can I say?"

"But good crazy. I'm crazy."

"I know."

"Want me to drive?" John asked in friendly tones.

"I can still drive. If you and LaRussa can trust me behind the wheel, I mean, with my tics and everything."

"I didn't say anything, Barry. Don't get on me."

Thinking about it, I couldn't help but squeak loudly, something I couldn't hide. John was kind enough to ignore it.

"You know what I'll do. I'll ask LaRussa if it'll bother

him," I said walking back to the car. I opened my door but before I could speak LaRussa said "Hey..."

"What?" I asked quickly before Frankie had time to say anything else. I heard John getting into the car. "I'm driving," I said.

"Hey, that's fine with me," Frank replied. I hoped that was his apology. I got in the car, started it up and, engine roaring, drove out of the rest stop getting back on the Turnpike South. The muffler damage didn't sound as bad once we were speeding along.

Big John glanced back and forth between the two of us. "Anybody want a beer?" He winked at me when I looked back at him. John wasn't school smart but would have been a great big brother.

"You are such a jerk," I reminded him laughing again. I heard him pop the top off a can and take a swig.

"What the fuck. Gimme one too," added LaRussa. We all finally relaxed and were seriously underway. We didn't need any gas and I didn't plan to stop again until we reached Haverford.

My interview wasn't until eleven-thirty so we decided to drive to the campus and walk around a little bit before my interview. I felt very out of place at Haverford as I did at most every other school I'd visited before. I was experienced now. I'd gone to my Yale interview first.

My interview at Yale was a particular nightmare and an experience I would never get out of my head. I had been the best swimmer on my high school team. But regardless of my status on the team, we still sucked and didn't win a single swim meet. My personal best finish was a second place in the fifty-yard freestyle against an all-black swim team from Queens. I think first place went to a guy swimming the dog paddle.

Nonetheless, before my interview at Yale University, I insisted they show me the pool and any other of the swim teams' facilities.

The great Yale Swim Team boasted no less than the world-record holder in all the shorter distance freestyle sprint categories, Donald Schollander. He was only a junior that year and would be swimming for Yale the following year as well, my freshman year.

Showing me around was an obvious inconvenience to Todd Weill, the swimmer who took me for a tour of Yale's swimming facilities. As we toured I squeaked, ticced and lied about my swim times in a desperate attempt to make Todd want me on his team. I couldn't resist the notion that a favorable response from anyone associated with the university, in even the most remote way, would help my admission chances. It was a childish, pathetic effort and I couldn't stop myself in spite of my transparency.

"What do you swim?" I asked. Todd was a tall, blonde with blue eyes. He wore a Yale Swim Team T-shirt and his pecks stretched the shirt in a way that made me feel even smaller and weaker than I actually was in comparison.

"Breaststroke," he replied.

"How's your time?" I asked trying to act his equal, already a member of the team. He seemed to shake his head as he unlatched an old, thick, dark, solid wood door. He pulled it open. It reminded me of the doors leading to the art room in the basement of my elementary school; the "good old days."

At least once a week while waiting for Mrs. Freeman to unlock the door to the art room we killed time ripping gray and white hunks of insulation from the exposed pipes as ammunition for our asbestos fights.

"This is the pool," he said pointing out the obvious.

It was an old pool but beautiful. It was the exact right pool to be in this stately, venerable institution. A swimmer was approaching the side of the pool swimming graceful laps. I *really* didn't belong here.

"Indoors," I said for absolutely no reason whatsoever. He

laughed quietly.

"You guys use an outdoor pool for the winter season?" he asked sarcastically.

"No, of course not. We don't even have our own pool. We have a deal with a private pool. It closes to the public when we practice."

"That must be a pain in the ass."

"Not when you really love a sport," I said trying to reclaim some dignity.

"I meant for them," he added.

"I'm the fastest on our team. Twenty-two six in the fifty free," I lied about my time adding a little less than a second onto Schollander's world record. "I've been a lifeguard at Jones Beach for the last three summers," I continued lying. "Best job in Nassau County."

I never even had the balls to go to the lifeguard tryouts. I was a strong enough swimmer. But I had always felt terrified that I'd be ridiculed if I'd tried out, tapping and grabbing my dick in those small tight black bathing suits that were an important part of their uniform.

"So. Is that it for us?" he asked me wanting to end the tour. "Is there something else you want to see? Because I have a class in about ten minutes and I don't want to be late."

"Oh. What kind of class?" I asked.

"Is there something else I can show you?" He asked again keeping us on track.

"Uh, the locker room. I'd like to see the lockers and, uh, do you have a weight room?"

He believed that I had used lockers before but not that I had ever lifted weights.

"Follow me," he replied looking at his watch. We walked alongside the pool, the room smelling of chlorine. Midway down the side of the pool we turned to our right and passed through a smooth tan brick entranceway and into the men's locker room. There was really very little extraordinary to see in there. I feigned great interest in the condition of the room even looking into the showers and at a couple of toilets. I noticed the door with a stencilled sign on a small translucent window pane which read training room. I let myself in unaware that a few guys would be working out.

"Hey, Todd," they said greeting my escort. One of them was tall like Todd but less muscular. He wore a loose, torn, foul looking Yale T-shirt and shorts imprinted with a Yale University Physical Education logo. The other guy was short, strong and needed a shave. They were men and I was a boy. "Thought you were working out with us?"

"Five minutes," he replied.

He had been lying about having to be in class in ten minutes and it added to my feeling estranged, self-conscious and unimportant.

The training room had free weights, a universal, and lots of mats for floor exercises and stretching.

"You're a swimmer?" the shorter one asked me pleasantly.

"From the sound of it, he'll be beating up on Schollander next year," Todd answered clearly letting his teammates know that he thought I was full of shit.

"My brother goes to Yale," I said trying to regain a connection.

"What's his name?"

"David. David Golden. He's in Calhoun College."

"Don't know him. But there are lots of guys I don't know. All that really means is that he's not on the swim team. I wouldn't know if he's in any of my classes 'cause I avoid them." He and his friends laughed. Their laughter wasn't meant to be cruel but it naturally excluded me.

"This is the weight room for the swim team?" I asked.

"And anyone else who wants to use it," the hairy one answered me.

"Listen, Barry," Todd interjected. "I don't mean to cut this tour short, but do you think that you can find your own way back to your interview so I could stay here and work out? It would be convenient for me if you could. I'm willing to walk you back if you think you won't be able to find the way."

"Oh, no problem," I said. "I've been on campus many times before visiting my brother. I know where I'm going."

"Great," Todd said extending his hand.

"Good luck with your application," said his friends already back on the weights. I turned and left, listening to my shoes on the tiles, hollow lonely sounds as I walked back alongside the pool watching the graceful swimmer who I knew I'd never see again.

Why did I come to Yale for my first interview? Why not start my interviews at a safe school where I could try and get a grip on my uncontrollable bullshit? The kind of bullshit that may have worked or seemed to work wonders on the dumb cops chasing us around the "Sweet Shop" back home.

I knew why. Yale University was my obvious first choice and I wanted to end this miserable process of applying to college and waiting to hear of my acceptance or rejection. I was hoping for a quick acceptance, a wink from my interviewer letting me know (unofficially, of course) that my admission was a lock, one which he would follow up for me personally, smoothing out any bumps or potholes he might encounter along the way. He would look out for me as if he were my mother because I was one guy he didn't want to see Yale lose.

The interviewer wasn't so young, late thirties I'd guess. Tweedy jacket I'd seen so many times before. They all must shop at the same place or from the same catalogue. Their clothing only added to the clubby atmosphere at the school. My brother used to refer to the people in New Haven not related to Yale University as "townies." I suddenly realized that I was also a "towny."

"I'm Jack Whittle," he said looking through a file which I assumed was mine.

"I'm Barry Golden. My brother is David Golden. He's a junior in Calhoun College." I felt like I was starting this interview with a voice begging for acceptance. No response from him so I continued. "I'm sure you realize that Yale is definitely my first choice."

He chuckled at this. "Yale is many people's first choice."

"I realize that. Hey, thanks for getting me that tour of the swimming facilities," I said trying to remind him of that little extra phony reason why he should want me.

"It was no problem. We do that sort of thing all the time but it's usually coordinated directly through the swim coach and not through our office."

"I kind of thought about it last minute," I replied, knowing full well that coaches knew who was who in high school swimming and sought after those athletes they wanted. "Our high school team was only just started and I was the fastest. No one would have heard of our team yet," I continued with my gibberish.

He looked up just as I was snapping my head back and scrunching up my features. He seemed startled. I squeaked in response and jerked my head from side to side. He watched my contortions but didn't say a word. I turned an open mouthed squeal into a peculiar guttural sound; a newborn sound apparently held in reserve for this interview. I sniffed in and out quickly and wondered what Jack Whittle was thinking. How much would he want me here at Yale?

The suit I'd changed into at Haverford, the one that my mother suggested, felt ridiculous and my head throbbed with anxiety. I knew that my father would have felt equally out of place on this campus but I still wished that he were with me now instead of LaRussa and Baker. I couldn't seem to remember why I had even applied to Haverford except perhaps that I was told not to. It felt anti-Semitic or rather no one seemed Jewish even though I'd heard there were plenty of Jews matriculated here. It was especially disconcerting because my father blamed almost everything on anti-Semitism. He even felt we had been secretly attacked by anti-Semites because of my dog Ditto.

Ditto had been adopted from the Bide-a-Wee Home across

from the high school when I was around twelve. Every dog there was a "shepherd mix" but this one only grew to thirty pounds, had floppy ears and a big curled bushy tail; quite an interesting German Shepherd. We used to keep Ditto tied to a chain next to our house. It was thick enough to hold a gorilla and didn't belong on Ditto. Sometimes the links on the chain would get twisted or he'd twist himself up around his gigantic doghouse reducing his movement to a small semicircle. He'd remain that way all day. No one seemed to untangle him except for me when I got home at the end of the day. We only seemed to love him at night when we brought him inside and, for the most part, kept him tied up on a long lead to the basement doorknob in the kitchen.

Ditto barked all day long while outdoors, probably begging to be untangled, but was silent once inside our house. He was certainly no watchdog, just an outside yapper. I'll never forget when one of our anonymous neighbors sent us a clipped out copy of a newspaper ad my parents put in the local paper. The ad listed all the reasons people should send their kids to our nursery school. The perpetrator wrote over the ad in big black Magic Marker "you forgot to tell them about your goddamn barking dog." I was very young and listened carefully to my father when he told David and my mother that the only reason they sent us that note was because we were Jews; those anti-Semites seemed to be *everywhere* we went.

As uncomfortable as I felt at Haverford, Big John and Frankie felt quite natural and relaxed as they made fun of our surroundings. We were quite a trio wandering around that day.

So far, as I said, my interviews were not going well and I felt under the pressure that had been laid on me like a curse by Mr. Bradford and the inaction and lack of guidance by my parents. I felt as if I was forcing these schools to interview me, like I was sitting at a table with people who didn't want me there. There was none of the welcome I remembered my brother describing as he bounced from school-to-school, interview-to-interview. And in spite of my companions I felt completely alone.

I hoped that I would do better at my interview here at Haverford, even though the buildings looked just as old and intimidated me as all the others had. But I was experienced now and knew more about the "tricks" to handle the pressure.

"You guys wait down here. OK?"

"We can go up with you," Big John suggested. "I'm sure a rich school like this has a waiting room, right? What're you embarrassed to have us up there with you?"

"Of course not," I said uncomfortably.

"You're so full of shit, Golden. I'd be embarrassed to have you guys come up and wait for me somewhere," John laughed. "Well, on second thought, I wouldn't be embarrassed with you being there, Golden. But I'd be embarrassed about little Frankie here."

"Oh, shut the fuck up. I would never wait for you anyway."

"I gotta' go," I said. "I'm already late. I'll be down as soon as I'm done."

I entered through two more grand doors and began to run up the stairs taking them two at a time. I was already on the second floor by the time I heard the heavy doors close behind me.

My interview was on the fourth floor but I stopped on the third landing to catch my breath. As I looked back down the stairs for a moment an impulse overcame me and I hurried back down to the landing between the second and third floors. I ran that flight one more time, this time touching each of the slats holding up the thick mahogany banister. Reaching the third floor I was trapped again convinced that I had missed one of the slats. I ran back down and did the flight one more time more slowly and consciertiously as I began to sweat. I finally made it past the third floor landing and was running up the two flights to the fourth floor slat-tapping the banister once again now adding a rhythmic squeak as I tapped each third slat.

I was exhausted by the time I reached four. My big feet had kicked my inside ankle bones so many times as I ran up the stairs I knew from experience that they were scraped and bloody underneath my socks. A salty droplet dripped into my right eye and I took out my handkerchief to wipe my face. My shirt was sticking to my back as I looked for Room 449. Once outside the room I paused to shake off my tics. I yelped and stretched my arms tight and straight at my sides. My wrists snapped up and back until they hurt. One by one I snapped and tightened the muscles in my upper arms against my torso then flexed each thigh and banged my knees together twice at first then another two times because the first two didn't satisfy my urge. My face scrunched and I sniffed out and in several times in succession. And, for my big finale, I squeaked in a loud high pitch and burst once again into my own strange song.

Two boys, Haverford students, suddenly approached in the corridor. I didn't know how they got there without me seeing or hearing them first. I was usually so attuned to that sort of thing.

I felt their eyes as they neared and glanced toward them hoping not to see their faces. I saw only shapes, not features. I couldn't see. I didn't know what to do with my embarrassment but instinctively grabbed the doorknob in front of me to escape. As I forced myself inside I heard them speaking.

"What the fuck was that?" A common question.

"I don't know, man." A common reply. And then they laughed a good laugh between friends.

"Can I help you?" asked Mr. McClinton's secretary. I was working hard, momentarily staving off my tics. I passed a small internal squeak, blinked my eyes and wiggled my nose. "Are you here for an interview?" she asked pleasantly.

I couldn't answer. Too much time was passing. It wasn't normal.

"Are you here to see Mr. McClinton?" she asked starting to look a bit concerned.

"No," I blurted out as if it were just another noise. Not another word would come out of me. I turned and left her and her questions behind me. My Haverford interview was over.

I sat alone on my bed at home, baby tears streaming, humiliated and ashamed. What would happen to me? What would I say when everyone talked about the colleges they were going to attend in the fall? I sat there feeling more rejected than I ever could remember, the letters of rejection in a pile on my hands; Yale, Princeton, Williams, Haverford, no, no, no, it was waiting list......at fucking Haverford, a school I didn't even want to attend, didn't even know why I applied to.

My only acceptance came from Tulane University, my bastard Uncle's alma mater, the "Harvard of the South", and my "safe" school at that. People down South must be awfully stupid. I only applied there because I was finally cajoled into it by Mr. Bradford and my parents. I cried, swallowing my squeaks and tensing my neck muscles. I tapped my dick. I could sense my father at my door but he just looked at me mostly hidden from view. I couldn't turn around. He was as ashamed of me as I was.

He disappeared as my mother came into my room. She sat alongside me on the bed. Affection was something rare in my house and I welcomed the gentleness of my mother's hand as she took mine.

My mother looked at me sympathetically. She was dressed in a rose sweater and a dark rose skirt. She was soft, overweight. She was round, soft and gentle.

"I feel so stupid crying," I told her between sobs. I peeked at the duck I made in woodshop in the ninth grade. It was stained light brown with a dark wing and it flew on the light peach wall above the ancient framed map which I never even looked at closely.

"Don't be silly. Even grownups cry," she tried to reassure me and I could remember her crying to my grandmother while tucking me in as a very little boy. My brother and I were still sharing a room at that time. I couldn't have been older than three or four and my mother cried as she spoke to my grandmother. I didn't know what she was crying about but I watched her feeling sad and I felt frightened, and helpless.

"What am I going to do?" I asked my mother. "Every

school rejected me. Nobody wants me," I said.

"Now you're being ridiculous, Barry. Tulane is a fine school. You know your Uncle Norman went there and then he went to their medical school."

"How can you think that's going to make me feel better? I hate him as much as Daddy does."

"Daddy hates everybody," she said smiling.

"He does," I answered. "So do I."

"You're just like him," she said.

I looked up into her eyes and started to laugh in spite of myself.

"You're just like him, as a matter of fact," she said wanting me to keep laughing.

"Oh, shut up," I told her gently. Was it really true? Were we really alike? But I knew the answer. I had disgusting tics and couldn't get into college. I think my mother meant that we were alike because he wasn't so normal either.

She reached out and wiped a tear from my cheek. I moved my head away and finished wiping my face by myself.

"What am I going to say to people? I'm ashamed, Mom."

"You don't have to tell anyone anything. You don't owe anyone an explanation. Don't tell them that you weren't accepted to the other schools."

"Oh, great. I'll tell them I got into Yale but decided to go to Tulane," I said sarcastically.

"No, you won't. Tell them that you didn't get into Yale."

"Oh, great. And Williams?"

"Tell them waiting list and that you don't want to wait. And that you were accepted to all the other schools and chose Tulane because you didn't want to be near home."

But I knew I didn't want to leave home. How far could I ignore the truth and still not tell anyone? I didn't want to go anywhere. I'd have rather stayed right there protected by my home's strong brick walls and within the fenced in square block of property that was the school. In that, I was like my father. He didn't want to venture far from our compound either. But I couldn't shame my parents further by telling them I was really only a child, not their fearless son David. I wanted to stay home.

That night I got drunk at the Club and told everyone I chose Tulane because Louisiana was the only other state besides New York with a drinking age of eighteen. A drinking age of eighteen...that, at least, was true.

THE GREEKS

Zeta Beta Tau

Two weeks before flying to New Orleans to start my
college days I broke the big toe on my right foot doing a
drunken handstand in a Chinese-Italian restaurant in Monticello,
NY. It was the only bone I'd ever broken and while they
couldn't put it in a cast they gave me a roll bar on the bottom of
my shoe and this great black cane.

It was all bullshit. I could have had no treatment for the toe
but I enjoyed the sympathy and thought it would be cool to start
out at Tulane with a limp and a cane. I never considered that
people would never ask me about it; that they would just
consider me lame.

About a month into the school year in September of '66, I
began to go around to all the fraternities I had been invited to;
the Jewish ones. The freshmen were being "rushed" and I was
probably the only foolish boy who felt that receiving an
invitation at my home on Long Island, seventeen hundred miles
away from any of the fraternities inviting me, actually meant
that I was being personally invited to these Jewish enclaves; that
they wanted me there, were indeed, waiting for me to arrive.

The first kid I met at Tulane, even before my roommate,
was Jeffrey Schwartz. He was skinny and weak with bad skin,
not the sort of person I would normally hang out with; too many
strikes against him. He had asked me if I would go with him to
the frat-houses during rush and I had made the commitment. I

was embarrassed just being seen with him and didn't want him to screw up my chances of pledging one of the top fraternities. I figured I would walk ahead of him and ditch him as soon as possible, before being directly associated with him as my buddy.

Rush week started on a Friday and ended the following weekend when the fraternities that wanted you to join offered you a pledge pin. Then you could decide which one you liked the most.

The first fraternity on my list was Zeta Beta Tau, the number one Jewish fraternity on campus. Jeffrey didn't even want to go to ZBT. He said that they were snobs, a fine cover-up coming from a guy who realized that the Zebes would never be interested in him anyway.

I had an "in" at ZBT. My mother's friend's second cousin was a sophomore at Tulane and already a full-fledged brother. Mom said that she spoke with her friend and that her cousin was expecting me. I was careful not to tell Jeffrey about my locked-in acceptance with the Zebes and secretly kept this guy's name on a piece of paper in my pocket in case I forgot it. I planned to look him up first thing and *not* with Jeffrey at my side.

The weather was still great in New Orleans as I'd heard it was supposed to be most of the year; rain, no snow. I walked a step ahead of Jeff but never turned around toward him even as we spoke during our walk to ZBT. Some of the fraternities we passed on the way looked wild, guys drunk, loud music, mostly Christian. I was always taught that Christians drank more than Jews although I could hold my own with anyone. I heard that the houses themselves were actually *owned* by the fraternities but couldn't figure quite how that worked.

Everyone in sight seemed so involved with their own great time that no one paid any attention to us as we walked by. I tried not to appear interested in what they were up to either and headed straight for ZBT.

Outside of ZBT were two large concrete lions on either side of the white steps leading up to the front porch and white front door. The door was opening and closing with the uneven rhythm of rush week at Tulane.

"I feel stupid even coming here," Jeffrey told me again at the bottom of their stoop. "They're all wearing shirts with button down collars. Look how neatly pressed their pants are. And the penny loafers! I've never seen so many penny loafers running up and down steps! They don't want us here, Barry," he pleaded.

Music blared from the frat-house, varying in volume as people laughed and drank on the porch and in the doorway. I watched a guy in a yellow oxford shirt and khaki trousers leaning on a column as he kissed a young girl. A mug of beer sat on the porch rail next to them. I rubbed the piece of paper in my pocket, my magical invitation, then blinked my eyes, once, twice, three times quickly in succession before answering Jeffrey.

"Don't come in if you feel that uncomfortable," I told him.

"Oh I see," he replied. "You feel so at home."

"I'm going in," I reiterated. "I don't feel at home yet but I am going inside."

"O.K.," he said resigned to the inevitable. "I'm with you." I so wished he wasn't.

I snapped my head back one more time and massaged it with my right hand. It was tense and tight against my shoulders. I tapped my white pants pretending to straighten an uncomfortably positioned penis. My pants were already slightly discolored on the crotch from so many previous taps. I moved from the sidewalk to the steps and ran up them at a faster clip than I normally would have hoping to create some space between Jeffrey and me before I reached the door. My invitation was in hand, out, open and easily accessible for the guy checking invitations at the door. I supposed they didn't want just anyone coming in.

"Welcome to ZBT," he said as friendly as can be. "Why don't you write your name on this nametag and attach it to your shirt right here?" he said touching my shirt. "Hi," he continued quickly turning to Jeffrey who had managed to stay close behind, "Welcome to ZBT. I need your invitation."

"I'm with him," Jeffrey said smiling. "I'm his date." I thought I was going to die. "Kidding," Jeffrey said still smiling, "I'm taking it cut now." He showed his invitation.

I stuck on my nametag and walked inside Zeta Beta Tau without waiting for Jeff. I felt like punching him. What a jerk he was, I thought to myself, as I began searching for my contact, my ace-in the-hole, Kenneth Henry Margulies, my mother's friend's second cousin, sophomore at Tulane, and a full-fledged brother here at ZBT. I shook my arms and then jerked them straight at my sides to relieve some tension. I tensed my thighs and clenched my toes inside my shoes. I knew that no one could see my toes.

ZBT was packed inside, the freshmen standing out with their bright white name tags plastered to their shirts. My neck snapped side to side.

"Excuse me." I was interrupting a quiet conversation between one of the brothers and a tall very handsome freshman. He was a freshman like me but with dark straight controllable hair and an outfit that made him look like he was already a Zebe. I sniffed more loudly than I wanted to and blinked, just once this time before opening my eyes wide in an effort at controlling them. "Sorry to interrupt," I said.

"Hey, where did you go?" Jeffrey asked, tapping me on the shoulder. I pretended not to hear him.

"I'm looking for Ken Margulies," I said as pleasantly as I could. The brother just shook his head. "Kenneth Henry Margulies?" I asked again.

"Who?" he replied over the noise.

"Kenneth Henry Margulies," I shouted back just as the music stopped so everyone heard me.

"Oh," he shouted back unnecessarily. "You mean Hank!"

People were still laughing at my shouting out a name as the next song began to play. They played a song by the Young Rascals. My friend back home, Diane, had introduced me to the group that past summer or I never would have known who was singing. I didn't really listen to much popular music; some, here and there. Instead I secretly played show tunes in my room at home singing along as if I was on stage and wishing I had been born with a great voice. I hadn't realized that the Young Rascals were a white group and Diane enjoyed tricking me.

"I don't see him," he told me.

Jeffrey tugged my arm to get my attention again. "Who's Hank?"

"Look for a little guy," the brother told me. "I saw him near the kitchen before. He's short, with brown hair. He's probably smoking a pipe."

"Thanks," I replied while Jeffrey poked me in the ribs this time.

"What?" I said to him abruptly.

"Who is Hank?" he asked again wanting to stick with me.

"Some friend of my mother's she wants me to look up. It's no big deal," I reassured him trying to downplay Hank's importance. "He's my mother's friend's cousin. She just wants me to say hello for her, that's all."

"You're mother's friend's cousin. He might as well be your mother's friend's cousin's second cousin once removed."

"What?"

"Do you think he's a connection or something?" Jeffrey asked hitting the nail on the head.

"Look, no one told you to follow me around here," I answered back.

"I thought we were hanging out together," he said.

"We're going to look stupid, Jeffrey. We'll look like a couple of kids."

"No we won't," he replied. "We'll look like friends."

"We should separate. We should mingle. That's what you do at these things. If we stand here together we won't mingle."

"What we should really do is leave. They don't want us here. Look around. Look what they look like. I told you this before we came here."

"Speak for yourself. I'm going to mingle. I'll see you later."

"Then how about we meet outside in around a half hour?"

"Fine," I replied. He was holding me back. "I'll see you later." I headed toward the kitchen without Jeffrey.

As soon as I reached the kitchen it was obvious which one was Hank. He was short as described, much shorter than me, at around five-feet four. He was thick with a short neck and muscular body. He looked like an ex-wrestler from one of the lower weight divisions. In spite of his apparent strength he didn't seem at all threatening and had a big smile and a crowd around him laughing. His unlit pipe dangled from his mouth, an appendage.

I approached and stood outside the circle of people gathered around him waiting for an opportunity to speak with him but it was taking much too long and I became impatient. I stretched my arm inside the circle squeaking quietly then quickly snapping my head down and jerking it out. I prayed that no one noticed. Hank turned slightly acting out the punchline of the joke he was telling and all I could reach was his elbow. I grabbed it a little harder then I meant too but at least I got his attention.

"Hi, Hank," I said knowing that I had screwed up his punchline about some Eskimos vacationing in China.

"Do I know you?" he asked, very obviously stopping to look at my nametag, "Barry." In one simple action he made it quite clear that he both did not know me and that I was merely a freshman. I pretended to be oblivious to his manner.

"Well, sort of," I replied. "I'm sort of a friend of, of your mother's."

"One of her mahjong pals?" He chuckled

"No," I said uncomfortably. Everyone around us was laughing at Hank's mahjong remark and I was already in too deep to simply walk away. "I'm supposed to say hello to you."

"From my mother?" he asked incredulous.

"Well, no. Not from your mother. A cousin."

A young girl interjected, "I didn't really get that joke about the Eskimos."

"Could I speak with you for a moment in private?" I asked as politely as I could.

"To say hello to me from someone?" Hank looked around at his audience, especially the other ZBT brothers. "Uh, oh," he added. "Someone must be pregnant." Another zinger. We walked several feet away from the crowd.

"Hello," I said stupidly.

"Is that the hello?" he asked.

"No, I mean, no, of course not." My mind was going blank. "I'm Barry, Barry Golden." I sounded as formal as my father did introducing himself at a business meeting. I stuck out my hand to shake his and he took it in spite of the fact that he looked at it first and seemed to think it was a peculiar thing to do. As we shook I tensed my fingers and he withdrew his hand quickly.

"What exactly do you have to tell me?" He asked. "Who says hello?"

"I forgot their name," I said blinking wildly and wiggling my nose. He just stared at me. "But I know it's one of your cousins."

"Oh," he replied in mock recognition, as if I had mentioned an old friend he hadn't heard from in years.

"Your mother's friend's cousin. It's your cousin too. I don't exactly remember. I feel so stupid. I know that this is the best frat-house on campus."

"Oh," he said helping me along.

"ZBT is my first choice," I told him as if the nightmare of applying to colleges had never ended. "This is really the fraternity I want to join and they suggested I speak with you."

"Who?"

"All of them, I guess."

"I see," he said. "Because I'm the most popular guy here," he added laughing. I wished I had a cold drink to wet my dry mouth. He put his pipe in his mouth. His arms crossed around his oxford shirt. "Let me get Dick," he added. "He's the vice-president. Let's see what he thinks about this." I sniffed in an out while he shouted above the noise to his friend on the other side of their eat-in kitchen.

"Hey, Dick! Dick! Come here," he yelled. Dick was speaking to two other freshmen and, what I assumed was a sorority girl. Dick had a deep tan and a great smile.

"What is it?"

"I need you," Hank yelled as if it was some sort of romantic yearning and not just to meet me.

"I need you too," Dick moaned back in a fun romantic tone as he excused himself and joined us at the kitchen counter. "Hi... Barry," Dick said as the other brothers had, reading from my nametag. I shook my head quickly and suddenly and pretended I had water in my ear so they wouldn't suspect a tic. It seemed as though Hank was looking wide-eyed at the vice-president alongside me.

"We have a little thing here," Hank began.

"Do we?" Dick replied as if they were already in the middle of a discussion. I pushed my hands deep down in my pockets so that any tapping I might do would be concealed.

"It seems, what exactly is that connection, Barry?"

I wanted to be a Zebe so badly that I pretended not to hear Hank's sarcasm. "It wasn't exactly a connection. It was a hello, someone said hello."

"Yes, I realize. But who was it again? My mother's father's cousin's friends' what?"

Dick laughed at Hank's remark.

"It was just someone saying hello," I told Dick. "And really not worth all this fuss."

"He wants to be a Zebe," Hank added pretending to be sincere. Dick seemed nicer than Hank who had an obvious mean streak. Dick's style was warm and friendly, his smile constant and natural. I wanted him to like me.

"I do want to be a Zebe," I told him. "I heard it's the best Jewish fraternity house on campus," I added wondering when I had suddenly become so Jewish.

"The problem is," Dick began, "that so many people want to join ZBT. Look around this party, Barry, and this is just the first day of rush."

I understood where he was going and felt like I was back at my interview at Yale. My eyes hurt as I blinked tightly and tried not to listen.

"We only pledge around thirty freshmen a year out of over two hundred who will all want to pledge."

Why couldn't I be one of them, I thought as the clarity of his words pierced the din of the stupid party. I wanted to be one of the chosen ones but realized that he was telling me instantly that I wouldn't be.

"You know what, though?" he continued. He looked over at Hank. "What about Jules over at Samy?" he asked Hank.

"What do you mean?" Hank asked.

"I think he should talk to Jules. Barry would be a great Samy," Dick said referring to me. He was referring to Sigma Alpha Mu, the wildest Jewish frat-house on campus.

"Jules could help you a lot," Hank reiterated. I didn't want to be a Samy. I wanted to be a Zebe. Another brother joined us. He was a cookie cut version of Dick with less of a tan.

"There's a kid I think you should meet," he told Dick.

"I'll be just a minute," Dick replied.

"He's got to leave and I think he's a great kid. We want him. Come on back with me, Dick."

"I think I'd rather be called Richard this year instead of Dick." They all laughed. I was afraid to join in. Afraid I would cry.

"Come on. Meet this kid."

"O.K.," Dick replied. He turned to Hank and me. "You tell Barry about Jules. You don't need me. Excuse me guys." And he was gone to meet a kid they wanted to pledge ZBT, one of the select thirty.

"So this is what you should do," Hank said. "Go to Sigma Alpha Mu and ask for Jules. You can't miss him. He's a real big guy with red hair."

I knew I didn't want to join a fraternity with red-haired members. I squeaked as quietly as I could but my squeaks were never as quiet as I wanted them to be.

"You tell him that Hank sent you and that I thought you'd make a great addition to Sigma Alpha Mu. It's his *sixth* year at Tulane so you know he knows everyone," Hank laughed, not unfriendly now. I felt like the first official ZBT rejection of the year.

I felt some tears and couldn't answer. These uncontrollable bouts of sadness and withheld tears reminded me of my forced summer camp vacations; the private penal colonies with the moneyed North Shore Jews. I was all alone and mortified at ZBT. I didn't want to add pathetic tears. That would be good for one of their laughs.

"You can stay here all evening if you like but, if I were you, I'd shoot over there.

I squeezed out some words "Yeah, sure," as my nose danced a jig in the middle of my face. I massaged the back of my neck pretending it was stiff and trying to cover up my jerking. I was sweating and felt nauseous.

"Can I get you a beer?" Hank asked as if we were celebrating something.

"Sure," I answered clinging to the hope that the longer I engaged him the greater the chance that he, then Dick, then all the Zebes would change their minds one by one and want me to pledge their fraternity. "Want to hear a joke?" I tried desperately to work on Hank as he gave me a beer. I remembered that Hank liked jokes and I knew a million of them. He handed me a plastic cup filled with flat beer from the bottom of the keg.

"Maybe some other time," he said. "I've got to get back to my friends, but I'll see you later I'm sure."

The music seemed to get louder and I looked for someone else to tell the joke to but didn't see anyone I thought wanted to hear it.

I found Jeffrey outside a short time later just as he had promised.

"So how did it go?" he asked innocently.

"Good. He was really glad to hear from me. But you never know. I mean he's not exactly going to ask me to pledge the first night of rush. I was surprised. Hank was a super nice guy. I kinda' hit it off with him. He was much nicer than you thought he would be!"

"Well I certainly don't claim to be an expert when it comes to fraternities or fraternity 'brothers.' I don't think of myself as an expert in much of anything, except maybe in life insurance and that's only because it's all my Dad talks about all the time."

"Why?"

"He sells it. I don't know which happened first, him talking about it or selling it," Jeffrey admitted with a chuckle. "All I know is I've listened to him talk about life insurance my whole life. He sells quite a bit of it. I think he just talks and talks until they buy some," Jeffrey said smiling and I wondered why he wasn't embarrassed that his father was just an insurance salesman.

SIGMA ALPHA MU

The next day I went alone to Sigma Alpha Mu, less confident than I had been going to ZBT. The Sammy house was noisier than any other frat-house I'd seen so far. Even though I was a block and a half away as they were first officially opening their doors for the evening I could hear their party at full swing.

As I approached the house I saw that unlike the neatly groomed and tailored Zebes, some of these guys were in T-shirts, others wore their shirts untucked and quite a few were wearing dungarees instead of chinos. From the looks of things it seemed they had started drinking hours before rush began. Some of them were already shit-faced and it was barely eight. Two guys, drinks in hand, were checking people at the door and they had hard stuff, not just beer.

I walked up the few steps onto their huge porch. The porch went three-quarters of the way around the house and there were two side entrances into their "party room" as well as the main entrance. While the ZBT house was tall and handsome, the Sammy house was flat, wide open and wild.

"You got a date?" the brother at the door asked me.

"What?" I responded.

"Can't come in without a date."

"I, uh, I,"

"We're just bullshitting. You don't need a date. We got girls inside."

"But we could always use a few more," his friend added.

I did like the Sammy's more relaxed focus. The Zebes had talked about the importance of maintaining your grade point average if you were a member of their fraternity.

"I have my invitation with me," I told him.

"No one cares," the first guy replied. "Don't forget to sign in and to stick your name on. By the way, what is your name?"

"Barry Golden."

He turned to his friend. "See, I was right. This is Barry Golden," he said.

"You knew my name?" I asked with hidden excitement thinking maybe Hank was really trying to be helpful.

"No, I did not Barry. Bullshitting again." He burped as he spoke.

"Pete's drunk," his friend said. "Ignore him and go head in."

I felt glad to be here.

It was even more dramatically different from ZBT once I was inside. There was a long table pushed against the wall on the left where a bunch of Sammy brothers were playing Whales Tales, a drinking game I knew from hanging out at Club Anthony's at home. I was a great drinker and thought about joining in but I didn't see any other freshmen in the game and didn't really know how to join in without feeling like an intruder. I could always play later. There was a live black band playing instead of them just playing records, which accounted for my hearing the music from so far away.

Given the state of things in the frat house it seemed more like eleven than eight. People were everywhere. They were not just packed on the dance floor and in the kitchen, they were lying all over the staircase which I found out later led to their bedrooms. They were a wild group. I could only imagine how crazy things would be in a couple of hours.

"Hey," one of the brothers was tapping me on the shoulder. He had a moustache, which was unusual by any standard here at Tulane. His long sleeves were rolled up one slightly higher than the other and his sweaty hair was combed straight back. I would have loved to have dark straight hair. My hair had thick waves that were always accidently curling. I also wished I had a beard or rather that I could actually grow one. Seeing hair on a face was a constant reminder that I didn't even have to shave yet. I did stand at the sinks and go through shaving motions every morning along with the other guys in the dorm but I never needed a shave. I was hoping that the constant shaving would stimulate beard growth. I wouldn't have felt quite so bad if I hadn't spent so much of my life awaiting physical maturity.

I'd been waiting impatiently for hair growth since the seventh grade and it didn't make it any easier as those around me matured. But here I was, a freshman in college and I still had no beard, little underarm hair, very little hair on my thighs, and worst of all I was missing a 'highway to happiness', the hair that formed a path from your navel to your dick. I had pubic hair but when I went to the beach there was no obvious trail to my pubes anywhere above my bathing suit. It was a real problem and always on my mind.

The brothers at Sigma Alpha Mu didn't pay very much attention to the freshmen who were trickling in and I was glad to not feel the immense pressure I did at ZBT. It was easy to spot Jules. I didn't need a roadmap. He weighed about a ton and was sitting on the couch with a superfluous guitar on his lap. He looked old and the young girl he was talking to seemed more like a prisoner of his than a friend. His red hair was sparse and his face blemished and pocked. I assumed that it must have hurt when Jules had to shave and was glad that I didn't have that problem. Here was a guy who'd be better off with a beard. As I approached I realized that he was just strumming the guitar but couldn't be heard of the over the band.

"Jules?" I offered my hand. He looked up at me through thick eyelids.

"And you are?"

" Barry Golden," I replied.

"Lucky you," he said sounding weird and a little out of it.

"Hank told me all about you," I told him. "We know a bunch of the same people."

"Hank? ZBT?" he asked.

"Yes," I said trying to smile through my tic eruption. "I was over at the Zebe house last night." I glanced at the skinny girl on the couch next to him and felt that she was staring at me.

"What'd old Hank have to say?"

"Mind if I sit?" I asked sitting down in an old tattered easy chair next to his couch. I leaned forward to keep his attention while secretly tapping myself and twisting my free hand in circles around my wrist. "Hank told me to look you up."

"What's that?" he asked through the din.

"Hank," I raised my voice. "We were spending quite a bit of time together last night planning my year and telling jokes. You know Hank loves jokes. Anyway, I spoke with him and met Dick. You must know Dick, their vice-president."

"Randall." Jules turned to the girl. "Dick Randall... asshole."

"Hey, I didn't think much of him either," I added squeaking quietly and sniffing in and out. I tried to breathe through my mouth to control my sniffing. "I think Dick could tell I didn't like him very much. But what the fuck, I'm not a Zebe. You know what I mean? And don't plan on pledging there."

"What?'

"I've always felt I belonged here."

"They're all assholes over there."

"I'm much more at home here than at ZBT."

"So go party. That's what we do here. Great meeting you. The beers are over there," he pointed. "Better stuff near the stairs."

"I stopped because Hank thought we'd really hit off."

"Yeah?"

"Hank...and Dick. I told you. Hank said you've been here longer than anybody. That this is already your sixth year."

"Those motherfuckers. They are such schmucks." Now I could hear him. Jules smiled and shook his head.

"So what do you want from me?" He asked growing a little impatient. It looked like he wanted to get back to the little stick sitting next to him.

"They said that you were the person to talk to, that you're influential." Jules seemed annoyed so I tried to change the subject a little. "Are you in grad school? I mean since this is your sixth year." I asked squeaking twice quickly after my question.

"What is that?" he asked. I didn't realize he could hear me over the noise. "Are you singing?" The girl giggled. "Is that you making those noises?"

"I have something in my throat," I replied massaging my Adam's apple.

"What? A whistle?" Jules was pleased with his great wit. The girl laughed. I didn't like her and I was embarrassed. I felt like mentioning his acne, his fat body and his sparse greasy red hair. He was a prick for pointing out my tics and I was now twitching with no boundaries. I squeaked again as my head snapped back and then jerked side to side. I tapped my dick so many times in succession that there was no way to hide it. They looked down simultaneously and probably noticed my pants were well worn in the crotch. I stood and turned quickly knowing that our conversation was over.

The frat house had become even more stuffed with people during our short conversation and everyone was having fun. I recognized some of the freshman I'd seen at ZBT the night before. I hoped they didn't recognize me. My eyes burned from the smoke in the room. I was so twitchy and uncomfortable that I headed toward the door trying hard not to run. I had to squeeze past a line of happy eyes waiting their turn to get in. As I moved down the block I knew I wouldn't be a Sammy or a Zebe. None of them wanted me but I still wanted them. What would I do? What would I become? I would be unaffiliated. And what kind of social life would that leave me? Who would be my friends?

No matter. I swore I'd never consider the other fraternities on campus. They were filled with nerds and losers. If I couldn't join the best then I wouldn't join any. Jeffrey wound up pledging TEP and, for him, I suppose it was O.K. TEP had the highest grade point average at Tulane but they weren't very well rounded people. Nerds.

I was outside the fraternity system, alone, jealous and angry. I became friends with an odd assortment of other unaffiliates from the dorm, each one tougher and meaner than the next. They respected no one. They were wise guys to each other as well but it was worth the teasing because with them as my friends I got to pick on almost anyone.

CHARLES C. CHARLES

I had my first and last official college roommate during my freshman year at Tulane. I purposely arrived earlier than he was scheduled to arrive to glom the best the room had to offer, and I did. I was unpacked, waiting, and as comfortable as I could be under the circumstances when he walked in, Charles C. Charles, III. from San Antonio, Texas. Charles Charles Charles!

I could understand Charles C. Charles, Sr.'s need to avenge his own naming. But what could Grandpa Charles have been thinking? I had spoken with Charles twice before heading down to Tulane and was not looking forward to meeting him in person. It wasn't anything in particular that he'd said on the phone but more my own anxiety over sharing a room.

Charlie was a nice enough guy, sort of goofy with a high voice and way too much school spirit. He smiled often and was thrilled to be at Tulane, "the Harvard of the South." I thought that phrase described southern sensibility more thoroughly than any other I'd ever heard. Tulane had as much in common with Harvard as a learning institution as Debbie Gibson had with Maria Callas as a singer.

Charlie did all the normal things students do except he seemed to purposely wait to jerk off until both of us were in our beds late at night. We had different friends and kept different hours. He would usually go to sleep at an hour that related to his classes the next day. I couldn't somehow. I had always scheduled my time with no regard to school and suddenly being on my own at Tulane wasn't exactly conducive to healthy scheduling. I would pop in to the room occasionally to grab a deck of cards or some extra change on my way down to Bourbon Street. Maybe I'd stop in to dig out a hidden bottle of Tequila. I tried not to disturb Charlie as he was usually sound asleep. What I could never figure out was what awakened Charlie when I finally did go to bed. I'd slide quietly between my sheets careful not to make a sound. What made him stir and why did I then have to listen to his quick breaths and quiet moans while he pulled his dick?

From his point of view, I was sure life with me was annoying. My tics were waxing when I started school and Charlie had to deal with a cacophony of sounds and visuals. I was squeaking, sniffing, and clearing my throat all the time. My face would contort, my neck snapped my head from side to side and I constantly tapped my groin adjusting my dick in an effort to find some nonexistent comfort zone.

Charlie and I were really a bad fit. He was neat. I lived in a mess. He seemed genuinely well adjusted and kind. I was self-conscious, confused, maladjusted and mean. Within a month after the fraternity fiascos Charlie and I were on each other's nerves worse than ever. What had been tolerable before was now unbearable.

Studying was never a priority to me but on this one particular day I was seated at my desk making an attempt. Charlie liked to play his radio while he studied. I needed silence. I was so easily distracted. I would try to concentrate but my brain seemed to whir all the time, thoughts flying by at speeds that rejected my attempts at any scholastic comprehension. I never felt a moment's peace. Even when I felt some control and things were still, I would hear a constant hum as my brain struggled, inhaling everything it sensed.

I would read one sentence over and over and over again but the words I read were in competition for my attention with such "jarring" sounds as the ticking of a clock, the small birds accidentally scratching the windowsill and the fly grazing on my forearm. I had no filter system. All sounds entered my head without priority and roared. My thoughts flew. My moods swung.

Charlie and I were sitting back to back at our respective desks. Charlie's radio was playing. The Turtles were "happy together" but "curious about the weather." To me the sound was overwhelming and soon the radio was all I could hear. I asked him nicely to shut off his *fucking* radio several times.

"Hey, Charlie. Last time I'm saying this nicely, shut off your fucking radio?"

"It's as soft as I can make it. If I turn it down anymore I won't be able to hear it at all."

"Well that's O.K. That's what shut it means!"

Charlie didn't turn it down. He was irritated and unresponsive. If he had only shut his radio off perhaps the din of constant stimuli would have followed its lead.

"Charlie! Shut that fucking radio off!" It seemed to get louder but I knew he wasn't touching it. "How many times do I even study in here, you little prick?"

"I was studying here before you."

"But I'm trying to study here now," I snapped back.

"Why don't you go to the library if my radio bothers you?" He spoke in a tone that infuriated me.

I pictured myself in the library trying to hold back my sounds, unable to study; unable to think of anything; just fighting my urges. My tics were like an itch in the middle of my back that I couldn't reach and wouldn't go away. It was driving me nuts. Eventually I have to find a release, a satisfying action to make it stop.

Charlie's mere suggestion that I put *myself* in that situation pushed me over the edge. I squeaked loudly and then quickly cleared my throat in a ridiculous attempt to cover the high pitched squeal with a more manly sound. He knew why I wasn't in the library, that son-of-a-bitch. His radio seemed to increase in volume again. It was the only sound in my brain.

"That's it!" I said knocking my chair over as I leaped from my seat to Charlie's desk. I pushed him aside and grabbed his radio on the shelf above him. Momma Cass was singing. I reached for its electric cord and yanked it from the outlet. The cord didn't break but snapped back and the plug hit me below the eye infuriating me further. I smashed his radio on the floor cracking its case.

"Get out or I will kill you!" I was practically screaming.

"This is wrong," He grabbed his books and left the room turning back to me from the hallway. "You can't do this," he yelled at me. "This won't end here."

I closed the door silencing my roommate.

I realized that I overreacted. He would rat me out to the floor advisor. And who could blame him? I was in the wrong. But no security or campus police came by for a visit. I think everyone knew I would never have hurt him. I was as frightened of fighting as he was, probably more so.

I couldn't study after all that commotion so I cleaned up the mess I'd made of his desk, lay back on my bed, turned my stereo on and listened to music instead.

Sometime later I stepped out for a few hours. Someone must have been watching the room because when I returned all of Charlie's things were gone. I checked to be sure that nothing of mine had been taken and lay back down on my bed hoping that Charlie was alright. I already missed him. I thought about how he drove me nuts and knew that there was no justification for what I had done but at the same time I realized that I couldn't help it. Something had just gone terribly wrong.

It was then that I realized that in our few months as roommates Charlie never once mentioned my tics, my unusual sounds; no odd looks and no questions. No teasing or secret discussions with others. He had the courtesy to accept and the ability to ignore. Charlie was a little silly but, all in all, he was a good guy.

No one else was assigned to my room for the remaining seven months of my freshman year. I had a private room. It was unheard of.

I didn't see Charlie again on campus for months and when

we did have a chance encounter we didn't really talk. I was glad he was still in school and he seemed none the worse for wear. And I have never again had a male roommate share my bedroom.

I told my mother what had happened between me and Charles. I could hear her disappointment but no surprise. She said she'd mention it to my father. JUST MENTION IT!

A catastrophe to other parents was worth a mention to mine. No discussion; takes too much time. Perhaps a mention while packing to visit my brother at Yale. But this time I was surprised.

A BIG SURPRISE

I left the lecture hall blank notebook in hand reeking from cigarettes. There were a hundred attentive students in class and I was the hundred and first. They kept a very shoddy attendance record so it was an easy class to skip and I often did. My parents were happy as long as I said I was pre-med. Facts and grades were irrelevant. Tulane was working out OK. There were lots of girls at Sophie Newcomb and more at St. Mary's Dominic College. St. Mary's was nearby so getting laid wasn't a problem. The girls were smarter at Newcomb, harder to seduce and far more intimidating. My "best girl" was a bisexual stripper who lived on Bourbon Street. I often visited her at work. Besides that, when I wasn't drinking with my friends or seeking out naïve young girls, I was plenty occupied being jealous and angry with my girlfriend back home. As I said, all in all, school wasn't half-bad.

I took the elevator in my dorm up to the fifth floor, looked into to the TV room to see if anyone I liked was hanging out. The TV was on but no one there so I walked down the hall to my room to catch up on my sleep. It was the only way I could manage to stay up so late at night.

Well … He was standing in my room when I got there.

"Dad?"

"Hello there." He seemed proud, not because he was visiting me but because he was here, in my room at Tulane. He'd actually left his compound and travelled somewhere on his own.

"I, I don t get it. What's going on?"

"You mean I can't visit my son?" I don't know how I felt

about that one. We awkwardly tried to hug each other. "So," he continued.

"I still don't really get it. Did something happen? Is something wrong?"

"Not a thing. I simply decided to visit. We don't really get to spend as much time together now that you're in school"

Like we hung out together when I lived at home, I thought, looking at him carefully. "Let's sit down," I suggested.

"Where?" he replied. "How do you live in such a mess?" That was a pleasant start.

I grabbed some clothes off Charles' old bed. The beds were constructed so when pushed in under the wall cabinets they were the size of a couch. I now kept Charles' bed pushed in and mine always out. It was one of the luxuries of losing your roommate; a dorm room built for two. My father and I sat down across from one another.

I spoke first. "So tell me, Dad. Assuming this isn't just a normal visit, what's up really?"

"It's honestly just a visit. I thought it would be nice. That's all." I couldn't tell if he was being truthful and, even if he was, I was certain that he had an agenda. This was very weird.

"That's great," I replied. "You're the first! No other fathers have popped in for a visit yet. I met some of them when they dropped their kids off at the beginning of the semester but I haven't seen any of them since."

"Well maybe this will start a trend," he suggested giving his best effort at being humorous.

"Don't think so. But it's great you're here." I tapped my groin and jerked around a bit. My eyebrows danced up and down. My father looked out the window.

"It's nice down here."

"Yeah, I like it. It's fun."

"It's supposed to be more than fun," he said.

"And a lot of work. You didn't let me finish," I lied.

"So school...you like it. It's pretty far from home."

"New Orleans is fun. Different. You know, they still have

some bars down here where black people can't enter. They have these windows open to the street to serve them and they have to drink outside. It's a terrible thing. I still drink there but I try not to watch what's going on."

"Why don't you try not supporting the bar?" He asked. We paused in silence. "Drink a lot?"

"On the weekends ... sometimes. You know we're hanging out."

"But there must be things to do on campus."

"I like to go out on the weekends."

"There must be lectures and things. You'd probably meet some nice people at those things."

I shrugged in response and shook my head like I'd just come out of the water. I squeaked and inadvertently farted. "Just so you know, that wasn't a tic."

"I didn't say a word," he replied defensively.

"Nonetheless."

I was being bold. I was confused about his visit and certain that my mother forced it on him. There was no way that this was his idea. I resented it; his being forced to visit. There was nothing for us to talk about. We had little in the way of shared memories except for our similar rectal surgeries and the incredible pain of recovery. It was that first bowel movement after surgery that brought with it the mind-boggling pain. It was a conversation for two old retired Jews in Florida not for a father and his eighteen year old son.

We made plans to have dinner at the Rib Room in the Royal Orleans Hotel downtown in the French Quarter. I couldn't afford to go on my own so why not take advantage of his visit. I still didn't get the whole trip. I thought about introducing him to my little stripper on Bourbon Street and could only imagine the look on his face if we ever walked into her club.

Later, back in my dorm room before he settled in to Charles' bed I drank a shot of Tequila to help me sleep. I didn't need it but wanted to show him that I could have it if I wanted to and no one could stop me. He didn't say a word. I started drifting. I was back in high school.

I was coming home from the our last high school swim meet of the year; my last forever. I had been waiting for my parents to arrive.

I wasn't good in most sports but I could swim. My parents had promised me that they would come to watch me swim, even if they were running a little late. Neither my father nor my mother had ever seen me compete...at anything. I looked around but couldn't find them in the stands.

My events were the fifty and the hundred yard freestyle and I had just been called to the blocks for the start of the hundred. It was my last event.

Just before the gun went off to start the race I glanced up into the stands one final time to see if my parents might have just arrived. I couldn't find them in the small crowd. At the shot I hit the water starting fast but finishing slowly, next to last. Another kid's parents gave me a ride home.

"I'll see ya' tomorrow Donnie," I said opening the back door of the Mahoney's station wagon and stepping out onto the curb. "At least there's no practice tomorrow, right?"

"We didn't have that bad a season. We did better than last year."

I laughed in response. "That's because we had one less meet."

"Goodnight Mr. and Mrs. Mahoney." I heard them say goodnight to me as I closed the door. I turned and walked up the icy driveway to the kitchen door. As I walked in through the kitchen, I had to pass Emma and her husband, Nathan, our housekeeper and maintenance man. I took off my coat as I entered the dining room. My family was in the middle of dinner.

"I thought you were coming to watch me swim," I said.

"We already know that you can swim," my father replied, trying to be funny.

"Some of the school buses got back later than we thought. The roads are very slippery and we have a lot of kids to worry

about getting home. One of the drivers was nervous driving on Merrick Road and Daddy went out because he was afraid she'd be in an accident. He was worried."

"How about worrying about me?" I asked.

My father looked up at me. "What would you have liked me to do? I'll leave our kids on Merrick Road and try to explain that to all their parents."

"They're not your kids. I'm your kid! You said you'd come even if you were running late."

"It was simply too late to go, Barry" mother added trying to convince me. "By the time all the kids got home it was well after six, and then your father first had to wash up, I had to make sure to get dinner on the table ..."

"Yeah, yeah, yeah," I said interrupting her.

"Don't cut your mother off like that. She does enough around here that she doesn't have to deal with that."

My eyes blinked tightly as I wiggled my nose and scrunched up my head into my neck rolling it around my shoulders.

"I'll tell you one thing," my father added sounding annoyed. "If I had been there, you wouldn't be coming home with a wet head in the middle of the winter?"

"Now that's probably true," I replied sarcastically.

"And when you get sick whose fault is it going to be?" he asked.

"Yours," I answered back. "Because you weren't there to remind me to dry my head."

"Let's not have this," my mother interjected, uncomfortable with confrontation.

"In two years neither one of you ever came to watch me in a single swim meet. I squeaked two or three times in succession. There isn't one other kid on the team whose parents never came to watch them swim."

"And there isn't one other kid on the team whose parents work as hard as we do. And what for? Not for us. For you, your brother and your sister," my father replied.

My brother was away at Yale at the time and my sister was trying to slide under the dinner table. Our arguments frightened her.

"That's enough," my mother added.

Dad continued. "You know what my father said when I told him that I wanted to go to college?"

"As a matter of fact, I do," I heard this speech before.

"He said 'that's great'." He was continuing compulsively. "He said that he was glad that I wanted to go to college and then he said that I should go to any college that I could afford to send myself. That's what he said."

"You've told that story three different ways already, Dad. Which one is the real one?

My mother jumped in more gently. "You should go grab the towel in the bathroom upstairs, dry your hair and then come back down for dinner. Everything is getting cold."

"I'll be right down," I said as I headed up the stairs to towel off and comb my hair for dinner.

I finally fell asleep staring at the ceiling in my dorm room now thinking about the sweet taste of the tequila.

My father and I got up the next morning, washed up in the communal bathroom and grabbed some breakfast at Bruff Commons, Tulane's cafeteria.

"I have to go to English at nine," I told him. "What are you going to do?"

"I don't know. Thought I'd walk around and get to know Tulane a bit."

"Then what? Want to meet me back at the dorm?"

"Let's do that. That sounds like a plan. What time?"

"I can be back around eleven. Want my keys?"

"I didn't need them yesterday. I think they realize I'm your father and not some cat burglar on the prowl."

"Here, take them anyway. Can't hurt to have them. Take them." I put them in his hand. I don't think he ever walked around the school but he did clean my entire room; folded clothes, made the beds, even dusted off the desks. He was so proud of his work.

"How's that?" He said on my return.

"Wow." I replied realizing it would now take me days to find all my shit. "Amazing."

And so went his visit, filled with these penetrating conversations bringing us closer by the minute. I still embarrassed him in public. We didn't even walk side by side. The day went by slowly with us both watching the clock and the following day I took him to the airport after a truly great breakfast at the Camelia Grill. I did want him to see the Grill. It was an amazing place, fast and delicious with its fat white owner at the cash register as the "coloreds" cooked and served.

We arrived early at the airport and sat awkwardly waiting for his flight There wasn't much left to say. I kissed him goodbye as he boarded the plane and hated my sadness as I watched it taxi down the runway.

SEEKING HELP

Later in the year some disciplinary issues came up and it was suggested by the school that I get some help. Having been in therapy since I was twelve I actually looked forward to a similar relationship here at Tulane. I felt close to my therapist back home.

"Do you see a story in this one also?" She asked.

I was trying to look at the inkblots but her good looks distracted me. I envied whoever she curled up with at night. She was older than I was, probably in her late twenties, and I wanted to impress her.

She had a resemblance to Sheila Thompson, who I'd had the good fortune to have sex with back in January. I was always obsessed with getting laid and considered it a fine obsession.

Sheila was my first and, at the time, my only divorcee. Given all the sex practice she must have had having been married, I figured screwing her had to be something quite special. Imagine her experience as a married woman being able to screw on a whim. Plus her tits were absolutely perfect for my fantasies. Everyone wanted to fuck her and that made me want to fuck her all the more. She was in my chemistry lecture class.

The class was gigantic, bigger than any class I'd ever been in and I sat all the way on the other side of the amphitheater from Sheila. But I really lucked out when Professor Corrigan asked everyone to write down any personal seating requirements. Only about ten had specific requests and I was one of the few people dropping my request in the drop-box outside his office later that afternoon. When he presented his seating chart two days later, sure enough, Sheila and I were side by side. I had written:

> Dear Professor Corrigan,
>   If you don't mind, would you please move my seat so that I may sit next to Barry Golden. It would mean a great deal to me. Thank you in advance and *please* don't mention this to anyone!
>   Sheila Thompson

I believe that I was the envy of many during those months; my own private room in the dorm *and* I was screwing the one and only Sheila Thompson.

"Excuse me. We only have a limited amount of time, Mr. Golden."

"What?" I was caught by surprise and felt awkward, like she'd been reading my thoughts.

"Please pay attention to what we're doing. We're almost done."

"How am I doing?"

"It's what you see. You can't do poorly."

"Right."

"Now, tell me what you see in this one."

I'd had some behavioral issues according to the school and was afraid that they would throw me out of Tulane if I didn't accomplish something constructive at this psychological evaluation. I was in a mess. I had caused a lot of trouble and felt that honesty was my best way out. But I had an advantage. Psychotherapy wasn't new to me.

I only briefly wondered whether or not I should be truthful.

I realized that lies would get me nowhere and only momentarily considered trying to bullshit my way through this evaluation. If I wanted into Tulane's free psychotherapy program, and I did, I would have to be truthful. I looked down at the inkblot.

"O.K. Here. This is a giant bird's head with its mouth wide open. I don't know; it looks like it's going to vomit on this guy who is this little girl's father. Well, she's either a girl or a little Arab boy. See. She's over here. She's swallowing some animal's tail. It's either a cow or a dog's tail. It's a cow's. See, it has an utter." I paused.

"Is that it? That's all that you see?" She asked as she was writing her notes.

"No." I decided to tell her everything I saw. "It might not be an utter. It could be a fetus. And there's the umbilical cord. And it's bleeding. The father, over here, is poking his wife in the chest. I'm not sure why but he's really pissed off. It looks like he's standing in shit. And on the edges, here, on both sides it looks like hair, pubic hair."

She was writing furiously on her side of the table.

"How many more of these inkblots are there?" She slid another one flat on the table in front of me. "Are there many more?" I asked again.

"Just this one," she replied. I studied the black smudges and let my mind wander.

"A butterfly?"

"What?" she said apparently astounded. It didn't look at all like a butterfly.

"Not really," I said smiling quickly. "Let's see." I studied it again. "It's like a civil war scene. Here's a soldier and he's loading this cannon in front of him." I squeaked suddenly, then sniffed in and out and wiggled my nose simultaneously. I had been rubbing my nose compulsively all year with this weird upward motion and had developed a crease straight across it dividing it into two distinct parts. It looked worse now since I had a slight tan; a sunlamp tan. It made my nose look like a map divided into territories.

I was very anxious as I studied the inkblot and suddenly realized that the cannon wasn't a cannon after all, but rather another soldier bending over in front of the first soldier.

"Is that all you see?" she asked me for about the millionth time.

"Not exactly," I replied adding a few minor observations. I hummed quietly to myself and then stretched my lips between my teeth and snapped them apart quickly making a popping sound like a freshly opened bottle of champagne. I sensed her eyes on me, took a deep breath and decided to go on.

"I don't really think that it's a cannon in front of him," I said. "It's another soldier definitely bending down." I couldn't believe what I was going to tell her. "He's bending down and the one behind him is shoving, I don't know, like a ramrod up his ass. I don't know what they called those things that they used to pack the powder in their rifles. I think it was a ramrod, but I'm not sure. Anyway he's definitely shoving it up the other guy's ass. I know that sounds weird but that's what I see." I looked up and saw that her mouth was agape as I finished. I really hoped that she appreciated my honesty. I knew she wouldn't get that kind of cooperation from most people.

"That's it," I asked.

"Yes," she replied adding to her already voluminous notes. "I'd still like to ask you a few more questions, Barry, if you don't mind."

"Sure. Go ahead." I let out a shrill little squeak like a tiny wild animal and snapped my head down toward my lap. I didn't really need my tics at this moment. They were absolutely ruining my chances of getting laid and I thought she was gorgeous. Her hair was shoulder length, black, straight and silky. Her features were perfect. She had large oval eyes, a straight thin nose and full red lips. Her blouse was white with a conservative cut, and the fabric was thin enough that I could make out her brassiere and I could sense they held a pair of perfect breasts with sensitive nipples that would be responsive to the slightest touch.

"Hello?" she said realizing my mind was wandering again.

I sniffed in and out loudly three times and hoped that I hadn't been staring. I adjusted my seat pushing my dick down between my legs to hide my erection. After the adjustment I tapped my dick three times matching my sniffing. "Earlier in the session you told me that you quit the swim team. My records show that you didn't actually quit, you stopped going. You never discussed it with the coach or the dean. According to my records it would seem that one-day you simply never went back. And you never took gym class instead, as you should have. Why did you quit the swim team?"

I was on a roll and I knew that regardless of how embarrassing it might be at the moment I had to tell her the truth. I knew that she was impressed with my candor.

"This is really gonna' sound weird," I said. I would never have a girlfriend as smart as she was, I thought; and so normal. The girls I went out with were stupid, they were easy to fuck. Not like her. She wouldn't be. And at that moment she was what I wanted more than anything and not just to sleep with, not her. I wanted to lay my head on her breasts and rest, to close my eyes and go to sleep.

"The truth," I said. "I have a phobia. I've talked about it before with Dr. Bernard, my therapist at home. It's gonna' sound stupid." I wanted to tell her all about it. I had to. "I'm actually frightened that there are fish in the swimming pool, predatory fish. And I'm afraid that they're going to bite my toes and my penis."

"You quit because you were afraid that fish were going to attack your toes and your penis. That's what you're telling me? That's your answer, your reason?"

I could tell she wasn't getting it.

"Well, not really attack them, just sort of nip at them, like piranha. They nip. Each individually takes a tiny bite but they attack in flocks."

"Schools," she politely corrected me. Now, I felt like an idiot.

"Look, I know that logically fish can't survive in

chlorinated water but that's my phobia."

"Then given your 'phobia', why join the swim team in the first place?" she asked.

"Because I'm a great swimmer and I'm not good at any other sport. I just have a phobia. I was trying to overcome it."

"I see." she said jotting more notes on her pad.

"And there was something else."

"And that was?"

"I developed this compulsion to inhale while my head was underwater." I squeaked as quietly as I could and sniffed again in and out as I thought of trying to hold my breath underwater.

"What do you mean?"

"Exactly that. It didn't matter if I was winning or losing or just swimming laps. I developed this compulsion to inhale through my nose, quick sniffs in, while my head was still underwater and when I inhaled, naturally, I would start to choke. So I had to stop swimming. But I wasn't about to tell the coach why. Do you think he would've been sympathetic? I was embarrassed, so I just quit. Plus, I really didn't enjoy swimming so many miles a week. I'd rather take gym."

"But you didn't. You did nothing."

"I know."

DANCING WITH THE DEAN

Three days later I was sitting nervously in the Dean of Students' waiting room. There was another kid there also. He looked like Ichabod Crane with a crew cut. His Adam's apple seemed to jump a good eight inches when he swallowed. I was half expecting a bell to ring each time it hit the top.

"Hi. I'm Steven. Steven Krause." he began.

"I'm Barry Golden." I replied, neither one of us offering to shake hands.

"Why are you here?" He continued.

"I got into trouble during Mardi Gras."

"For what?"

"For nothing, really." I was uncomfortable discussing what had happened.

"What did you do?"

I didn't want to be rude to him, so I answered. "I rode a friend's motorcycle up to the fifth floor in Monroe."

"I heard about that! I live in Monroe too! I'm on the second floor. What floor are you on?"

"The fifth. That's why we rode up there." I replied. I snapped my head down toward my lap, twice in rapid succession and then rubbed the back of my neck and twisted my head around in a circle to mask my tics. I had been twitching a lot and my neck hurt from all the snapping. I flexed my thighs, first one then the other. I made a fist and twisted that in circles around my wrist. Everything seemed to hurt.

I continued the conversation with Steven in an attempt to

divert his thoughts away from my ugly tics.

"What are you here for?" I asked.

"As I said, I live on the second floor and I want to be moved to a higher floor. It's too noisy on the second. I don't get enough sleep and find it very hard to study."

"I can imagine." I replied, wishing I too was waiting for the Dean for as innocuous a reason as that.

"Didn't you have to go before the Student Council?" He asked me.

"Yup. And now the Dean. The Student Council found me guilty. What a bunch of assholes."

"I heard that you broke into the trophy case," he said. I felt like I was on trial again.

"It was during Mardi Gras. We were drunk. And I didn't break into the trophy case. It was locked in the front but easy to open from the back. It was just stupid. We held a fake awards ceremony and awarded the trophies to our friends on the floor. Everybody went along with it. It wasn't just me. I can't even remember whose idea it was in the first place, but I got in the most trouble."

"I heard some of the trophies were never returned."

"I returned the ones I had."

"Oh." We sat there in silence for a while. I hoped that he had finally run out of questions and I squeaked, maybe in delight.

"Didn't you hide someone's dissertation too?"

"He got it back. It was a joke."

"But I heard that…"

"Look," I interrupted him. My patience was running out. But before I lost my temper and before he had a chance to discuss every other little charge against me the Dean entered the room.

"Mister Golden?" he asked pointing at each of us one at a time.

"I'm Golden."

"Well won't you please come into mah' office."

We moved quickly and quietly into his office. The Dean's leather chair was burgundy, just a few shades darker than his pudgy, pockmarked face.

"Have a seat, Mr. Golden." He spoke more pleasantly than I had anticipated. I watched him flip through what looked like my psychological evaluation.

"Well, well," he said while looking it over. He reached for a tissue on his desk and I pushed the tissue box closer to him so that he could reach it more easily. "I can reach it, son."

I withdrew my hand quickly and watched the Dean remove his reading glasses and exhale powerfully on the lenses before wiping them clear with the tissue. He rocked back in his chair. I wondered if he was a father and what he was like with his children.

"Well, this is something to read, Mr. Golden." His tone of voice was non-committal, which was good. At least he didn't seem angry.

I sensed that this meeting wouldn't be all bad. She'd told him how candid I had been with her, how I wanted to go into the psychotherapy program. Maybe I would call her and ask her out to dinner. I could say it was as a thank you. The Dean peered at me over his reading glasses.

"You don't much like people from the South, do ya' boy?"

"What?"

"You figure we're all stupid, right? Cause we tawk funny an' everything. Well, you'd be surprised, Mr. Golden. We're not all that dumb."

"I don't think that."

"Do you know that in Hot Springs, Arkansas, we've been sellin' plain ole' tap water in jugs to you Northerners for years. Years!" He paused.

"I don't know why you have the impression ..."

"Shut up, boy! You're not jus' in the South now, son. You're in my office! You'all don't say another word unless I'm askin' you a question."

"Yes, sir."

He flipped through a few more pages of the report, pinched his nostril and secretly admired the small bit of snot he'd discovered. He flicked it off his pinky onto the carpeting behind his desk. "So you think some ole' fish is gonna' bite your dick off in the swimmin' pool."

There was silence. It lasted too long as he peered at me over his glasses.

"Yes, sometimes," I replied. I swallowed, shocked at his abruptness and fought to control my tics. I didn't want him to realize how much he frightened me.

"And you saw a woman in a frilly dress bein' butt fucked by a unicorn. Do I have that right, there? You saw all that in one iddy-biddy inkblot, Mr. Golden? Lotsa' butt fuckin' in your visions aren't there, son?"

I didn't answer. That piece of shit! She didn't simply give the Dean an evaluation. She gave him all her notes; my words, verbatim! I thought that was even against the law.

"Our young therapist says here, you'll love this. She says that you have transvestite tendencies but you repress them. Don't do that, son. Don't repress. You gotta' let your feelings out. Get yourself some panties; maybe those panties with the day of the week printed on each one."

That cunt, I thought, remembering her apparent kindness.

"Now we're not as liberal as you folks up North, I admit that. But we'll try to understand your tendencies, son, 'cause this is a modern institution'."

"I don't really…"

"You shut up! That's what you do really!" The color of his face now matched his chair.

"Please allow me to go on." He read further into the report. "You were not very cooperative. I can see that."

She never heard my candor, my sincerity. She hated me!

"She says that you were tryin' to shock her, makin' things up and bein' generally and negatively reactive. It's all here."

"It isn't true, sir. She misunderstood."

"It says you were sayin' bizarre things to 'cause her

discomfort. Listen here, and I quote: 'This comes from Mr. Golden's inability to deal with the reality of his situation. He is beset by intensely violent and poorly controlled aggressive impulses and can overreact sharply in this area. His complete disregard for our testing indicates that he cannot be helped through psychotherapy at this time.' Then she goes on and on. You're nuthin' much but a problem for us down here now."

He was taunting me and there was nothing I could do about it. I tried to figure out what was going on in his head. Was he just plain mean or an idiot? Did he really understand so little? And what about my lovely psychologist with the great tits? I supposed that I wouldn't be seeing her again.

"I don't really know what to say. I think you have it wrong, sir."

"I don't," he went on opening his eyes wide to feast on my discomfort. "The most despicable character I have ever encountered in life or in literature would be Iago from Shakespeare's great tragedy *Othello*. That is, until I met you. Mr. Golden, may I say that if you so much as spit on the sidewalk, anywhere in the State of Louisiana, I will personally see to it that you are thrown out of this fine university. Am I making myself clear? I am putting you on disciplinary probation for the next two semesters. That is *all* of next year. I don't like you, Mr. Golden, and I suggest you not find yourself back in my office again. Now get yourself up and get outta' my sight."

As I started to stand my feet slid out in front of me and I fell back into the seat. I was afraid the Dean would think that I was being a wise guy and that I purposely sat back down so I jumped up, a bit too quickly this time. The Dean hopped up as well moving slightly backward as if he thought I might attack him. I let out a grunt and a throat clearing bark that only made matters worse.

"You try somethin' smart with me and you'll find yourself in jail! Don't fuck with me boy!"

"I'm not. I slipped."

"Don't fuck with me you little bastard!"

There was nothing left to say. As I opened the office door to let myself out the Dean continued shouting and the other kid in the waiting room was gone. I assumed he heard the commotion and decided that this was not the best day to put in his stupid room change request.

I was physically homesick now and felt it from my throat to my belly. My cheeks were painful in the fresh air and I grimaced and scrunched my face as tight as I could. I pursed my lips and pressed the bottom of my nose against my upper lip. I cleared my throat and grunted several times snapping my head backwards trying to squeeze it tightly between my shoulder blades. I turned, blinking many times and tapped and tugged at my dick as I walked on the grass along the side of the building. I hoped that no one was watching. I had no one to talk to and I ached for the year to end so that I could go home.

PART TWO

MANHATTAN, 1970

It's easy to get lost living in Manhattan in every sense of the word. I was enrolled at NYU, a huge university dwarfed by the city around it. I lived off campus, campus being limited for me to Washington Square Park.

I owned no books, rarely attended classes and no one seemed to care what I did with the exception of Dr. Littell, head of the Education Department who was easy to get around. My parents still never reviewed my grades and I lived in a world without consequence. When I graduated I still didn't know anyone in my class except for Anne Garafolo, a tiny black-haired Italian who I was screwing infrequently and some black kid who was always wearing thick black-rimmed glasses and a smile.

I never even knew where NYU held its commencement exercises but soon after the graduation, on July 15th, 1970, I received a call from my mother that my diploma had arrived. I remember the date because I was ashamed that I didn't stop fucking my date while speaking with my mother. I should never have done that to her and I later marked my calendar so as not to forget this great shame.

She was upset that our last name had been spelled Goldin instead of Golden on my diploma and I had to promise her several times that I'd definitely have it corrected by NYU and would have a new diploma sent out *no matter what the cost*. My mother was convinced that the degree wouldn't count if the correction wasn't made.

My roommate was a schoolteacher by the name of Michael Warner. Michael was beating the draft by teaching elementary school in Bedford-Stuyvesant. He taught kids from the slums with names like Leander Sanders, Cadillac and Tangerine. It was fun for him; very unsupervised.

I even went to visit him one day at school and we told the kids in his class that I was Pete from the Mod Squad. It was one of the most exciting days they ever had, asking me questions and listening to my fantastic lies. No one at the school seemed to care who came and went.

Michael and I lived in a newly built high-rise on Fourteenth Street and Fifth Avenue. The area was a sort of no-man's land without the distinct identity of a Greenwich Village or a Chelsea. Bi-lingual discount stores were everywhere, crowding the sidewalks on Fourteenth Street with clothing racks, and boxes of sandals and sneakers. There were cheap shampoos and conditioners, and bargain electronics that you knew would never work.

Our favorite late night restaurant was also on Fourteenth Street, two blocks east, named Tad's Steak House. We'd go there often, usually stoned. It might as well have been a warehouse for monosodium glutamate given the amount they put on their food. But mostly we liked to eat at Max's Kansas City on Park or the new Steak and Brew which had just opened on Fifth Avenue and Twelfth Street.

I was proud of my new friends. First of all they weren't anti-Semitic. As a matter of fact they were Jews. They just didn't seem it, or sound it for that matter. I think that was because they came from Jersey and not Long Island. There was always something about "the Island" that stood out. My new friends were older than I was; the youngest of them already twenty-three.

Michael and I couldn't have afforded this expensive apartment if it weren't for our selling drugs to supplement our meager incomes.

We primarily sold high quality pot to other drug dealers and were in the enviable situation of having more suppliers than customers. We would make our sales calls four or five hours before we copped and then we sold everything from our apartment within hours after that. We made enough money to pay our bills and keep ourselves in drugs but it seemed never enough to accumulate.

We were friends with other drug dealers who seemed more farsighted than we were. As a matter of fact, Michael's girlfriend, Elizabeth, was Richie Greenberg's little sister and he was the most farsighted of any drug dealer we knew. He used to have Elizabeth fly the pot he was selling at the University of Buffalo in one of those small commuter airlines in exchange for letting her have as much in drugs as she needed for her head.

I think that Richie also monitored the amount he was giving her to make sure that she wasn't taking extra for Michael and me, not that we needed any extra. Richie was very cool, funny, intelligent and particularly confident. For me, he also had a powerful and intimidating presence. I was secretly embarrassed by how much I wanted him to like me.

"You must have some coke?" Richie asked me one evening as we sat in our living room on Michael's bed smoking pot and getting ready to snort some heroin. I was possessive of my cocaine and didn't always share it.

I had only done heroin three other times and I was always a little nervous beforehand. Just the word, heroin, sounded so serious. It lacked the recreational sound of pot or Quaaludes. It was one scary sounding drug.

When we did heroin we bought it in a very pure form and would enjoy it from Friday afternoon until Sunday afternoon throwing out whatever was left at that time. We figured that that was one way to avoid becoming addicts (or at the very least it would prevent us from starting our week off under its influence).

"I wish we could do speedballs, man," Fred reminded us for the fifth time. Fred Godfried was one of my best friends as well. "You want a Quaalude?" I asked Fred.

"Fuck no," he answered. "Are you fucking nuts? I'd never take Quaaludes with smack."

"You think it's dangerous?" I asked.

"No," he laughed, shaking his head. "It's a waste of a 'lude." Fred was also one of my most knowledgeable friends. He was an aggressive guy which I admired. He loved to get into a fight. He wasn't as big as a lot of my friends but Fred was strong and muscular, never taking shit from anyone.

He stopped to re-light the joint going around the circle we formed on Michael's bed. He almost singed his handlebar moustache in the process.

A giant squeak jumped from my throat. Two quieter more melodic squeaks followed in rapid succession.

"What song is that, Golden?" Greenberg laughed at his great joke. I ignored him. These remarks about me were not my favorite jokes.

"So, no coke as a mixer?" Fred chimed in. I shook my head.

So after snorting our Friday night drug of choice we spent our evening under its effects, staring at our shoes and nodding off. We slept where we sat, waking periodically but seeing very little. It was a joyous time.

"Anyone up for breakfast?" Elizabeth asked soon after sunrise.

"Nope," We all seemed to answer simultaneously and then laughed as though this were the funniest thing that had ever been said by any of us.

"None of you are hungry at all?" Elizabeth continued. "The bakery on Greenwich opens in about an hour. They have great croissants. I'll go get them." Richie looked at his watch.

"I've got to go," Richie said.

"What are you talking about? We thought you're hanging out with us for the weekend," I replied, making sure to hide my disappointment.

"Can't Thought you knew. I've got to pick up Virginia and the dog. We have to go up to Connecticut."

"What s up there?" I asked.

"We're looking at a place to buy. Tom's going too."
Virginia was Richie's girlfriend and Tom his best friend.

"For what?"

"A small farm. I told you about it before."

"I don't think so."

"We're thinking of growing our own," he said.

"What?"

"Alfalfa...idiot.."

"A pot farm?"

"I'm sure I told you about this, Barry."

"You knew about this," Michael said.

"You can be in on it? I told everyone that." Richie said as if reminding us. "But I can't tell you where it will be or anything else.

"How much to buy in?" I asked wanting to be included and desperate for some serious attention from Richie.

"Fifteen-grand each. I've been reading about growing pot and been saving the seeds from the best pot I've had for over six months."

"Who else is in on it?"

"Tommy, of course. Virginia's brother wants in on it."

"I had no idea. When exactly are you doing all this?"

"We're doing it right away. But contingency money is always good and I'd cut you in for a full share if you have the money. But I can't wait for you to raise it."

"I know." I once again regretted that Michael and I lacked the foresight and will power to put away money for good investments like this.

"I'm not going in on it," Michael added in a suggestive tone.

"What about the winter?" I asked Richie.

"The farm we're buying has greenhouses and we're planning to start growing the pot indoors late fall. That way we can transplant them outdoors in the spring and they'll be ready to harvest by summer. We're going to transplant in the woods where the plants can't be seen and I'm keeping my dog up there to protect the farm from intruders. Someone's also going to stay there all winter as well. Have to really care for the plants."

Richie seemed to have it all figured out and I really wanted in. They were talking about making a small fortune the very first year and then selling the farm for another quick profit. My father was always a believer in real estate as a good investment.

"I'm not doing it," Michael reminded me. "I don't have the money and I have nowhere to get it."

"I'm getting most of the money from my father," Richie said. "Your father has money, Barry."

"Not to give to me for a pot farm."

"Why would you ever tell him it's for a pot farm?" Richie asked before giving me step by step instructions on how to secure the financing from my Dad to go in on his project.

UNE DEUX TROIS

I tried to not think about my future "fundraising" issue and to instead concentrate on this evening. I liked to take downs during the day and did quite often. I could relax with them. They would calm me down. And today they helped me look forward to my evening date. My sister had fixed me up.

I could never understand why Ellen couldn't learn to disregard personality when judging someone's physical appearance. Both my mother and my sister seem to have this fixation about wanting me to be with someone vivacious and seemed to not understand that I didn't care about vivacious but I did like nice tits. I'd rather save vivacious for middle age. After all, I was only twenty.

I pushed up my left shoulder and tried to rub the back of my neck with it. I then jerked my head to the right quickly and tapped my pants again three times quick succession and tugged my dick gently, sliding it over so that it would point down my other pants leg. When I reached Une Duex Trois I hopped up the four steps leading inside.

I felt completely out of sorts, so average. I was average everything; average height, average weight, average looks. My hair was curly but not too curly and my nose was sort of large, not too large, but for some reason it felt larger tonight. I wiggled it as if checking that it was still there. I was dressed in all black and I eyed the beautiful women at the bar wishing that any one of them was my blind date, Hope. I was told that Hope was my sister's best friend's sister-in-law's college roommate's sister and naturally assumed that if she was accepting this blind date that she must be a dog.

I realized immediately that my selection of Une Deux Trois as a meeting place was a mistake. It was so wide open. The interior decorator had the ceiling painted with clouds that looked like huge cotton balls; the only thing missing was the Calamine Lotion. I wore Calamine way too often as a kid. I felt closer to Calamine than to any moisturizer on the market.

Une Deux Trois was very trendy and I felt more and more out of place as I squeezed my way through the crowd at the bar to get my drink. Can I buy you a drink? I smiled to myself pretending to talk to the woman next to me. My name is Barry Golden. Would you like to fuck?

I ordered a scotch and the bartender took care of me without looking up. I took a quick sip from my lonely drink and shook my head again with a quick jerking motion. Une Deux Trois was one of New York Magazine's recent Best Bets. But so was a Vietnamese restaurant just off Canal Street where all they served was fish head stew. I imagined that people must be lined up all around the block for that!

I turned my body toward the bar to rearrange my privates and sneak in a quick tap. I looked around for Hope and squeaked. The people near me glanced around trying to find the source of the peculiar high-pitched sound they'd just heard.

Hope did sound attractive on the phone but, then again, I'd had more than my fair share of experiences scheduling dates with voices, none of them satisfactory. They had been learning experiences and so I had asked Hope for a more detailed description.

She described herself as a green-eyed brunette with an hourglass figure. She said that she was adventurous and creative. Her answers sounded practiced. Ellen told me that she once met Hope and that she was extremely nice and that Ellen thought she was very attractive. My sister also told me that if I didn't like her taste in women then I should stop asking her to fix me up with her friends.

I jerked my shoulder up again and twisted my tight fist around in circles. I tensed my fingers around my glass being careful not to spill it. I saw an angel exiting the ladies' room; gorgeous. It wasn't Hope.

"Are you Barry?"

This on the other hand, was definitely Hope.

"Hope?"

"Yes."

"I didn't see you come in."

"But I did,"

"What?" I asked.

"Come in. I mean I'm here, aren't I?" she replied.

I wondered if any woman would be willing to describe herself as overweight and plain looking before accepting a blind date. Her hair was black and in tight curls. Her face round and deeply tanned. The good news was that the two large moles on her face, one on her cheek and one above her right eyebrow, were hairless. If her shape was indeed an hour-glass and I flipped her onto her head it could easily have timed six or seven hours.

"Were you waiting a long time?" she asked.

"No. I always come to restaurants two, three hours before dinner. It gives me a chance to wash my hands, have a drink, you know, relax a little."

She looked mortified.

"Didn't you say seven-thirty? How early did you want to meet? I was at work."

"I'm kidding," I replied. "I just got here myself. Would you like to have a drink before we sit down?" I asked.

"I'm not a big drinker. I'll have some wine with dinner."

"C'mon then," I replied chugging down what was left of my scotch and leaving the glass on the bar. "Let's sit down." The quicker we sat, the quicker we'd leave, I said to myself.

As we followed the maître d' to a table, Hope hooked her arm through mine. She was strong. I tried to gently swing my arm out of her grasp to disclaim her but couldn't loosen her grip. We took our seats.

"And monsieur. Something from the bar?"

"Yeah," I replied. "How about the blonde in the second seat from the left?"

I looked at the maître d', then at Hope, back at the maître d', then back at Hope.

"I was kidding, Hope. It was a joke."

Hope didn't crack a smile. "It really isn't polite to be with one woman and then to look around at others."

"It was meant as a joke. My timing was off. That's all. I don't know ... I thought it was funny." I looked up at the maître d' but there weren't any smiles there either.

"We'll have a look at the wine list, please," I said.

"Very good, sir." He turned and walked away.

I closed my eyes for a moment and tried to relax my face but failed. My chin jutted out first straight ahead and then it led my head flinging off to the side. I massaged the left side of my neck trying to mask my next tic.

"So how did you know it was me?" I asked trying to mask my peculiar mannerisms with some light conversation.

"You described yourself very accurately. You said that you'd be dressed all in black. You said you had long curly brown hair and that you would be wearing glasses with red frames. It's usually very hard to picture people from their own descriptions, but how many people in here are dressed in black with red eyeglasses? Besides, your sister said that you were very cute and she's right."

It's hard not to like a girl who showers you with compliments.

"She's prejudiced," I replied.

"She didn't have to say you were cute. I'd have gone out with you even if she hadn't said that."

I knew she spoke the truth.

"Monsieur." The wine list had arrived.

"So, what kind of wine would you like?" I asked opening

the list and going straight down the prices.

"I like anything," Hope replied. "For me it's the fun of sharing with a friend. What kind do you like?"

"Red."

"Oh…"

"You don't like red?" I asked.

"Red's fine," Hope replied sounding disappointed.

"Look, I'll order white. It's not that important to me whether I drink red or white."

"Order whichever you prefer."

"A bottle of Beaujolais, please." I closed the wine list.

"Is that a red wine?" Hope asked making the cutest disagreeable face she could muster. I wanted to punch her.

"Yes," I replied.

"Let's get a white wine," she begged.

"Make that the Pouilly Fume," I said to the maître d' mentioning the only white wine that came to mind.

"Very good, monsieur. Your waiter will be with you in a moment. His name is Walter."

I looked back at Hope. She had large teeth and a toothy smile. I knew she was eating almonds on the way to Une Deux Trois because she had a sliver stuck between her two front teeth. I couldn't stop looking at it and hoped that a sip of liquid would dislodge it.

"Here," I said picking up my glass of water. "To a pleasant evening."

"That's sweet," she replied lifting her glass and taking a sip. It didn't work and I considered that the almond sliver would be with us for most of the night. I pictured her in a taxi on the way here stuffing her face.

My eyebrows jumped up and down and my eyes blinked tightly. My nose seemed to leap quickly left and right and I tucked my lips between my teeth as if blotting lipstick. Then, forcing air against my trapped lips, they exploded outwards making a loud pop. A small wet particle of bread flew from the warm comfort of my mouth and made a splash landing on

Hope's cheek. It was time to forgive almond sliver.

"I'm sorry," I said reaching over to wipe the wet bread away. I was mortified.

"I can't believe I spit on you."

"That's alright," Hope replied taking her napkin and wiping her own cheek clean.

My head jerked side to side like an Egyptian dancer. I didn't even know how I learned to move my head that way.

"Why do you do that?"

"What exactly?" I answered quickly.

"Those tics. Why do you do them?"

"I don't know," I said uncomfortable with the question. I would have ignored her if I hadn't just spit on her face. Then again, if I hadn't spit on her she probably wouldn't have asked such a stupid question. "I don't know, Hope," I continued. "I don't do it because I enjoy it. They're habits, bad habits, that's all. I've been doing things like that since I was little. I don't know why. Nobody knows why."

"I go to a therapist," she said.

"That's really great," I said sounding defensive and sarcastic. "Look, I've been in therapy too, for years as a matter of fact; psychoanalysis. They originally thought that I had an anxiety problem, but the truth is I'm just not that anxious."

"So what do they think it is?" she asked again.

"I just told you. They don't know." I must have been raising my voice because people at the table closest to us were looking at me. "What?" I asked the table with the nerdy guy right next to me. "You want to join us?"

"They don't bother me," Hope said trying to draw my attention back to our conversation.

"Fuck them," I said.

"I mean your mannerisms. Tics don't bother me, Barry. I was just curious."

"Yeah, well, most people don't make it the topic of conversation," I said.

"They don't bother me a bit. A girl I roomed with for over

a year had tics."

I looked away from Hope, first glancing around the restaurant and then down at my plate. "Did you ever try to stop?" she continued.

"Of course I tried to stop," I snapped back. "What do you think? That I do it on purpose? Jesus Christ. You think I just never considered trying to stop?" I squeezed the words out in a hiss through my teeth. My head jerked around again and this time it was Hope averting her dark eyes; big and bloodshot, encircled with dark lines of black mascara. They were like bulls-eyes, little targets.

The sommelier came back with the wine followed by the waiter and I rushed us through the meal. The disturbing fact was that Hope's company wasn't half bad. Of course I didn't see us together in the future. "Would you want some dessert?"

"Something light," she replied tight lipped.

"How light?" I asked.

"I don't know what's on the menu," she replied.

Anger seemed to surface again for no reason. I fought with anger all the time. *She wants something light. Something small. Something on the side. How about a side of beef? That should do the trick, I thought.*

"You order for me, Barry. Something small. Something we could share."

I pondered over the three choices on the menu, kumquats, rainbow sherbet, or chocolate mousse.

"Let's share a little moose," I said, laughing silently at my little pun.

After dinner we went back to Hope's apartment on East 56th Street. I sat in her living room while she moved into the bathroom. I hoped she was freshening up to fuck.

The apartment was tastefully decorated all in earth tones with a large R.C. Gorman serigraph over the couch. The apartment seemed to have been touched by a decorator so I assumed Hope did pretty well working at Bergdorf's. I considered living with her just to stay in her apartment.

I sniffed in and out several times and tapped my dick. My head jerked and I let loose with my loudest and longest squeak of the evening.

I wondered ... if I had to stop twitching, if a revolver were held to my head, could I stop? I played this game a thousand times before. I pretended some assailant was holding a gun to my right temple.

"O.K. motherfucker! Don't move!" I would say to myself as I imagined being both mugger and victim. Like a volcanic eruption my features would explode in a wild dance on my face. I'd squeal several times successively trying to release my fear and tension as the hammer on the gun cocked and I prepared for the fantasized stillness of death to follow; the last tics of a dying man.

I heard the toilet flush and Hope joined me in the living room.

"I love your apartment," I told her. "Have room for a boarder?"

"I did all the decorating myself," she replied. I assumed she was lying.

"It's great," I reassured her.

"Thank you." I could tell that Hope had confidence in her apartment. The apartment must have worked wonders for her in the past. "So..."

"What?" I asked.

"So what do you do for fun? What's your place like?"

"It's a regular apartment. I mean it's not as well appointed as yours."

"I didn't mean that. I meant, you know, do you and your friends do drugs and stuff."

"Doesn't everyone?" I asked.

"You want to do some coke?" she asked.

"You have coke?"

"Oh, it isn't mine. My girlfriend left it here."

"Sure, I'll do some," I replied.

Hope returned swinging a plastic bag. Inside the bag she had what looked like a small cylindrical wad of aluminum foil that wrapped a small vial of cocaine containing tops a half gram. A tiny silver spoon was attached to the plastic top by a chain. "Wrapped for freshness," I said smiling.

"I don't do coke very often," Hope replied but her expertise at filling the spoon and stuffing it up her nose belied her claim. I watched her take another hit then she handed me the vial. I took a few hits as well and it went right to my brain.

"Good coke. Thank you."

"You could do more."

"Thanks," I replied taking two more quick hits before recapping the vial.

"What would you like to drink?"

"What do you have?"

"Almost everything. I never used to have anything, just like gin and Southern Comfort. I was going out with a guy who liked Southern Comfort. I had never tasted it. Then one night after we split up I tried a little on the rocks. Much too sweet for me."

I had difficulty believing that anything was too sweet for Hope.

"Do you have any cognac?" I asked.

"I don't know. Probably." Hope knelt down to look in her liquor cabinet. Her ass was quite a target. "Anyway, what I was saying was that my mother and father stayed here for a week recently and my father couldn't stand it. I mean that I had nothing here for him to drink. They don't understand that we don't entertain like they do. You know what I mean. We're not exactly a part of the dry martini generation. Is Canadian Club a kind of cognac?" She asked.

"No. Remy Martin, Courvoisier, even Hennessey," I replied. The cocaine was exacerbating my tics. I sniffed in and out for what felt like a hundred times. Every tic snapped in an amazing number of repetitions. My head swung side to side. I was sure if it hadn't been so well attached it would be pivoting on axis like in *The Exorcist.* I tapped and pinched my dick again and again. I spread my hands open, stretching the fingers out stiffly and then clenched them into tight fists. I snapped them up and down above and below my wrists. I clenched my thighs and banged them together as I squeaked a few bars of *Yankee Doodle.* I was glad Hope's head was in her cabinet.

"Anyway," Hope continued. "So Daddy went out and bought up the whole liquor store."

"Except, perhaps, for cognac," I said with a laugh trying to gain some control of myself. My head shook downward, chin to chest, and I hoped that Hope wouldn't turn around too quickly.

"I don't even know what I'm looking for. Come here. You look with me. At least you'll know it if you see it."

I took a deep slow calming breath and moved to kneel beside her peering into the liquor cabinet for the cognac. She moved back a little giving me the better view and leaned on my back as if waiting for a whistle for us to start wrestling. Her breasts, held in tight by her brassiere, pressed down on my back and I got hard.

"Do you see any cognac?" She asked as coquettishly as possible. She moved her head next to mine, cheek to cheek, as if helping me in the cabinet. Her hair was thick and slightly stiff against my cheek and her perfume far too sweet.

"Maybe your father hates cognac?"

"Could be," she replied seeming to not want to talk any further. Never say no, is what I said to myself as I turned my head around to face her. Our lips met.

As we kissed, Hope's mouth opened wide and her tongue began to dart back and forth like a lizard catching flies.

This was no way to kiss. I moved my head slightly to avoid her stabbing tongue and wrapped my right arm around her sliding it underneath her sweater and up her back. I unhooked her bra. The tension suddenly released and I could feel her breasts billow out like dough rising in a bread pan. I loved her huge tits but had to get away from her tongue. My defense was to create a wall of teeth and lips. It was impossible for her to pierce my armor. She moaned. Her moan lacked the sincerity a moan deserves. I hadn't yet earned that dramatic a response. I slid my hands down behind her and pressed her into me.

"Remind me to thank your sister," Hope said in husky tones.

"Shhh," I replied far more sincerely than Hope must have thought.

"Oh, that feels good," she continued.

"Don't talk," I replied. We rolled over on the floor as we humped. Hope drove her hips forward rubbing herself tight against me and simultaneously reaching for my belt. I unfastened her pants as well and we slid each other's pants down in tandem.

"Wait one sec'," Hope said reaching for her purse.

"What are you doing?" I asked.

"Better safe than sorry," she said handing me a condom. There is just no cool way to give a man a condom. I tossed the condom on the rug beside us.

"Mmmmmmm," I lied as I stroked her.

"Nice," she replied holding my dick in both hands. She began to rub her hands back and forth as if warming them up on a chilly day. It felt good. I wondered if she was at all concerned about how I would report on this date to my sister the following day.

I knew of only one sure-fire way to avoid her annoying kisses and after removing her panties, I snuggled my mouth in the curly hairs between her legs.

"Oh, God," she said loudly once again at what seemed to me an inappropriate moment. Her moans were in anticipation and not in response to my love-making.

My hands roamed her body. She had mountainous breasts which were great. I liked that. I squeezed one gently but she was unresponsive. She seemed to prepare for action as I donned the balloon and entered her.

"Oh...Uh, Uh...Uuuuh!" She gurgled driving her hips up hard against me over and over again but without any human rhythm. We were completely out of sync and she was way overactive. She threw her hips wildly up and down and up again. I was on a bucking bronco in this rodeo on East 56th Street. Our hips slammed together. I was getting bruised and it hurt. I held her hair like reigns so I wouldn't be thrown but I wanted off and fast.

"Ohh...yesss," I said faking an orgasm for the first time in my life. I made it brief and to the point. "Oh, yeah man." It was over quickly.

"How was it?" Hope asked me proudly. "We were really going there for awhile, weren't we?"

"We sure were." I couldn't imagine what tragedy in her life had caused this complete misinterpretation of fucking. I felt my pelvis checking for damage. I wondered whether or not I could sue if I were really injured in a sexual encounter. Everything seemed to check out. All my features scrunched toward my nose and then every part of me above my shoulders seemed to shake simultaneously. I squeaked once first then two more times quickly. The sounds came from deep inside my head. It was a different sound.

"Was that you?" Hope asked.

"Yes," I replied. "It's from the coke. That was good coke."

"You were great," she said but again I knew that she was lying. I had faked my orgasm quickly. It was over too quickly for her but it served her right for not knowing how to fuck; for going berserk.

"Yeah," I smiled grabbing my underwear and hopping up trying to hide my dissatisfied erection. I didn't want her to see that I really didn't cum. "I'll be right back," I said walking quickly to the john. Hope sat up watching me and seemed much fatter than before.

Alone in her bathroom I slid her mirrored medicine cabinet open quietly as the purposeless prophylactic swirled down the flushing toilet. Aspirin, Tylenol, Midol, dental floss (Butler's Unwaxed), Erythromycin (prescribed by her father, the doctor?), Ban Roll-On Unscented, Crest, Gilette Foamy, Comtrex, Valium and something unlabeled. Diet pills, perhaps. I thought about stealing a few of her Valium but since I was standing there naked holding only a pair of underpants, I had nowhere to hide them.

I took a washcloth from the tub and wiped my dick off with cold water my erection shriveling down. Curiosity still had the better of me. I opened the top drawer in her vanity and saw a hair brush filled with long black hair and dandruff flakes. There was an old band aid and a powder blue diaphragm case. It was empty and sat alongside a tube of spermicidal gel. So what was the big deal about the rubber, I wondered?

In the second drawer I saw a familiar sight; Quell. I immediately started to itch and sat down on the toilet looking down searching myself for crabs. I thought about Hope and wondered if I inadvertently ate any of these small crustaceans. I hoped she'd only used it long ago and checked the date on the tube. It had expired two years ago. She should throw it out.

I looked in the mirror staring back at my bloodshot twitchy eyes. I no longer had any plans to try and stay here. I wiggled my nose and shook my hands at my sides.

As I returned to the living room Hope was wearing her panties and sweater.

"I have to get home," I said.

"If you'd like to stay here," she replied as disinterested in my staying at her apartment as I was.

"No, but thanks," I replied dressing quickly. I imagined waking up next to her. I thought of her without make up. "I have to get home."

"I'm a terrible night driver too," she confessed.

"I never said I was a terrible driver. I'm on Fifteenth Street. Only the cab driver has to drive well."

"Oh, I forgot that. I'm sorry. But I am a terrible driver," she added quickly. "I always get sleepy." There was an awkward pause in the conversation. "Why don't you do a little more coke?" she suggested.

"I'm fine," I said. "Ahh, O.K. What the hell. I'll do a

couple of hits for the road. Just a little more," I hit each nostril once again. "I had a great time," I lied.

I knew that if I asked Hope for another date that she would turn me down.

"You could take the coke," she said. "There's not much left anyway."

I wondered if she meant that I already did too much of it. "No. It's yours," I replied.

"Don't be silly," she said. "Take it with you."

"That's very nice of you. Are you sure you don't want one last toot?" I asked her.

"No, you keep it." I tossed it into my pocket.

"Well, again," I said. "I did have a wonderful time. You were a lot of fun." I leaned forward and kissed her gently on the lips. I felt that my insincerity was transparent. "I'll call you," I lied again.

"Say hello to your sister for me," Hope replied.

"I will," I said gently smiling as I closed her door behind me.

EXTORTION

Two days later I was at home with my parents to execute my mission.

"So what's so important that I couldn't relax for two minutes after dinner?"

I looked at my father and doubted for a moment that I could go through with my plan. I thought that having a pot farm in Vermont was a great idea and I wanted to be a part of it. Without the money I was sunk. I wasn't planning to be an active partner, living on the farm and growing the crop. I could only imagine getting busted, how embarrassed my family would be. And forget prison. There was no way I could survive a trial and a prison term no matter how short it might be. The thought of being raped made me squirm. Prison was definitely not for me. So I realized the smartest way for me to participate in this deal was as a silent partner, an investor in the farm, an entrepreneur.

"I need some money, Dad."

"If you want to work here this summer speak to your mother. You know I would never object to whatever she says. She handles the nuts and bolts of the camp, Barry, not me."

"I don't need a job."

"Then I don't understand. You just need some money. I thought you were working as a waiter."

"I am." I never told them that the amount I earned as a waiter was just a pittance compared to my earnings as a drug dealer.

"Business is that slow? You said the restaurant was doing well. What the hell is the name of the place?"

"Steak and Brew. It has nothing to do with my job Dad, or any other job for that matter. Would you please just let me tell you what my problem is?"

He sat back in his easy chair now for the first time during our discussion, his arms resting on the stiff round arms of the chair. The chair had been in our den as long as I could remember and it was my father's favorite. He would sit in it every day after dinner to read Newsday and the editorials in the New York Times. It was where he seemed to study for his conversations the following day. At the dinner table, when David and I lived at home, my father would review and rehash that day's current events in spite of our lack of interest. It seemed the he was trying to perfect his recollection for his future conversations. It was his pre-test.

For his comfort my father had a table to the left of his chair. It was round with small drawers beneath the tabletop. These drawers contained all the dangerous things that children shouldn't touch like lighter fluid, books of matches and my father's utility knife. The table could rotate but no one ever turned it except to show people how easily it could turn. Behind the chair was a built in bookcase painted white and filled with books about World War II and the Nazis.

Dad was totally obsessed with the war and the "Rise and Fall of the Third Reich." He spoke about Hitler all the time, about how Hitler was suspected to have Jewish blood and what a mesmerizing speaker he had been. He told me that Hitler could hold his arm out in a Nazi salute for hours as the German army marched in front of him. He went on and on about world-wide anti-Semitism, using the United States continually as an example. "If it hadn't been for Pearl Harbor we never would have even gotten into the war. Lindbergh 'that Nazi bastard' had been poised to take over here in the US if the Germans won the war." From the way my father presented the story I couldn't tell if he was frightened by Hitler or if he secretly admired him.

My father was afraid to serve during the war and had been terrified by the draft. He was actually asthmatic and would have been excused from service anyway but, nonetheless, he and my mother devised a secret plan for their own reassurance. As the story was told to us, my mother handed my father a brown paper bag filled with Dentyne chewing gum as he boarded the bus on the way to his physical. He had a violent allergy to Dentyne and proceeded to chew as many as fifteen packs during the bus ride to induce an asthma attack. By the time the bus arrived he needed emergency care. They didn't have to take his word about his condition or even take the time to read the thick file of doctor's notes he brought along.

This was one of life's great adventures for my father and he seemed to enjoy telling the story to friends. But other times he seemed equally embarrassed by the tale. When it came to serving in the armed forces we were a family of cowards, not pacifists. I believe that no one in my genealogy had anything to do with the military all the way back to the Iron Age, forget the World Wars, Korea and Vietnam. We were the gatherers not the hunters.

"Please just listen to me, Dad," I said, unable to hide my discomfort.

"All right," he said looking hurt as if I'd just told him to shut up. "What's the problem?" I finally had my father's undivided attention. He spread his fingers out and gripped the arms of the chair.

"I owe some money."

He was expressionless and waited for me to continue. I knew that like me, he had a fairly constant urge to speak.

"I need to borrow money. I lost some money and I have to pay it back to some people."

"How much do you owe?" He asked. "And how did you lose it?"

This was much harder than I anticipated. He was already uptight and I hadn't even begun to tell my biggest lies. I couldn't look him in the eyes.

"Fifteen thousand dollars," I told him quietly.

"What did you say?"

"I said fifteen thousand dollars."

"Fifteen thousand dollars?"

"Yes," I said gaining some strength and looking up but still avoiding his eyes.

"Do you know how much fifteen thousand dollars is?" He asked incredulously.

"I think so, Dad. I mean, I'm the one who lost it."

"Fifteen thousand dollars?"

"Please, don't say it so loudly. I don't want Mom to know. I'm talking to you now, not her."

"Do you think for even one minute that I would loan you fifteen thousand dollars without your mother knowing? How does someone your age owe fifteen thousand dollars, and to whom? I want to meet the idiot who loaned it to you in the first place."

My heart was racing and I ticced mercilessly. But I had to go on.

"I was stupid."

"I imagine that. But maybe you can be a little more specific."

"I borrowed it."

"Don't talk to me like I'm an idiot too. Who loans a kid fifteen thousand dollars?"

"I'm not a kid."

"OK," He replied. "Just a stupid young man. Let's not talk in circles. I don't like this."

"I realize that."

"Why did you need this money in the first place and who do you owe the money to?"

Even though I was telling him lies, I didn't want to answer his questions. This was brutal for me and I considered backing out. I squeaked and grimaced, snapping my head back and forth. I waved my hands, shaking them loosely on my wrists. It was apparently a new tic and it felt as though I was waving good-bye to any remnant of decency or principals I had left. I squeezed my words out.

"I lost the money gambling and I owe it to the bookies who loaned it to me. They want their money and they've threatened me. I'm frightened and I don't know what to do."

I don't know where I found the balls to say this to my father. He was expressionless for a moment just rubbing the side of his nose with his index finger and staring at me. I felt as though I'd struck him; that I'd struck my own father hard and in the head. He removed his eyeglasses and leaned in close to me, his eyebrows inching down toward the bridge of his nose. He had soft dark brown eyes with small sacks beneath them that had begun to show age on his otherwise wrinkle free face. He needed a shave. I looked at the black and gray stubble on his soft cheeks; cheeks I could never get near.

"I can't believe you're that stupid," he said.

"Well, I guess I am." There was no retreating now. "I have to bring them the money or they said … you know what they said." My father didn't answer. "I have to bring them cash." I squeaked a few notes, blinked my eyes and popped my lips. He was probably more disgusted by my tics now than ever but I couldn't stop. I felt awful. "They want small bills." I said, thinking that this sounded believable. "And I've only got two days to pay them."

He paused and studied me carefully.

"You know this sounds like bullshit." He looked me directly in the eyes trying to read me. "How could any sane person lose fifteen thousand dollars gambling? How? Explain this to me."

"You don't follow any sports," I said thinking I could ease him into my story. None of us Goldens were athletically inclined but I was the best pretender. As a young child, when I wasn't alone in my room singing along with Gordon MacRae to the album "Oklahoma," or dancing in ballet class with my cousin Carole, I could shadow box quite well and pretend I was tough.

"Fifteen thousand dollars!" He repeated. "You're that stupid?" We sat for moment in silence.

"I suppose so." I felt ashamed of something I hadn't even

done.

"Rose!" My father shouted calling my mother. "Rose!"

"Upstairs." she replied from the distance.

"Please come down here."

"We don't have to include Mom in this," I pleaded.

"You think not?" His voice was cold. "She shouldn't know what an idiot she has for a son?"

I sat in silence, my tics as always getting the better of me.

"Do you think I have to understand all about sports to realize that you were betting on which team would win or lose? I don't have to grow my hair as long as yours in order to know how it will feel on my neck. What do you think?"

"I'd rather not think about it," I replied.

"You mean you'd rather not think? Makes sense. Why change direction mid-stream?"

I heard my Mom's footsteps as she came downstairs.

"Why don't we forget the whole thing? Leave Mom out of this and just forget it. I know what I did was really stupid and I can figure a way out of it. I can."

No comment from my father. He was looking past me, waiting for my mother to join us. He didn't even hear what I just said. He didn't want to look at me anymore. My mother arrived.

"Rose, pull up a chair and join us. You should participate in this. You should listen to what Barry has to say."

"Forget it, Dad."

"No," my father was emphatic. "Unfortunately I can't! I can't leave things here."

"What is going on?" My mother asked sitting down on a hassock. "Are you two fighting?"

" Barry owes someone some money."

"That can happen," she added.

"Rose. Your son owes some 'gangsters' fifteen thousand dollars. This is the good news he's been sharing with me."

"What are you talking about?" My mother focused on me as I squeaked and snapped my head. "That's not true. Is it?" I was in too deep. I didn't know how I could back down now. I swallowed and squeezed my eyes tightly shut. Was this a tic or an effort to disappear?

"Your son has been betting on sports games, losing money and apparently borrowing from some bookie thugs to cover his losses. Assuming that this is true, Rose, your son is an imbecile!"

At least he got part of it right. I did feel like I was her son and hers alone; especially right now.

"Is this true, Barry?" My mother asked me.

I didn't want to answer. This was my mother for Christ's sake. But I had to go on.

"Yes, it's true," I replied.

"Fifteen thousand dollars!" My father reminded us all.

"How will you ever pay them, Barry?"

"Oh no, Rose. That's the good part. He'd like *us* to pay them."

"I have to pay them back, Mom." I was looking down at our gray low-piled rug. "They, they threatened me," I lied.

"Oh, my God." She replied.

"I can almost buy a new Cadillac for fifteen thousand dollars!" My father chimed in.

I looked at my parents and felt unwanted. They never wanted me. My mother wanted a baby girl and who the fuck knew what my father wanted. I'm what they got. My brother made them boastful. I embarrassed them.

"I'd like you to leave mother and me alone now to discuss this. That is, unless, you've left out some salient information that we should consider."

I could see my father thought I wouldn't know the word salient. I did.

"I have to pay them the money and I have to pay them now. They're serious and I'm afraid. I'll pay it back to you. I promise I will."

"That must be some job you have as a waiter at Steak and Brew if you'll earn enough there to pay back fifteen thousand dollars. I'd like that job."

I wanted to tell them waiting tables was a cover. I enjoyed it but it was a cover. I did very well as a drug dealer; just didn't save. I should have. They tried to teach me to save but I never did.

"I'll go upstairs. I'll go to my room."

"Oh, Barry," my mother said with gut felt disappointment in her words. I was in a bad place with no wiggle room. I got up from my seat and walked upstairs passing another bookcase filled with ageing books and their torn yellowed covers. I took hold of the banister and pulled myself the rest of the way to my room. I had no desire to eavesdrop on the frightened conversation my mother was engaged in.

The room I grew up in had never taken on any personality. I'd contributed to the lack of style in my room in the same way that I'd contributed to the lack of style in my life, through inactivity and thoughtlessness, real care-less-ness. I didn't seem to care; or rather cared about the wrong things. I never had an opinion about decor. I accepted what was given to me and that was that. I had been an opinion-less child who was now up to no good.

Other kids tacked up photos of their friends and posters of their heroes. Their bed linens and covers had themes. They probably helped select them. The only difference between my room and a guest room was my small single bed, and frankly, that was just an inconvenience as I had been having sex in it since I was sixteen. *"Better at home in a bed than in the backseat of a car in an alley somewhere"* was what my mother told me before I brought Andrea home to fuck. Skinny Andrea with her blouses damp with perspiration. Thursday nights she'd come over to "study." *It's nice to meet you Andrea,* my parents said the afternoon they first met her. They knew our plans as we walked upstairs.

I looked down at the light blue bottom sheet on my bed and the thinly striped red and green one folded neatly around a brown quilted cover. I plopped myself down and was thankful for the two pillows that smelled of childhood safety. There was nothing hanging on my walls and there never was.

There was, however, a ton of childhood clutter all over the desk, in the drawers, and on the shelves. I'd sworn to go through that stuff many times. Everything was a mess, complete disarray, except for the pencils and pens which were always neatly lined up, touching side by side, all perfectly parallel to one another and perpendicular to the edge of the desk. This had always been the way. I had outgrown the room but didn't want it to go away.

My father built my desk and shelves as he had most of the cabinets and shelves in our house. And as was his wont, nothing was quite complete; desk drawers that fit but were difficult to open and no doors on my cabinets (which is why they were shelves). In our kitchen, the cabinets had simple doors and hardware but lacked the magnets to keep them closed. They were swollen shut in the summer from the humidity and swung open unpredictably all winter long. That was one quality we shared, Dad and I. Neither of us ever fully completed a task.

I was restless because of what I'd just done to my parents. Would I get the money? What were they saying? I got up and looked through the shelf over my bed and found a note hidden carefully under some magazines. My father wrote it and slipped it under my door after an argument we'd had several years ago. It was the only thing I had in his handwriting and I overvalued it. I remembered the occasion. I couldn't remember what the argument was about but I did remember the hurt that turned into rage. I think my Dad was too busy to come to some crappy school concert. I accused him of never caring, of not participating as a father. Then came this note; the same sentiment I received periodically throughout my life.

Dear Barry,

I must tell you that I was very disappointed with our conversation. I wanted to and would have come to see you but I had a very important meeting with Ira Cohen about some difficulties we are having regarding the renewal of one of my insurance policies. But I must tell you this, Barry. I may not have been the kind of father who would take you to ballgames or play football with you and your brother but it is with great confidence that I tell you that there has been no time in my entire life that I didn't act in my full capacity as your father with regard to any and all decisions about your upbringing and your welfare.

Love,
Dad

PS Mother reminded me that your birthday's coming up soon and I also want to be the first to wish you a very happy birthday.

"Barry?"

They were outside my door. I jumped up off my bed quickly stuffing the note from my father back under the magazines. He would never know I kept it.

"Yes."

"It's us; mother and Dad. We'd like to come in?"

This was it; the shit was about to fly off the fan.

"Would you rather I come downstairs?" I answered quickly sitting down in my chair so that it would look like I had been busy doing something. That was a habit I couldn't break.

"It's time to talk," my father said opening my door.

"We want to talk to you," my mother added.

"I know this is a terrible thing." My head jerked back and my hands flew up. They flailed. I must have looked like I was trying to mimic a horse rearing and was embarrassed because my parents had never seen my hands flail like that. Shit! I never did. However, being used to sudden motions from me, they pretended not to notice this new tic.

"I'm not sure that you do. This is very difficult for your father and me."

"If you don't have the money…"

"The money is the least of it, Barry." I took her statement as a sign that they would come through and help me out of the jam they thought I was in. "It's how could you get involved with something like this? Is this how you've been spending your time?"

I wondered how they would feel if I told them that I wasn't really a gambler but a drug dealer instead. "No," I answered.

"Well if it isn't, Barry, why do you owe someone fifteen thousand dollars?"

"It just happened."

"Just happened?" my father interjected, shocked by the ridiculousness of what I'd just said. "What did you do? Bet fifteen thousand dollars on one horse? One race?" He asked, never considering that I might have bet on anything besides horse racing.

"I don't watch horse racing let alone bet on it."

"And don't be a wise guy!" he snapped.

"Did we do something, Barry?" my mother asked. "How could you have such poor judgment?" She turned to my father. "I wouldn't mention this to anyone," she told him as an additional indication of how humiliating this would be for our family. At least this time I understood why.

Our family never mentioned anything even moderately negative about ourselves. We lived as if isolated on an island. My eyes closed tightly and I squeezed my forehead with one of my hands. I wanted to sit still and I tried to imagine how my mother felt.

How do you talk to your greatest disappointment in life? Your greatest embarrassment? What do you tell it? How do you make it go away quietly? My sudden squeak was loud and shrill. It repeated itself three times and I started tapping my dick finally pinching it over to one side of my pants. My head shook side to side and my hands swiveled around my wrists.

"Move over to your bed so that we can sit down too." My father spoke to me in a tone that clearly said I should have thought of this common courtesy first. I was being rude in addition to everything else. "We'd like to sit as well if you don't mind."

I sat on the edge of my bed and my mother dragged my straight backed desk chair over the vinyl tiles and sat down. My father completed our triangle sitting down on the only plastic Papasan chair in the Western Hemisphere. He wouldn't look at me as he spoke. His eyes could slide away from me like he was a blind man.

"I'm not going to discuss why you did what you did or how stupid I think it is or what an embarrassment this is for your mother and me. I'm going to take care of this thing." I never knew when my mother was included in his thoughts as he randomly jumped between the subjects I and we in his conversation.

I hated what I was doing but it seemed I was getting the money and this is what I was trying to accomplish. Was this the feel of success? I was a prick but a prick who was about to make a lot of money.

"We'll get the money, but there will be changes. You will repay every cent that we give you."

"I understand that." I would be able to pay it back with an awful lot of interest but I couldn't say that! I was hitting a home run. "What do you want me to do?"

"We haven't decided all of that yet but don't dare think that things won't be changing. You act like a stupid kid and you'll be treated like one!"

"We have to make changes, Barry," my mother added. She seemed unsure of how to participate in this. She seemed in shock.

My tie-dyed T-shirt felt sticky and my jeans too tight in the crotch. I could look my parents in the eyes now. I wanted to hear the rest. I was excited.

I knew my plan. I'd never go to the pot farm. I'd stay far away, reap the rewards and never get busted. The door downstairs slammed shut and we knew it was my little sister coming home from school. Mom got up.

"I'll keep Ellen downstairs." She looked at me now, no longer worried about me, but angrily for the first time this afternoon. "Your sister will not know anything about this! Do you understand me, Barry? She's not to know anything! She looks up to you!" My mother left the room to head my sister off at the bottom of the stairs.

Ellen did look up to me. She'd have wanted to say hello right away. I loved her too. She was still too young to be aware of all my flaws. I lit a cigarette and pulled my ashtray closer to where I was sitting.

"Can't you wait to smoke until after this conversation?" my father asked.

"I haven't smoked in hours." My head snapped from side to side. I blinked, squeaked and scrunched my face. I took a few quick drags on my Winston and stabbed it out in the ashtray. I exhaled and forced any excess smoke out of my lungs.

I rolled my wrists around and around. I felt like Art Carney warming up at the piano.

"Even one cigarette a day is too many. You might as well dig your own grave."

"Oh." I replied. We'd had this conversation many times before and I suppose any conversation was better than the issue at hand.

"You heard me," he added.

The remarks that formed the foundation of our home were weird threats that became repetitive comments and meaningless sayings. *"If you don't stop teasing her I'll cripple you." "Touch that and I'll break your fingers." "If I hear anything like that again I will beat you within an inch of your life." "If you're that thirsty, swallow spit."* While we all hoped these expressions and threats weren't true it was hard to feel certain when you were only a child.

It was obvious that neither my father nor I were eager to continue our conversation about the fifteen thousand dollars.

"Mother is very worried about you, Barry. It's not simply the money. It's about your lack of judgment. No one in our family gambles."

"Grandma and Grandpa," I responded compulsively. It was almost impossible for me to leave well enough alone.

"Grandma and Grandpa play cards. They play bridge! You want to know who bets on sports? Christians do. That's who. And God knows that's not how we raised you."

"Raised?" I thought. My head jerked back and forth then snapped down hard, chin to chest. I felt as though I pulled a tendon or something behind my neck and rubbed it with my hand as my nose wiggled and I squeaked three times.

Some evergreen branches tapped against my bedroom window and my father looked outside. He was stuck with me; this kind of a son.

"Just stupid," he said quietly this time.

"I'm not stupid." I replied. I pinched my nose and forced air into my ear canals. Maybe I was getting a cold but I was sure it looked like a brand new tic to him.

"You want the money," my father said again more quietly than usual.

"I need the money."

"O.K. So I have the money," he replied. "Now, how do you plan to pay these, these men?"

"I can take care of that."

"Very good," my father said with a hint of sarcasm. "May I ask how? How will you take care of it? What do you mean when you say that you'll simply 'take care of it.' You'll simply pay them?"

"And within a few months I'll pay you back."

"How could you be so stupid as to get involved with people like this?" He wondered aloud.

"I don't know, Dad," I replied, snapping my head and sniffing in and out a few times.

"Well, here are the facts. *You* won't be giving them anything?"

"What do you mean by that? You just said that you're giving me the money? What am I supposed to do with it? I can't mail it in." I was very confused.

"Do you think I am so stupid that I would hand you fifteen thousand dollars in cash?"

"They won't take a check."

"I don't plan to give them a check. But I don't plan to give you the cash either."

"Then I don't…"

"*I* am going to give them the money. I know some people too and I plan to go with the people *I know* and give your 'friends' the money personally."

"You can't. They don't know you! They don't want to meet you."

"Well that's the only way they're going to see any money from me. I want to make sure that when I pay them that it's over!" He was starting to raise his voice. "I know how this stuff works, Barry, and I want to know that when they get this money that that is it! I want to go to them with the people I know and make sure this is over! I don't want to hear about additional interest from them or any other nonsense."

"It will be completely over when I give them the money, Dad."

He spoke emphatically now. I never heard him speak like this before; quietly but emphatic. This wasn't my Dad. "You will *never* be giving them the money personally. You will give me names, addresses and telephone numbers and I will handle it from there. *You* will not be paying them. I will be."

He was crazy. I didn't believe my father knew any tough guys, not my Dad.

"They'll never do it. They don't want to meet any new people."

"I find that hard to believe. In the first place I have a hunch that they'll be glad to meet the person giving them the money you owe them."

"They'll think that you're a cop. That it's a set up. They could kill me."

"And in the second place," he interrupted, "they are businessmen like any others. They want their money and, who knows, maybe they'll think I'm a future gambler; an idiot, like my son."

I ignored this angry insult and tried not to take it personally especially since I hadn't really lost the money we were discussing.

"They want *me* to pay up. They don't want to meet my father. Jesus, Dad."

"Don't you have any idea how much fifteen thousand dollars is? You don't just pick this kind of money off trees. It's a lot of money. Barry. I don't know where these ideas of yours come from but you don't seem to have any concept of money."

"I can't pay them like that. You might as well not be giving me the money."

"It's the only way I will give it to you. I can have it for them as early as tomorrow. Let me know what you want me to do."

"Who's your friend?" I asked mildly suspicious.

"What?"

"Who's your friend? The guy you plan to go with."

"No one you know. Remember," he said refocusing the conversation. "I need some names and a way to contact them."

He was finished with the conversation. He got up from his seat and looked me directly in the eyes.

"Whenever you decide, let me know what you want to do." He seemed bold and confident with his decision. He left my room closing the door behind him without even so much as a glance back at his second son.

We spoke no further about it before I left for the city.

I chain-smoked home to my apartment and was still smoking cigarette after cigarette as I sat with my back against my kitchen wall. I couldn't believe my father! Did he see through me? Was I so obvious in my lies? There was no way he "knew somebody." Maybe he was calling my bluff but that wasn't like my Dad. And if he didn't think I was bluffing he must really think I'm dumb; *really* his idiot son. I couldn't tell him I was making an investment. That's what I should have told him. That it was for a real estate investment. But then I knew he'd have wanted to get involved. He'd want to know every detail, after all, that was his thing. He loved to buy houses. Buy 'em and rent 'em. That's what he did. He never sold them, just kept buying and renting. He had a lot of houses and collected a lot of rent.

It seemed that getting the money from my father wasn't going to be as easy for me as it was for Richie and the others. Their Dads believed in them. They didn't have to check their every move. This whole situation I was in really stunk, and worse, I did look stupid. I rolled a joint and took a few hits before lying down to take a nap. Fuck me! Fuck me, Jesus.

I woke up a few hours later and saw darkness outside my window. I got up, went down to the kitchen and ate some pound cake and ice cream before getting undressed and going back to bed. I would have toasted the pound cake but even lacked the patience to wait and stand by the toaster oven.

I thought about giving Michael a call but knew that Michael wouldn't be home. These were the crazy hours that we 'roamed the streets'. Besides, speaking with him would be a waste of my time. I could count on him to have some crazy inane solutions that would undoubtedly make things worse and sink me deeper into the hole I was already in. This was not my finest hour. I smoked another cigarette and then some pot. I took a Quaalude and went to sleep even before feeling its sublime effects. I left early in the morning leaving them a note that I'd call later in the day.

CONFESSION

By the next day in my apartment I was freaking out. I anxiously called my mother who thankfully was the person who answered the phone. She was in a panic and I was desperate to help her but too deep into my plan.

I needed time to think and tried to reassure her that everything would eventually work out. I knew it would since I wasn't in real danger anyway. Obviously, I was in this shit so deep I couldn't share that with her. Her description of my father suffering about this was over the top and I popped my first Quaalude of the day.

"Your father is frantic, Barry. He's barely slept."

"Who's his friend? I asked sincerely. He told me he had some tough friend to go with him to pay the money." I asked. I was so curious and found it difficult to believe him. My father wasn't the kind of guy who could have survived 'the old neighborhood.'

"Can you hear me, Barry, or are your ears stuffed with cotton!"

"I hear you. I'm sorry, Mom. I hear what you're saying."

"Where is Daddy now?"

"Upstairs He's trying to nap. He's frightened, Barry. He's frightened for you. He's frightened for us. You're forcing him to meet people he doesn't want to meet. I don't care what he told you. I can't live with this hanging over my head. We don't know what to do."

This was bad. Worse than I ever thought it would be. It was

torture. How could I not have anticipated so dramatic a reaction? "Fuck me," I murmured quietly but apparently it wasn't as quietly as I thought.

"Don't talk like that."

"I'm sorry…" I said. I was going to have to forget about the farm. I wasn't going to be able to work this out with the money. My Dad had outsmarted me whether he "knew people" or not. My heart was beating fast and it was difficult to take a deep breath.

"Please…" The words came out but they had no meaning. "Please, Mommy."

"Please what?" She asked.

"I don't know. I can't do this to you guys." I was in distress and felt like dirt.

"We will work this out, Barry. It's just such a terrible thing; to be in this position…your Dad…if you could only see him."

I was at a loss, out of things to say. Just get out of this, I thought. I was speaking with my *mother* and wringing out her love.

"I've never seen Daddy like this, Barry. I know it will work out in the end but it's killing him. I can see it."

"Tell him that it's over. I know how to handle it. I figured something out and I don't need money from you guys. Please go tell him it's over. Tell him to get some sleep."

"I will do no such thing. Don't simply tell me that it's over! That doesn't help. Daddy's going to take care of this. I told you that. It's just that……"

"No, Mom. Listen to me. I really have a way to make this all go away. Please trust me."

"We did, Barry. We trusted you. But this is simply much too much. It's frightening; too much to handle."

I was light-headed and unclear, my heart raced and my eyes tightened. Stop, stop, stop.

"I have to call you back," I couldn't even make eye contact with the phone!

"Don't do something stupid, Barry. Something more stupid than you already have getting into this mess."

"Let me get off the phone, Mom. I'll call you right back. I promise. Please let me call back."

"This can't go on and on, Barry. Call me back as soon as possible." My mother said...loving, irritated, frustrated, frightened and in pain.

"I will. Let me go." I pleaded.

"Call me back," she said as she hung up the phone.

My eyes were closed and I tried a deep breath but my throat sealed it off. In a moment or two I managed to breathe but couldn't slow down my heart. Deep breaths, eyes closed, head down...I tried to gain some composure.

It was time. Six minutes had passed and I could see her standing by the phone waiting for me to call. There was no chair by the phone and she had to stand there shifting her weight from one foot to the other, watching the phone as if she'd see it ring before hearing it; standing and waiting for my call.

I lifted the handset, dialled, and sat up stiffly when I heard the click. It didn't ring, I thought. It caught me by surprise. I rested my elbows on my thighs supporting my head in my hands, telephone pressed to my ear.

"Hello."

"Mom?"

"Yes, it's me."

"I know." We were silent. Perhaps I had nothing to say. She couldn't say anymore to me. I was certain of that. "Please, Mom. I'm so sorry."

"I know you are. We're going to take care of this," she gently tried to reassure me. "We'd never let you down. We love you, sweetheart."

"Jesus," I said to myself. "I know that, Mom. I do... I do. It's not that."

"Will you please tell me who they are and how to get in touch with them? And what we have to do? I have to tell Daddy.

And you're right. He doesn't have a tough guy friend. He wishes he did. We're going to go together, the both of us. They'll be happy to get paid. It will be over and we won't even tell them who we are. We're going to ask them for some sort of receipt, some kind of proof that we paid the debt. They'll give us something."

God forgive me. "It's not that," I repeated. "You don't have to go."

She was firm but still loving as she said "Daddy will not give *you* the money. He will not. He has to be sure that this thing's over."

"I can pay them myself."

"What will you do? Borrow the money from someone else? No. You will not!"

"I don't owe them any money!" I spoke too loud. She said nothing. "I don't owe them any money. I don't owe anyone money."

"What are you talking about?" She was thoroughly confused. "What in God's name do you mean by that?"

"I mean I lied! *I don't owe anyone any money,*" I sounded loud, angry, as if I were arguing with her. This was all wrong. "I just needed the money, Mom. I wanted the money. I don't want it now. There are no evil men. I don't gamble. I'm not that stupid."

"I don't understand what you're saying, Barry," she said unconvinced and bewildered.

"Listen to me, Mother. I don't owe the money to anyone. O.K.? *There are no me! No gangsters. No loan sharks. No gambling!*"

"I still don't understand?" She asked now as uncomfortable as she was sincere.

I had to reach down deep. I don't know how deep but I had to find the sound, the sound of truth. It was a pathetic truth; an evil truth I'd buried from my parents but gleefully shared with my friends. It was an ugly truth.

"I lied," I finally told her choking on the words. Still she was silent. I wanted her to say something, something angry and nasty to show her disgust for my cruelty, for what I did to my only parents; to show disgust in me.

"Please Mommy. Talk to me. Whatever you say I deserve it."

She still didn't speak. A dead dreadful silence, and then, a dial tone.

I spoke with her again a week later but it barely touched on what I had done. We mentioned it and she told me how shitty she and Daddy felt about me, that it was despicable. I was despicable. My father never came to the telephone. We barely spoke for months.

PART THREE

I-6

PSYCHOANALYSIS

March, 1984

When I had first graduated from NYU I taught elementary school for six months but, for some reason, it only felt like a few hours out of my life. As I said, I still sold drugs but also worked weekends for Eleanor Cody at the Eleanor Art Company. I managed large art sales and after a while filled in as an auctioneer when necessary.

I was a wild auctioneer. Fearful that the audience would focus on my tics I was active, moving about, gesticulating all over the place, figuring if I just kept moving no one would notice a slight dick tap, head snap, wrist twirl or facial scrunch. Audiences enjoyed the most "animated" auctioneer anyone had ever seen and I was funny to boot! It was working out well.

I was thirty-two and deep in psychoanalysis with a physician named Dr. Brady. Four days a week, flat on my back. My drug phase was practically over with the exception of a few Quaaludes, a gram or two of cocaine every now and then which I shared with my girlfriend: Quaaludes, cocaine and a bottle of champagne every Sunday afternoon taking baths in our Jacuzzi and watching the Giants or the Jets on TV.

Deidre and I were as happy as happy can and in a comfortable routine. We lived together along with her two children who I was very fond of. It was difficult enough for me to experience anything close to what I imagined love to be. It's hard to love and be loved by two children who left the horror of a 'stepfather's prison' and traveled to a land of candy and elves at their father's home on weekends.

My mother liked Deidre and her kids but always fell back on the expression "I'm happy so long as you are happy." My father gave Deidre his opinions as well but shared little of his heart with them either. Then again I don't know that he ever uttered an emotional, unmeasured comment in his life.

It was virtually impossible for any 'outsider' to be genuinely accepted into our family. Shit…it was hard enough for my parents to bond with their own kids, my brother, my sister and me, so lots of luck to the strangers floating in and out of our lives. My personal relationships never smacked of permanence for me anyway so why should they for Mom and Dad?

I had originally tried to get accepted into Columbia Presbyterian's Psychoanalytic Institute. Dr. Albert Howard was my interviewing psychoanalyst.

I remembered staring out the window to steer him away from my tics. A thick moment of silence passed between us. "Is there anything else that you'd like to tell me?" Dr. Howard asked sincerely.

"Not really. That's about it." I replied. It was my third session with Dr. Howard. "So, what do you think?" I shrugged good-humoredly.

"Well, I don't think that you'd be right for our program."

Fuck you, I thought as I stared at him, but not because of his decision. It was a 'fuck you' for my situation. My life wasn't right and I needed to see someone.

He went on. "You're so angry, Mr. Golden, hostile, and clever. You need an experienced analyst; someone with more experience than the doctors training at our Institute."

I had very mixed feelings about this. On the one hand I was

obviously very fucked up. On the other he was telling me that I'm clever. I took that as a compliment.

"If you want me to look around, I'm certain that I can find someone with more experience to take your case. But it would be on a private basis, not through the Institute."

"How long would that take? I mean until you find someone."

"Perhaps a month. No more than six weeks."

It was longer than I had anticipated. I shrugged again not having any good choices.

Dr. Howard made some notes as I continued.

"There is one thing," I began lying through my teeth and shooting for the moon. I've been very anxious what with everything that's going on in my life and I have a lot of difficulty falling asleep. My friends have Tuinals and Seconals but they're barbiturates and addictive, plus, my friends obtain them illegally. They'd give me some if I asked for them but, to be honest, I don't want to take them." I paused. "There is a new drug on the market. I'm not sure what it's called but I think its chemical name is methaqualone or something like that. My girlfriend's physician prescribed it to her 'cause it helps her sleep but it's not habit forming. Maybe I could get a temporary prescription for that. I really don't know what they're called commercially," I continued as he, unbeknownst to him, was looking up Quaaludes in his PDR. If I couldn't get a shrink yet, at least I could try to score.

Dr. Howard found them in the book and they were still considered safe on the market. The PDR described Quaaludes as a fairly innocuous medication, a soporific. With my guidance on quantity, he wrote out a prescription for one hundred, three-hundred milligram Quaaludes renewable three times. The drug was not yet publicly abused enough for doctors to be clear about their recreational use. It was addicts and drug dealers who really made it their business to stay on top of these things. Quaaludes were already big business. Now, armed with the prescription I could carry around a bottle of as many as a hundred without the fear of getting busted.

The analyst Dr. Howard eventually recommended to me was his office mate. His name was Dr. Brady. He was a Yale University graduate who had then attended Harvard Medical School. He was a practicing psychoanalyst at Columbia Presbyterian Hospital and was exactly the WASP I could never be.

What won me over even more than his background was an incident during our first session. I tried the same stunt I'd pulled with Dr. Howard, but Brady was all over it. I remember him saying, "If you're having so much trouble sleeping what you should do is spend that time thinking about why you can't fall asleep. You'l eventually fall asleep. But there is no way that I will write a prescription for sleeping pills to a drug addict."

"I'm not exactly a drug addict." I said responding to his melodrama. He replied with a shrug. "You really won't give me a prescription?" I asked again.

"That's right."

"Even though I can't sleep?"

"I will not write a prescription for you at this point in time for anything."

"O.K." I said. "Then fuck it. I might as well tell you the truth. I don't need them anyway. I never had a problem sleeping. I was just trying to score. What the fuck, right? You win some. You lose some." I smiled first. Then he smiled a small one back. And that was the beginning of our relationship, a relationship that lasted for years but ended very abruptly.

It was three and a half years later. Brady was running late and I was in his small waiting room for almost fifteen minutes. I was really pissed when Dr. Brady finally got around to calling me in.

"It's already fifteen minutes into my session." I said.

"Sorry," he replied.

"Will you be able to run over at the end?" My jaw felt tight. I wiggled my nose and twisted my neck. My eyes blinked over and over.

"Not today." He was slightly out of breath. "I'd rather you sit on the chair today instead of lying on the couch."

"Why is that?" I asked trying to mask my anger.

"I want to talk to you."

"That's good. About what?" I said, getting up from the couch. There was a sharp edge in my voice.

"Sit down, Barry."

"I am!" I sat down as if sitting was an act of aggression. I sniffed in and out and twisted my hands around my wrists. I tensed one thigh then the other and tapped my dick a few times harder than I wanted to.

Dr. Brady looked at his watch.

"What? Are we running out of time?" I asked sarcastically.

"There are things we have to talk about. I want you to listen to me because this has nothing to do with you," he said. "I've decided to go back to school."

I didn't believe him. "So? Why are you telling me this? What are you going for your GED?" I laughed.

"No," he smiled.

"I don't think I was joking," I told him.

"I'm sure you weren't. But the truth is I don't want to continue in medicine."

"Good one," I said.

"This is so very important to me."

I was nervous now.

"I was accepted at Parson's School of Design. I've been sidetracked by medicine for too long now. It's not what I want."

He was in his fifties! I was certain he wasn't starting his life over. "So what are you planning to do? Go nights?"

"No, Barry. That's what I'm explaining. I'm going to go full time. I'm taking the summer off and then I'll matriculate in the fall. I'm giving up psychiatry."

My throat turned leaden; my stomach queasy. I couldn't even squeak.

"You're just leaving? You can do that? What about all your

patients?"

"Don't you really mean what about you?"

"Fuck you!"

"I can understand your anger."

"I've been coming here four times a week for the last three years," I said barely squeezing out the words.

"You'll be fine. If you find that you're having difficulties I'm giving you the name of another psychiatrist. Dr. Polakine. He continued. "He sees patients both privately as well as in group therapy. Group therapy might even be good for you at this point in time."

"Are you fucking crazy?!"

"You might want to try group," he repeated. "I think that might be good for you." Brady looked at his watch again. We were apparently out of time. Now that was a very quick session. He graciously didn't bill for it.

So I took a few years sabbatical having been weaned from four visits a week to none in a matter of minutes; cured by Dr. Kevin Brady with the simple stroke of a pen.

A few miserable years later I was back in therapy, but luckier this time. This guy didn't seem artistically inclined. My new therapist seemed fully devoted to his work. He wasn't pretending to listen to me while secretly dreaming about finding a future job in graphic arts.

He had also studied at Columbia. His name was Jonathan Wohl. Dr. Wohl was tall, much taller than I, and very kind. His only obvious difficulty seemed to be matching his socks. He chuckled when I told him about my early psychological evaluation and having been diagnosed as schizophrenic. He even knew the clinical psychologist who tested me.

Apparently at the time I was diagnosed as schizophrenic, schizophrenia was a catch-all diagnosis which really meant "we're not quite sure what's wrong with him but he's certainly all fucked up."

Over time I was diagnosed with clinical depression in addition to my hopeless tics. This neuorologic condition had its horrific, terrifying onset about a year into my treatment with Dr. Wohl and it was no joke. My tics were as bad as ever. Soon after throwing a few aggressive fits at total strangers with little provocation, I was additionally diagnosed as suffering from manic-depression. I tried Lithium but it made me stutter. So I was put on Depakote.

I was now taking 80 mg of Prozac, 15 mg of Valium, and 1500 mg of Depakote daily; enough meds to treat a horse. It was just too much and things still didn't seem right. Because of the amounts and levels of the medications I was taking Dr. Wohl suggested a drug washout at Columbia Presbyterian's mental health facility; its institution, the I-6 unit.

He felt that it would be safest there, especially if I fell into a serious depression during the process. But it was made clear to me that I would be going in as a voluntary admission. I was not being committed. My art business was slow and I had no other plans at the time so I agreed to go. Plus I needed the vacation.

CHECKING IN

I-6 is located in a building that specializes in diseases of the eye. I wished I were there for an opthalmalogical problem but I was not. There are six floors in the building. People with certain neurological or psychological problems are often put in buildings with innocuous names so that you can tell people you're in the hospital without telling them that you're playing a part in a real life version of *One Flew Over The Cuckoo's Nest*. The sixth floor in this building, I-6, is a "nut" house.

Of course, in my case, it was a voluntary admission. I wasn't dragged in off the street in a strait jacket or brought up from emergency but, nonetheless, I was frightened, anxious, and apprehensive.

As I entered the building I was in a stately, turn of the century atmosphere. Original solid mahogany paneling was everywhere. Paintings of the dead benefactors hung with great formality on the walls and watched me wander in. The lobby was furnished with old stuffed vinyl furniture that could no longer pretend to be leather. The colors were wrong, the seats cracked and torn. It was the same cracked vinyl we had at home when I was a boy; the kind that pinched bare skin when you got up. The stuffing was exposed on most of the pieces and in some cases oozed out along its beading. Reupholstery seemed a lost art. It's an odd mix when a hospital marries the Friars' Club.

My insides jumped as a little girl ran past me from behind, her tiny footsteps echoing in this grand room. Her mother followed carrying an infant in one arm and a shopping bag in the other.

Complete silence returned after they passed by. I felt even more alone but I had a secret security blanket with me: the cocky reassurance of knowing that my voluntary admittance somehow set me apart from the others upstairs.

While the others were nuts and belonged in I-6, I was merely a visitor for safety's sake, for a "washout". I was to be weaned off my plethora of medications and then, perhaps, set on a different more successful path of psychopharmacological treatment. It might be fewer medications or smaller doses of the same. Or I might wind up taking different, newer medications. But one thing was certain, I was a special case and that's the feeling I needed in this grand old lobby. It was as if I was entering some staid, private, restricted club, the basis for acceptance was a troubled mind.

A hospital employee sat at the desk to screen visitors and answer questions.

"Can I help you?" she asked.

"Yes."

"What?" she said too quickly.

"I-6." I replied.

"Visitor?"

"No."

She scrutinized me as if I was suddenly morphing. She studied me with a combination of fascination and pity, a newfound curiosity and, perhaps, just a dash of fear. Why was he checking into I-6? She probably thought I was entering as a regular patient. I wouldn't bother to explain.

"Name, please."

"Barry Golden."

All she had on the desk was a list of names. I knew mine was on it. She handed me a permission card and looked back down at her "work."

"You take the elevator to your right," she pointed with a jerk of her head in the direction of the elevators. "I-6," she said, her voiced rising suddenly as she notified the large black security guard in his neatly pressed uniform standing at full alert when he heard my destination.

Turning back to me she said, "When you get up there, you'll see a telephone to your left on the wall. Pick it up and then hang it up quickly. A buzzer goes off inside. Don't keep the phone off the hook for a long time because the buzzer stays on inside and they get rightfully annoyed. Just up and down. Someone will come to let you in."

I would remember to not anger "them" and to wait for "someone."

The security guard watched me closely as we boarded the elevator. These were the few unpredictable moments that made his days exciting. The elevator doors closed slowly and he pushed six. I could feel him watching me on the elevator as it ascended. My arms flung out slightly and my head pushed down as if an invisible stranger had just put me in a full nelson. I squeaked. He stepped back a bit as my teeth snapped together like a turtle snapping at fish. I felt a small piece of enamel break off one of my molars.

When the elevator stopped it took me a moment to step out. The doors closed and I was alone once again; alone in a cubicle with dirty white walls, quite different from the lobby. I wanted to be young again and living at home, my parents' responsibility.

My heartbeat quickened and I tried to relax by breathing more slowly. Straight ahead was the white entrance door with a small glass and chicken wire window. It was a type window that was impossible to break. I squeaked and snapped my head from side to side. I sniffed in and out and squeaked three more times quickly. I stood tall and peered through the glass, my hand over my head blocking out the bright fluorescent light above me. All I could see was another dirty white wall.

As I looked around the tiny security booth I was in, it looked more and more filthy with fingerprints and other dirty smudges all over the whitewashed sheetrock. The door to enter I-6 was old and needed painting as well but it was also thicker and stronger than the walls. It was all steel.

Just as I'd been told, the telephone was on the left wall near the door. I lifted the receiver and put it to my ear. It was cold and dead. It sounded so black I knew immediately that it hadn't been spoken through in years. But I did hear a buzzer go off somewhere inside. Why use a dead telephone as a signal that someone was in the box? Realizing the telephone receiver was in my hand and off the hook too long I quickly hung up. I peeked through the indestructible porthole window again and still saw nothing.

I waited a reasonable period for a response; about twenty seconds. Now irritated and impatient, I held the receiver off the hook and let the damn thing buzz away inside. An annoyed nurse and yet another strong black man, this one practically bursting through his crisp white uniform, unlocked and opened the door. He didn't seem like a security guard to me, and so, not knowing his role, I found him all the more intimidating.

The little nurse looked at me unpleasantly. "You only have to pick the receiver up once! We hear you immediately. You're the new patient?"

I noticed that the lock on the door had a keyhole on both sides and always needed to be opened with a key. I was at first surprised but then it made good sense. No doorknobs on exit doors here and the keys to everything were always securely fastened to a strong belt around someone's waist.

"You're the new patient. Golden, right?" she asked again even more unpleasantly.

"Yes. I'm Barry Golden. I'm a voluntary admission."

"Well, you'll have to wait until lunch is finished to be checked in. They're almost done," she responded without changing her tone. She certainly didn't seem to care or even grasp the distinction between voluntary admission and being committed by someone who had decided you were nuts.

"I'm a voluntary admission," I reminded her.

"I'm sure it's all in your chart. You can stand over here," she continued, moving me out of the way.

I didn't feel that I was off to a good start, but I was finally inside I-6.

I had thought about my stay quite a bit before my arrival. I planned to keep to myself as much as possible. Let's face it. I wasn't here to make friends, just to have my medications reevaluated and get out. The other patients were here because they were crazy.

A whole bunch of them; men and women, young and old were finishing their lunches around a large community table. Many of them looked my way and smiled. I returned a polite smile, but broke eye contact with them as quickly as possible. I would be polite in here but on my own. Dr. Wohl said he could probably get me a private room. He told me I would be in I-6 for three or four weeks, a maximum of thirty days. That was fine, just get in and get out. I had my books, my laptop, relaxing clothes and some toiletries. What else could I need?

I watched as the inmates deposited their empty styrofoam trays on removable shelves in a large rolling metal cabinet. Some of them were laughing together as if they were friends. Some were silent and some half asleep. Some were in wheelchairs. Some sat alone. Some were dressed and some were still in morning robes. The food they ate was hospital food and looked like shit.

"Remember; when you've finished your food put your trays on the cart."

"There's an extra pudding," a nurse near the food cabinet announced. Maybe they weren't all nurses but they were dressed in white uniforms and seemed like they were.

"What kind?" asked a tiny little man dressed in a tee shirt and grease stained khaki trousers.

The nurse looked at the label on the container. "Vanilla."

"I'll take the pudding," he replied.

"Would you please pass the pudding to Mr. Casell?" the nurse asked another man who didn't seem to want to be disturbed.

"I will!" said a young, eager female patient in her flowered housecoat jumping up to help.

"Thank you, Emilia, but I asked Mr. Martin."

"Let her do it!" Mr. Martin replied.

"I asked you," the nurse answered him calmly.

"I can't reach it," he answered.

"You don't have to reach it. I'm giving it to you. Now, please pass the pudding to Mr. Casell." She paused. "Mr. Martin?"

Mr. Martin caved in and silently passed the pudding to Mr. Casell as many of the other patients moved out of the lunchroom and on to whatever else they had planned for the remainder of their day. Some of them disappeared, entering corridors I hadn't yet seen. Others went directly into a large community room directly across the hall.

The community room had an old television set which was turned on with no one watching. The room could seat many with its worn, pilled, brown plaid couches and bright orange plastic chairs. The more I stared into the room the more it became a perversion of June Cleaver's home where I had spent so much of my youth.

When only a couple of people were left in the lunch room, a middle aged pear-shaped black woman was filling her pockets with all the left over sugar, sweet n' low, ketchup, mustard, jelly, and salt and pepper packets she could get her hands on. She kept looking over her shoulder as if she were on a secret mission although everyone could see what she was doing.

I smiled inside as I watched her squirreling. Our eyes met.

"No one else wants 'em," she said. "If no one else wants 'em, I'll take 'em. I can use them. You know how much sugar costs in the store?"

"Hey, I don't care if you take it all." I smiled as I spoke.

She smiled back like a guilty child who'd gotten caught, wasn't punished, and made a new friend. "My name is Doris."

"Mine is Barry."

"Are you coming in?"

"Yes, I am." But I'm not nuts like you, I thought.

"I also have some fruit in my room. Would you like a banana or a' apple?" She even had the voice of a child.

"No thanks."

"The bananas go bad so they's gotta' be eaten the quickest."

The little nurse, name tagged Barbara, turned to me. "Now we can get you settled." I'd now been waiting for about twenty minutes. The nurses had watched over their brood until the last was finished with lunch, that is with the exception of Mr. Casell who was both protecting and eating his vanilla pudding a quarter teaspoon at a time. I couldn't tell if he was enjoying his extra dessert or simply trying to make the meal last all afternoon.

I had brought with me one soft bag for my clothes and an attaché case with my laptop, associated paraphernalia and about a dozen CD's. The black man who had originally unlocked the door and had made me so wary was actually a nurse and he walked toward me now to begin the check in process. He was called Big Dave.

I had watched this very large man during lunch. He stood by the food carts and never smiled as the patients put their empty trays away. With his dark black skin and massive chest stuffed inside his sparkling whites, he was something to behold. He was like a tough staff sergeant. Big Dave was not there to smile. He was not there to have fun. It seemed that his sole purpose on I-6 was control, to keep everything orderly. I clung to my thoughts about what voluntary admission meant like it was my last canteen on a vast desert plain.

Big Dave moved alongside me near one of their cheap dilapidated eight foot dining tables. Nurse Barbara stood to our right.

"Would you toss that bag up here on the table?" he said.

"Sure," I replied. My meager rebellious act was to only half toss my bag onto the table. It balanced precariously on the edge of the table. Big Dave caught it before it could make up its mind. He unzipped it and dug his hands deep inside randomly pulling out anything he deemed suspicious or couldn't immediately identify.

"What is this?"

"It's the cord to my razor."

He looked at Barbara who O.K.'d the short cord. She was holding my secret chart. I felt like I was going through customs in Jamaica.

Big Dave removed an empty plastic bin from a locked cabinet overhead; high quality Tupperware. He dumped the contents of my dopp kit on the table and began sorting them. I felt like I was standing naked in an employee's lunchroom. "You won't be needing any of these." He was putting all my medications in the plastic bin. I reached forward.

"But those are just eye drops. My eyes itch."

"If your eyes itch you can always speak with one of the nurses. They'll give you eye drops if you need them."

"But these are the eye drops I like."

"We can always get them for you from the dispensary."

What was the point for keeping my eye drops? The medicines I carried were special to me. I needed them on a daily basis. Granted I was always carried away in that I kept any medicine ever prescribed for me during the past five years; unctions and ointments for almost any condition as well as stale dated extremely unnecessary pills. But my dopp kit helped me feel safe. It was the little red dog that I slept with as a child, my most treasured possession disappearing for a second time and I had to stand by helplessly as it was disemboweled. By the time he'd completed the initial inspection all that was left for me to take to my room, aside from clothing, was my toothpaste, my toothbrush, my hair brush and my electric razor.

"Could you put your case up here now?"

I was a fucking voluntary admission. I didn't have to be here at all and I clearly didn't need this fucking dehumanizing process. I wasn't planning to lead a rebellion in this nut house.

Big Dave was opening the case and looking inside. He was about to launch a new invasion.

"Look. This is my laptop, my discs, my books and a few

other things that I need for my work." I already knew what he would focus in on. "I cannot work without the wires and accessories that bring these things to life and, unfortunately, they utilize that recent phenomenon we call electricity."

Barbara intervened. "He's right. He's not a regular admission and he can have these for his work." She turned to me. "But please keep the wires hidden. We normally don't allow any wires, chords, even shoelaces to be in many of our patients' possession; nothing that can be tied. I'm sure that you understand. We wouldn't want some of the others on the floor to find them in your room."

I pictured someone dangling in their room from my Toshiba computer cord.

"I'll be careful."

Finally, my first voluntary admission perk. I would wallow in it every time I plugged the cord into a socket

"Would you please empty your pockets, Mr. Golden"? Big Dave knew his job and stuck with it like a pit-bull; a hired mercenary, focused and well trained. My back pockets were empty. I emptied my most important pocket, the one with the credit cards and cash. I placed them on the table. I pulled out a snot stained handkerchief from my other pocket.

"You want me to spread this open on the table?" I asked pointing to the handkerchief.

Big Dave wasn't fazed. He was a tough man who couldn't be provoked by words alone.

"Won't be necessary but you ought to put your valuables in the cabinet. That is, if you want to be sure that you'll have them when you leave.

"O.K.," I replied, "but not the cash. I'll hold onto the cash."

Barbara stepped in. "No one here would ever touch your things. But, if you'd feel more comfortable, security can come up and hold the money for you," she suggested.

"That's fine with me."

Big Dave was finished with his job. Barbara had me give

her a rundown of the medications I was currently taking, both the dosage and frequency, assuring me that these would not be altered in any way until I had been seen by a physician. "Let's get you into your room."

I followed her with my lightened bags in hand. Other patients watched us as we passed them, a few whispering gently, others smiling harmlessly and still others watching us with a vacuous stare, as if they were looking through us, as if we were invisible. A few nodded or said a quick hello. My defenses were wound tight around me but I couldn't find meanness or hostility in any of the patients I saw. I was surprised. It put me at a momentary loss until I realized that they were probably all heavily medicated.

The first room we walked up to was a bathroom and she walked me inside. It resembled my high school locker room but was smaller and done in pink. Both men and women used the same showers, but, of course, one at a time. There was no lock on the door but, when in use, staff conscientiously stood guard to guarantee privacy.

All the walls in I-6 were dead; dirty enough to not want to lean against them but not dirty enough to warrant a paint job. I assumed that the hospital was on an austerity budget.

My room was the last room on the right side of the corridor. Next to it was a small community room, much smaller than the living room I'd seen earlier. It included those same plastic molded orange chairs along the perimeter and had an "eclectic" style to match the I-6 mindset. It had a few wood-toned Formica coffee tables, a thin rug and a television. I imagined that a single television in a room which housed so many nuts could be the scene of some serious battles.

Two residents were in this television room; Emilia, the "wannabe" pudding passer from lunch and a skinny male deaf mute in his mid-thirties. She was working hard to communicate with him and suddenly pulled up her sweatshirt exposing her small breasts.

"Emilia!" Barbara exclaimed. "I don't want to have to tell

you again!" Emilia, slightly disappointed, fell back on some other possible ways to communicate.

SECURITY

My room in I-6 was small. I had a single bed, a small metal night table with two drawers and one stiff-backed wooden chair. It must be relaxing to sit at attention and read. I also had a traditional hospital table; the kind you swing over so you can sip your drinks with a curved plastic straw. I peeked into the bathroom, saw the toilet and sink, then sat on the edge of my bed.

"This will be your room," Nurse Barbara told me, I suppose trying to clear up some impossible confusion about why she had brought me in here. Several large chunks of plaster were chipped from the walls high up near the ceiling. I pointed them out to her.

"Who was the decorator?"

She seemed to be ignoring me now.

"O.K." she said. "While you get settled I'll send up security to make sure that your money will be safe."

I was tired and lay back on the bed. I repeated, "you need a new decorator."

"O.K., then." She smiled, turned and walked away.

Once she was out of sight I got up and looked out my window. Naturally, it was a window that could only open several inches but I still felt the fresh air. If I pressed the left side of my face hard against the window I could see the Hudson River and I liked that. I swallowed my sadness and looked around the room once again. It hadn't changed.

I was most curious about the bathroom. In general people want to love their bathrooms and I went inside mine to check it out more thoroughly this time. It was the safest bathroom I'd ever been in. They had thought of everything for our protection. The mirror over the sink was like a fun house mirror distorting my reflection. I tapped it and realized it was made out of a thin almost soft plastic. My stress had made me thirsty so I sipped some cold hospital water from the sink faucet. I looked up and threw a kiss to myself in the mirror not knowing why.

When I had turned seventeen, I considered myself an adult and decided to kiss my father as a greeting whether he liked it or not. Not known for his affection he would stiffen, not knowing how to react when I put my hands on his shoulders, leaned forward, and kissed him on the cheek. My father's cheek was soft like Mom's but, of course, unshaven. Eventually through forcing these kisses on him I hoped that some affection could pass through that softness, the mere softness of contact. Our cheeks would touch and I would hold it there just a moment longer than necessary. It might have been no more than a second, but it was a second of affection. I knew he could have forced us apart sooner.

Some real satisfaction came to me a few years later when I overheard him boasting to a friend "how his son would kiss him every time we said hello or good-bye." I would miss things like that in a hospital room.

I started to rearrange the room slightly, moving the wooden chair next to my night table in an effort to convince myself I hadn't lost my freedom. Enough people knew where I really was and, more importantly, Dr. Wohl knew what was happening. We were doing this together. He said he would come by and I was sure he would; as soon as he could. I was sure of it and so I began to wait.

As I took out my computer I thought I smelled something in the air. I was very sad and I think it was the smell of Death; Death as a solution. And to think I had the tools in my room. My electric cords and cables were the stuff; tools of death in I-6. Maybe it was Nurse Barbara's dark concerns that made me carefully hide all my electric cords when I put my computer away so that if someone did hang themselves, it wouldn't be on my account.

I kicked back on the bed and was dozing when security arrived, officially escorted to my room by the ubiquitous Nurse Barbara.

"Hi." The guy from security carried a small manila envelope.

I sat up slowly in an effort to let them know that they had disturbed my relaxation. I extended my hand "How ya' doin'?" and he shook it politely. He was about my age, same height and weight but balding. He seemed more muscular than I in the way his polyester blend light brown security uniform sports' jacket fit. His ID badge was neatly clipped on, hanging properly and very visibly from his chest pocket. Yep. No question in my mind. This was security, all right. I squeaked and snapped my head up and down.

"You have some valuables you'd like to check with us?"

"So I'm told. It's money."

"No problem. What you do is to fill in the information on the face of this envelope. Then we'll count your money, put it in the envelope and return it to you when you leave."

Sounded fair enough. I took the envelope and began to fill in the blanks with one of the felt tip markers I brought with me rather than with his ball point pen. Rejecting his pen was a bold stroke of my independence. I figured I would give him four hundred dollars and keep sixty just in case. Just in case of what? In case I needed it. For what? Who knows? Maybe to bribe someone. To get special food or something like that? I'd obviously watched too many movies and taken them too seriously, I thought silently.

I completed the form and was about to count my money while security watched when I decided to first read the small print on the envelope. So often we ignore this rule but I was going to be here for a while and I wanted everyone to see that I was nobody's fool. I wanted them to watch me read boilerplate so they'd understand that I'm neither stupid nor unaware. I wanted to be clear.

"Tell me something," I said pointing to the envelope. "It says here that if I give this to you, the maximum that you'd be liable for is fifty dollars. Am I reading this correctly?"

He looked at the envelope. "I'm not sure. Truth is I never read it," he chuckled and it was obvious that no one had ever reviewed this with him before.

"It's says it right here. Look at it."

He looked closely at the envelope.

Through the doorway, Nurse Barbara chimed in. "No one is going to take your money. It is always safe with security."

"It seems to me that if I sign this that they're only liable for fifty dollars," I told her.

"You don't have to give us anything if you don't want to," security reassured me kindly. He was a man lost in an area never covered by his training. Nurse Barbara was not in a reasoning mood. She had other patients to see to.

I ignored the noise of her irritation and continued with security. "I'm sorry I brought you all the way up here."

"I don't mind ..."

"I'm going to keep my money with me."

"You'd get it all back," he seemed unsure if he should take a side; Nurse Barbara's or mine. "No one will touch this envelope downstairs. It gets locked up."

"That's not the point," I replied.

Nurse Barbara said "you know, if that money is taken from your room, the hospital's not liable!"

"Oh, really. Somehow, I think you're wrong. You're telling me that if this money is stolen from my room, or, better yet, say that my laptop is stolen! You're telling me that the hospital isn't liable."

"That's right. Only what you give to security."

"I guess, in that case, I'll have them run my underwear up here every morning."

With that said, security was out of my room and heading down the corridor toward the exit. Barbara was moving backwards slowly, still warning me. "The hospital isn't liable. I want you to know that. What's in your room is not the hospital's responsibility!"

I stepped into the hall as she moved away.

"You're a nurse! Not an attorney!"

Our conversation was over and she disappeared from sight.

I waited a few minutes after they were gone and then snuck quietly down the corridor to the only public telephone. I was glad it was enclosed; an old fashioned wooden telephone booth. It looked cozy. I called my attorney to check if I was right, having already taken so strong a position on liability. Even though it was glassed in, I knew the telephone booth probably wasn't soundproof so I spoke quietly. I didn't want to be embarrassed with my need to call. I left a message for him but I was nervous now, wondering if Barbara was going to withhold some of my pills when I needed them later that evening; a chance to get even.

Not realizing how exhausted I was once back in my room I passed out on my bed.

It seemed only moments had passed when a nurse I'd never seen awakened me. It was dark outside my window.

"C'mon now. You gotta' go to the meetin'."

"What?" My head wouldn't clear.

"They started the community meetin' and everybody has to be presen'."

"What about dinner?"

"Dinner's over. You slept right through that."

"There's nothing to eat?"

"Everythin's gone, far as I know." I figured that was Nurse Barbara's fault. "But you gotta' get up and go to the meetin'."

Nobody cared that I didn't eat dinner but I couldn't miss some meeting. I threw on some sweats, wet my face and hair and stumbled down the corridor.

THE COMMUNITY MEETING

The community meeting was already in progress as I joined the rest of the ward. There was a moment of quiet as most of the inmates watched me turn the corner and enter the room. I moved along the wall to avoid being an even greater distraction. Everyone, except for the three nurses present, was seated around the same collection of tables used for lunch and, I assumed, breakfast and dinner as well.

"I believe we have someone new joining us."

I was suddenly bombarded with hey's, hi's and hello's. I couldn't be both late and inconspicuous. I acknowledged their greetings with a few quick self-conscious glances and a tight lipped smile as I moved back even farther, as far to the rear of the room as possible. The cabinets which held my valuables were there and a few women were standing close together inadvertently blocking my way.

"Excuse me," I said.

Their smiles were warm and friendly which only added to my discomfort. I had to pass in between them and didn't want to accidentally rub up against them. God forbid they should misinterpret my actions. I wanted to reach the cabinets and, hopefully, no longer be noticed.

"I'm Rose," one of them said kindly as I passed by.

"And I'm Mildred," the woman next to her chimed in stepping on Rose's words. I could tell they were close friends. Mildred's smile was gigantic, toothsome, and never-ending. I thought of a horrid clown as I struggled in a stressed attempt to act friendly.

" Barry," I replied. I couldn't stand being there.

The gentleman who announced my entrance sat at the head of the table apparently conducting the meeting. Although dressed simply in chinos and a white dress shirt, his manner made it clear that he was in charge.

"I think that's nice," he lamely announced. "Since we already know one another and Barry ... that is what you said, right? Barry."

I nodded.

"Well, this is obviously Barry's first community meeting and since we all know each other already, I think that we should introduce ourselves to Barry. Barry ... we hold these meetings every Wednesday evening at 7:30 here in the dining area. This is where and when we discuss our community problems. Next Wednesday, unfortunately, will be my last meeting. I have other patients who need me very badly."

There were more than thirty people seated around the table. It was standing room only.

"I'm Dr. Frank Winters," he continued.

So, at last, a physician was in the room. I was wondering when a physician would finally appear. Up until now I had only dealt with nurses.

It was a tedious process as, one by one, they introduced themselves. I would glance at each of them as they spoke but I had difficulty listening. I was mentally overloaded and couldn't follow their words.

All in all, the only names that managed to break through to me were the names of two young female Hispanic patients, Emilia, the exhibitionist, and Graciela. I liked Graciela. She was heavier than most of the women I'd had sex with in my life with but she was dark, with dark eyes, dark hair, white teeth and great tits. Graciela turned and spoke with some guy whose name I didn't remember. They seemed to be around the same age and I could hear them speaking in Spanish. When they began to laugh and she touched his arm I grew increasingly jealous.

Primarily concentrating on not displaying my tics, I wanted to be ignored by almost everyone but had no luck there. I let out a sharp little squeal, scrunched my head back into my shoulders twice and then shook it as if I were simply loosening up muscles before a workout.

I noticed Mr. Casell all the way across the room almost directly opposite me. I could barely hear him say his name. But I could see that gripped between his tiny hands was another vanilla pudding. My first genuine smile appeared.

It was finally my turn to introduce myself. "I'm Barry, Barry Golden."

A small delicate and very refined woman in her late sixties had evidently missed her turn. She was seated in a metal folding chair directly to my left.

"My name is Caroline," she said quietly.

"I'm Barry," I repeated to her softly.

"What do you do, Barry?" Dr. Winters asked loudly interrupting my attempted escape from the goings on.

I didn't want them knowing about me but I couldn't think of anything to say besides the truth. I made it sound as simplistic as I could, a first for me. I sell wall décor, inexpensive artwork.

"That's great, Barry. It's great to have you aboard. But now let's get back to business. I believe that Mary had the floor." Dr. Winters continued the meeting.

"Mary," Dr. Winters went on. "You were saying?"

"I was saying that the shower curtains are disgusting. I have a real problem with our bathroom and it's mostly with the shower curtains. There is mold or mildew or whatever that greenish stuff is all along the bottom."

"It's like that on our side too," someone added.

"It's disgusting," Mary went on. "Why can't they simply have one of the janitors clean it off?"

"I heard a commercial about some stuff called Clean Away and that's just what it's for; that mildew stuff. You spray it on and that's it. It works all by itself. No scrubbing. No rinsing. Nothing. I seen it on T.V." This was Jimmy. He was a tall fireman who worked in the Bronx. I remembered pieces of his introduction and was surprised at how skinny he was for a fireman. He wore jeans, a tee-shirt and an open long-sleeve shirt over that. The shirt hung limp and wrinkled from his shoulders.

"It's what they tell you on television and it's all a bunch of crap," Mr. Martin said offering his opinion. "All that stuff they show you on TV is crap. They sell junk. The stuff only works in the commercials. It's a set up. It won't work here. They get rich and we buy their crap," he added.

"Well, I don't think it's too much to ask for the shower curtains to be cleaned," said Dr. Winters glancing at one of the nurses, obviously looking for some additional input.

"I'm sure we could get someone to clean the shower curtains," the nurse replied.

"They're garbage too! They're not real shower curtains. They're junk. What do you think? We're in some fancy hotel?" added Mr. Martin emphatically.

"We can definitely look into it and do whatever needs to be done. Am I right on that?" Again, Winters looked toward the nurse.

"Yes. I think it's a fair request," she said.

"I should say so," Mary replied in an effort to get in the final word.

"If you're going to clean them, then just use plain old Chlorox. That's all you need, plain old Chlorox and some old fashioned elbow grease. That's all you need. But what d'you know?" Mr. Martin added, dismissing everyone with a wave of his hand.

The nurse looked at Dr. Winters. "I think we should move on," she said.

"All right. Is there any other new business?" He responded quickly.

I couldn't believe this was why the nurse awakened me. It was idiotic. They weren't discussing a single thing of importance. And I was hungry. I thought of stealing the vanilla pudding from Mr. Casell.

"No new business? Then, I guess that's it," Dr. Winters said.

A homely woman, chubby with bad skin, stepped forward. "I'd like to let people know about the schedule," she said. "First, just to mention, I haven't seen many of you in the exercise room. Please remember that it's open every afternoon except for the weekends from two to three-thirty."

I looked around the room at the shabby, out of shape inmates and thought of them in a fancy New York health club and laughed silently.

"Gym has been switched from Monday to Wednesday next week so instead of gym we'll have an extra arts and crafts class. Other than that, the schedule stays the same."

"Oh, Christ," I thought, "arts and crafts." My parents' offered arts and crafts as an activity at their day camp. Arts and crafts, nature, woodworking, softball, swimming; the list went on and on in my head.

"Barry," she said. "The schedule is posted here on the bulletin board every morning. The sign-up sheets for each activity are next to it. You can sign up for anything except if the sheet is already full. Then you have to choose something else."

"Thanks," I replied.

She looked over the meeting. "That's really it for me," she added. "Oh, by the way," she was looking my way again. "My name is Phyllis for those of you who don't know who I am."

Again there was silence in the room.

"So is that it now? Does anyone else want to add anything?" Dr. Winters asked conscientiously. He glanced at the nurse and she nodded his way.

"Any questions?" he asked.

The group suddenly seemed edgy awaiting his final words.

"Then I think the meeting is officially adjourned," he said.

Most everyone moved quickly away from the room as if a corral gate was suddenly opened and the unbridled horses were set free. Some were quicker than others, and a few stood still as did the nurse and her two cronies.

I was one of those standing still. If I moved I'd have to weave my way through so many inmates and probably have to add some more personal introductions. I didn't want to speak anymore. I wanted to do my time here, straighten out my meds and get out.

Dr. Frank Winters got up slowly and headed for my corridor. As he got up I noticed his soft brown boots. When I looked closer I noticed that Dr. Winters had no shoelaces! He was going to his room! He was one of the nuts!

I sat down at the big table in disbelief. Was he really a doctor or was this a game they let him play? And even if he was a doctor, he was also a nut. He lived down the hall and they took his shoelaces from him!

Caroline was still in her seat and we were seated near one another.

"Excuse me," she said softly. She touched my arm. I don't like taps and touches. I moved my arm tight into my body. "Excuse me," she said again. I turned her way.

"Yes." I responded as gently to her as she spoke to me.

"Could you tell me something?" she asked quietly.

"I don't know," I said. "I'll try to."

"I don't really understand," she said. "What kind of club meeting is this?"

BREAKFAST

"Mr. Golden," one of the nurses said knocking on my door. "You'd better come on now. Breakfast is almost over."

Food! I was up in a flash, throwing on the same sweats that I wore to the community meeting the night before. I washed my face and brushed my teeth in record time.

As I walked into the dining area I saw that I was catching the tail end of breakfast. Most of the inmates had already eaten and their trays of garbage were neatly stacked on several shelves in the ever-present large metal shuttle. I noticed Emilia, the flasher, still at the table. The housecoat she wore seemed borrowed from an old *I Love Lucy* episode but even that couldn't hide her odd shape. She was a very short girl with a normal size head and a huge cylindrical body, Humpty Dumpty with a real head. I was looking at her from behind as she had an animated one-sided conversation with the same young deaf mute she was with yesterday. I didn't remember his name but, then again, he'd never *said* it.

I wasn't familiar with morning protocol and my hesitation must have been obvious. Someone tapped me on the shoulder and I jumped, whipping my head to the right in surprise.

"You have to go see Dave first," she said. It was yet another nurse. This one was round and red-headed with puffy cheeks and freckles.

"And then come see me," my old friend Barbara said as she leaned out of the med room.

"Don't you forget about me," I replied. "I need my pills."

"Go see Dave," she said sounding more than one day

friendlier. I was glad.

Big Dave sat across the dining room with a blood pressure machine by his side. He was just as massive as I'd remembered but looked more relaxed and less threatening with a stethoscope around his neck.

"Sit right here," he said pointing to an empty wooden chair alongside the machine.

As I sat down Emilia noticed me.

"Hi," she said with a grin. Her genuine friendliness gave me the creeps.

"Hey," I replied trying to muster up some friendliness of my own. Then I looked away.

I watched Big Dave put a new sterile tip on the thermometer he was holding. The thermometer was modern, baby blue with a digital readout. As the plastic thermometer goes under your tongue you can watch the readout climb. It shoots up rapidly at first, in tenths, and then slows down as it approaches your body temperature. A tiny beep signals when it's peaked.

When I had the thermometer in my mouth I noticed that no matter how hard I bit down on it, it wouldn't break. That was because of the soft thickness of the plastic. At worst my biting down would leave a tooth mark or two. I remembered when thermometers were made of glass and filled with mercury.

There was a morning when I was eight and I woke up feeling sick. I was sweating and felt hot and cold simultaneously. I was dizzy and didn't want to go to school. I wanted to go back to sleep.

At the time there were two basic criteria in my house in order to miss a day of school due to illness. You had to both feel very sick and score high on the thermometer. If your temperature wasn't at least one hundred and one "by mouth" you failed and had to go to school.

As I mentioned, our thermometers at home were made of glass and contained a visible line of mercury. Once I held the thermometer up to the lamp by my bed to insure a high reading.

I was caught easily when the mercury climbed to one-hundred and eight and the thermometer had to be thrown out because the mercury wouldn't come down no matter how hard my mother shook it. The "punishment" was monumental. We had to use the rectal thermometer.

"Mommm!" I shouted from my bed. "Mommmm!" Then I waited to see if she heard me. "Mommm!"

"What is it?" she said. She was already at my bedside. "You know I hate it when you scream, Barry."

"I'm sick, Mom. I'm all sweaty and I have a fever. And my throat hurts when I swallow." That last part wasn't really true.

"I'll get the thermometer," she said as she left my room. She was back in about two seconds.

"And I'm dizzy and I think I'm nauseous."

My mother shook the thermometer swiftly downward three or four times driving the mercury below normal.

"Let's first see if you have any temperature," she replied. She gently placed the thermometer under my tongue.

"Now close your mouth slowly and keep it closed. You have to leave it in for three minutes with your mouth closed," she said. "I'll come back in three minutes." I watched her walk out of my room. I knew she wouldn't be back as quickly as she said. Something would come up. It always did.

I took the thermometer out of my mouth and tried to read it. It was shaped like a triangular tube. To read it I had to turn it slowly in order to catch a glimpse of the mercury inside. I was proud of having learned that skill. Most kids couldn't do it. My mother could read it in a snap. It read ninety-six degrees so I knew that my mother had shaken down the mercury with great success. I put it back underneath my tongue. I knew I had fever anyway and didn't have to lie. I looked at my clock to begin timing the three minutes.

If you sit and watch the second hand on a clock go around it really starts to creep, even more so when you're young. It's unbelievable how slowly it seems to move. Within fifteen seconds I was uneasy.

I tried to relieve the compulsion to open my mouth by tightening and then relaxing my lips around the glass thermometer. I wiggled my lips all around it and pressed them together as if blotting lipstick, but the urge to open my mouth and breathe in was unbearable and the second hand on the clock seemed to be slowing down. I was trapped in one of my recent nightmares; a game of "Simon Sez" in which I was both leader and the only player. It was like trying to stop a sneeze.

I thought of a compromise. I opened my mouth at its corners, breathing in fresh air but keeping my tongue pressed down hard on the small enclosed ball of mercury at the bottom tip of the thermometer. I thought about biting the thermometer and closed my teeth tighter 'in order to keep the thermometer in place under my tongue'. I knew I didn't have to close my teeth on it but couldn't help it.

I was in one of my terrifying places where no one else ever seemed to be. I *couldn't* ignore my thoughts. They were commands that couldn't be denied.

Less than a minute had gone by. My teeth closed a little tighter around the glass tube. They began to grind back and forth on the thin glass. I was losing control and was going to bite it! I quickly pulled the thermometer out of my mouth and read it. It hadn't even reached a hundred. It was just beginning to respond to my body's warmth. I thought that maybe by pulling the thermometer out of my mouth and then putting it back in slowly as my mother had, this urgent need to bite the thermometer, this spell on me would be broken.

Less than two minutes had gone by and I was right back where I had left off, breathing through the corners of my mouth and tightening my teeth on this fragile glass tube. I was way behind the three minute timing and my mother might be back sooner rather than later. Why couldn't I stop this urge? I pulled my top teeth inward creating additional pressure and the thermometer crushed in half between my teeth.

I immediately opened my mouth, grabbing the protruding half and then holding up my tongue, head facing the floor allowing the other half to fall out along with some crumbs of broken glass. A small piece scratched across my inner gums and my mouth had a metallic taste. I spit and watched the mercury roll around my floor in a way that dared me to try and pick it up. Some glass was stuck in my lip! How big was it? It felt gigantic! What if I swallowed it? I breathed in and out holding my tongue up high so I couldn't inhale the glass and wouldn't die. The thermometer was all over the floor.

I hopped out of bed and began picking up the big pieces of glass first. What would I say? What would I tell my mother? We didn't have another oral thermometer and I didn't want to use the one that would be stuck up my ass with that big gob of Vaseline. We didn't even need to own that one. Everyone knew that your temperature was always one number over the oral one. I picked up more glass and put it neatly on the table near my bed. I tried to feel the glass inside my mouth with my tongue and couldn't find it. But I knew it was there and was afraid to swallow.

I heard my mother coming down the hall and sat down quickly on my bed.

"So let's see how high your temperature is," she said.

"I didn't do it on purpose," I started to cry. "The thermometer broke in my mouth!" My bare feet dangled off the side of my bed.

She saw the pieces of glass on my night table and the mercury rolling on the floor.

"What happened?" she asked. She seemed to be raising her voice.

"I bit down on the thermometer and it broke."

"Did you get cut? Are you alright? Let me look inside your mouth! Where's a flashlight?" She wasn't pleased.

"On my shelves," I cried back. "I think there's a piece of glass in my gums!"

"Where on your shelves, Barry? Tell me where the flashlight is."

"The second shelf." She looked on the wrong side. "No!

It's up there," I pointed.

My mother found it.

"What if I swallowed some glass?" I said wagging my hands in a panic.

"You didn't swallow glass. Now open your mouth," she said as she turned on the flashlight."

"What if I did?" I repeated, tears streaming now.

"Stop it!" She replied. "Stop it and open your mouth! Come on, Barry. Open up." I opened my mouth and she shined the light inside.

"It's in my gums!" I yelled mouth open.

"Where?!"

"Under my tongue!"

"Then lift up your tongue," she said scolding me. She shined the light around inside my mouth. "I don't see any glass."

"But I feel it," I replied.

"You have a tiny scratch on your gums but there isn't any glass," she sounded relieved.

"I feel it," I said still crying.

"Things feel bigger and different in your mouth. There isn't any glass," she replied.

"What will you do?" I asked still frightened.

"Nothing. I'll buy a new thermometer. Things break. I'm not angry with you."

"I don't know why I did it, Mom. I just bit down. I couldn't help it," I said.

"I'm not angry," she replied.

"I'm really sick, Mom. Do you have to take my temperature with the other thermometer?"

"You're lucky you weren't badly cut," she replied. My mother already knew how hard it had become for me to keep still.

"I do have fever, Mom. I swear it. I'm really sick."

"Let's see," she said leaning down above me and placing her soft lips on my forehead like a reassuring kiss. "You do feel warm."

"I'm sick."

"You don't have to go to school today. Get into bed and stay there. I'll buy a new thermometer and take your temperature later but you stay in bed today. It's not just a day off from school. You'd better rest! I'll call the school and find out what homework you have and I'll send Emma to clean up the little bits of glass and the mercury so you don't cut yourself. Thank God there's no glass splinter for me to remove. That's all I need today. Do you want Emma to bring up some orange juice, and maybe some toast?"

"O.K.," I gratefully replied.

My mother tucked me back into bed and left my room.

"Ninety-eight point five," Big Dave said as he wrote my temperature next to my name on a list with all the other inmates. "Now hold out your left arm."

I moved my right arm.

"Your left arm," he repeated wanting to get on with his day. My blood pressure was a little high. I watched him complete his notes.

"I didn't order any breakfast. What do I do?" I asked Dave as I got up from the chair.

"Oh, there's always extras sent up for people who don't order special so just look on the shelves over there." He pointed to the metal cart. "Top shelf on the left. Grab any one of those," he added.

I took a seat at the corner of the community table as far away from everyone as I could. I drank some orange juice and opened the main course of scrambled eggs and *something*. It was even more tasteless then I'd imagined.

I looked down at the thick Styrofoam plate and poked my scrambled eggs accidentally uncovering a short curly black hair. In a hospital! But I was too hungry to lose my appetite. I unpacked a muffin from its sealed cellophane wrapper and opened a small container of orange marmalade to spread on the muffin.

I saw Nurse Barbara coming over with my pills. "So here."

I began looking them over carefully.

She started pointing to each pill. "You have 60mg of Prozac down from 80. Then you have 15mg of Valium, .15mcg of Synthroid, and 2000mg of Depakote. We also have your inhalers in the med room if you want them. Tornalate and Vanceril, right?" I nodded as she continued. "Do you want them?"

"Yes. But can I take the inhalers after breakfast?"

"I'll get them for you now and you can give them back to me later. I have to lock up the med room. Actually, I was supposed to lock it up about ten minutes ago. Just give the inhalers back to me when you're through with them."

"Sure," I replied.

"The only thing is that I take 1500mg of Depakote and your saying 2000mg."

"Well, that's what it says on your chart," she replied.

"No one told me anything about an increase. I'm not sure that I should take that much especially since I'm here for a washout. They're supposed to be decreasing things, not increasing them."

"You can check on the dosage later when you speak with your doctor."

"My doctor?"

"The doctor who has been assigned your case here in the hospital?"

"Who is my doctor here? What do they do? Draw names out of a hat?" I asked, never having been given a name and having no clue as to how they were assigned or, frankly, anything about them at all.

"I think that it's Doctor Genovese. She's a very good doctor. But they all are," she said covering her ass in case she was mistaken.

"Oh, I'm sure," I replied politely.

"How's your breakfast?" Barbara asked before walking away. It was a rhetorical question.

I raised my eyebrows, cocked my head and snapped it down into my chest. "It's pretty bad." I'm already talking to myself, I thought. I watched Nurse Barbara disappear into the "drug commissary" to get my inhalers and lock up.

I wiggled my nose then pinched it like it was itching to try to mask my tic.

DR. GENOVESE

After breakfast I took a nap. I had nothing else to do and this environment was draining through its boredom. But the nap didn't last very long. I was awakened by a knock on my closed door.

"Mr. Golden?"

I stirred and opened my drugged and groggy eyes.

"Mr. Golden?"

"Yes, yes," I replied.

"I'm Dr. Genovese. May I come in?"

My own newly assigned special doctor, Dr. Genovese, had come to get me for our first appointment. I felt far superior to my surroundings.

"One second," I replied, hitting the bathroom sink to see how I looked before having company. I ran some water in my hands and slid them back through my hair. Why shouldn't my first appearance be a good one? I opened the door.

Dr. Genovese was about my height and heavy which made her a very big woman. I'd guess somewhere between one hundred and seventy and one hundred ninety pounds. She wore a solid black blouse and loose fitting cashmere cardigan. She had dark hair cut short making her face look particularly round. Her skirt was long and huge in black and gold, and seemed carefully selected to hide gigantic legs.

Accompanying her was a young girl dressed in medical whites with a stethoscope curled and stashed in her deep medical jacket pockets. She looked like a child dressed up as a doctor for Halloween. I couldn't tell if she was a medical student, an intern, or a resident but she was clean scrubbed, young and cute. I realized that this first session was going to be between the three of us.

I wasn't sure where we were headed and the way they walked in silence down the long corridor on either side of me gave me a very weird feeling. I felt like I was going to be punished for something I didn't do. I snapped my head down and pinched my dick two or three times. I rolled my eyes as if I were trying to look through the top of my skull and then closed them tightly. I blinked like this several times then tried to swallow a squeak, but it managed to escape in spite of my efforts. If they heard it, they didn't react.

As I walked down the hall with the two of them I was apprehensive about our meeting. They had to know I was a voluntary admission? So what was this for? I accepted the fact that I was going to be staying in I-6 but I didn't need to talk to a doctor. It suddenly dawned on me! This was probably about the meds; my washout, of course. She was overseeing the washout and it had to be reviewed. I felt better about this perp walk now. I squeaked inward a few times quietly and scrunched my features when I thought they weren't paying any attention. I clenched and unclenched my fists.

"Where are we going?" I asked.

"There are some rooms to talk in on the other side," Dr. Genovese replied.

"On the other side? I've never even been to the other side," I said. I almost thought of the other side of I-6 as a separate community, one half of a bi-polar world, one side manic, the other depressed.

We turned left at the end of the corridor and walked through the dining area. The "playroom" was to our left and several people were milling about, some shooting pool, some watching television, while others just sitting, doing nothing. It was rest time in this school of craziness, most of them probably in their rooms still digesting that horrid breakfast. I imagined hearing burps, farts and giggles as we walked the hallways. I tried to make myself more comfortable by acting like an equal with Dr. Genovese and her little pal.

"What are you?" I asked the kid. "A resident?" I was trying to flatter her. It never hurts to have an ally anywhere, especially in a nuthouse. She blushed and looked up at me. Her brown hair was pulled back off her face and she couldn't have been taller than five foot one.

"No. I'm a medical student. I start my internship next year."

"Here at Columbia?" I asked, already knowing the answer. She nodded.

I figured that at this stage in her medical career her knowledge was still limited to what she memorized from textbooks and learned from lectures. I was certain she had little hands on experience. This might be her first trip to I-6. I wondered what she was thinking.

"Well, you're in a great school." I hoped she realized that I hadn't been committed to I-6 but was admitted voluntarily.

"Thank you," she replied.

"Wait," I said to both of them. "I want to look in here for a second." There was a door with a sign that read Health Club. I had never been inside so I peeked through the small window in the door.

On the few interior doors on I-6 that even had windows, the windows were puny and didn't seem to serve much of a purpose. The only exception was the window in the nurses' office which made it easy for the nurses to watch us floating around the public areas. As I looked through the little window in the health club door I saw some cheap gym equipment squeezed into a tiny room.

"That's the health club?" I asked smiling. Dr. Genovese didn't react.

"I was hoping for Nautilus equipment. I want to do some special work on my lats while I'm here. I suppose I can't requisition a special piece of equipment, can I? Maybe with your connections?" I still got no reaction at all. "I'm just kidding," I said.

"Let's go in here," Dr. Genovese said opening the first door on the right.

"Hey! What's going on? Someone's coming in," yelled a panic stricken voice from inside the room."

"I'm so sorry for the interruption," said Dr. Genovese.

The hysterical voice inside the room continued on. "You said that this was private! She just walked in. How long has she been there?" Dr. Genovese quietly closed the door.

"We'll try the next room," she said.

"You might want to knock first," I interjected. Dr. Genovese didn't reply but her little student with the name tag 'Dr. Klein' pinned to her chest smiled as I winked at her. After no one screamed from inside the second room we walked in.

The room was as sterile as all the others in I-6 with bare white walls and four gray cloth chairs on stick-like chrome legs. I sat down across from the two of them watching and waiting as they prepared, opening their pads and files. I wondered if I was a name, a number, or both; probably both.

"So," Dr. Genovese began. "It's nice to meet you, Mr. Golden."

"Call me Barry," I winked again in Dr. Klein's direction suddenly wondering if she realized I was being playful and not ticcing.

"As you know already, Dr. Klein is a student here at Columbia and I'd like her to handle your initial interview."

"My pleasure," I assured them both, realizing that this meeting was going to be a complete waste of my time. I was a practice interview for a medical student.

"Dr. Klein," Genovese gave her the floor.

"Mr. Golden," she began.

"Call me Barry, please."

Glancing nervously in Dr. Genovese's direction, Dr. Klein then said "Yes, Barry. I'm going to ask ..."

"She's going to ask you a few simple questions," Dr. Genovese said on top of Klein's words.

"Yes. There are just a few simple questions," Klein repeated.

"Now, you go ahead," Dr. Genovese reassured Dr. Klein.

"The questions are simple and I will ..."

"She will ask you the questions one at a time," Dr. Genovese interrupted her again.

"Can I answer two at once if I want?" I asked.

"What?" Said Dr. Genovese.

"Can I like save up some of the questions and then answer them all at once?" I focused all of my attention on Dr. Klein as Dr. Genovese made a few notes on her pad. They were completely unresponsive to my attempt at humor.

I sniffed in and out and in and out, my head jerking sideways like I had a crick in it. "What's your first name?" I asked Dr. Klein.

"Joanne."

Dr. Genovese threw her a look trying to teach her not to cross that professional therapist's boundary line by putting this entire interview on a first person basis.

"Doctor Klein. Please continue." Genovese wrote a note on her pad. "Do you know what day this is?" Dr. Klein asked.

"Yes," I replied. "Thursday, September 20th."

"And what year is this?"

"So the questions are already getting tougher," I said dumbly trying to make our session more enjoyable and a little less idiotic. "I've got it! 1984. How's that?"

She wanted to go on and I was acting foolishly. I talked on. "There was a book about this year. Who the hell wrote it? George something or other. Orwin? It was something like that. 1984, right? Oh well...I can't think about that right now. It'll come to me. Tomorrow is another day," I said dramatically, trying to sound like Vivien Leigh in *Gone with the Wind.*

"Do you know where you are, Mr. Golden?"

"Does anybody, really?" I knew I should be taking this

interview more seriously. "Of course I do. I'm on the sixth floor of the Edward S. Harkness Eye Institute at Columbia Presbyterian Hospital."

"Barry," Dr. Klein continued. "I'm going to give you three words and I want you to remember them. I'll be asking you to repeat them back to me in the same order later on."

"Shoot."

"Music, red, and sad."

"Can I commit them to memory or would that be like cheating?" I asked still rejecting this conference. "No, music, red, and mad." I said opening my eyes wide and rolling them around the room. "Just kidding again. I know it's sad. The third word I mean. It's sad, not mad."

They took some notes as I finished my riff.

"Do you know who the President is?"

"Give me a minute on this one. Kennedy's dead so it can't be him. Let me think. He was an actor. I know that; an American actor which cuts out all the British, the French, the Italians, blah, blah, blah. Foreigners can't be presidents, am I right? I mean of the United States." No response. "Let's see. Pinky Lee was a fine actor."

I closed my eyes and pretended to be deep in thought. My tics flared. My head snapped down, then side to side. I snorted and squeaked, flexed my thighs and twisted my hands around my wrists. I shrugged quickly then opened my eyes embarrassed as I realized what a weird spectacle I had just made of myself. Dr. Klein was staring at me while Genovese continued with her copious notes. I wanted to stop her from writing.

"All right, all right. It's Reagan. Ronald Reagan. What are you writing? I'm joking around. I obviously can answer these questions. Listen. Look at me, Dr. Genovese. I'll answer seriously, all right?"

"You can answer anyway that you like," replied Dr. Genovese in what seemed a slightly ominous tone.

"You know I'm kidding around. And I hope that you realize that I can stop."

"Stop what?" She replied as Dr. Klein went on. Genovese was being a real fuck.

"How do you spell 'world'?" Klein asked.

"W-O-R-L-D." I replied still watching Dr. Genovese taking notes.

"Can you spell it backwards?"

"Yes, I can."

We paused.

"I'm sorry. D-L-R-O-W. I should warn you. I'm an excellent speller." Fuck them both I thought. I didn't need this shit.

"I'd like for you to count backwards for me in sixes from eighty."

"O.K. Here goes. Eighty, seventy-six no four! Sixty-eight, sixty-two, fifty-six, fifty, forty-four, thirty-eight…do you want me to go all the way to one?" I asked.

"That isn't necessary," she replied.

"Gotcha!" I said with feigned excitement. "You can't count down to one that way. You can only go to two. Did you know that, Dr. Klein?"

Dr. Genovese looked at me seriously now.

"Tell me how you feel, Barry? How do you feel about being here in the hospital, here in I-6?"

"It's alright," I replied.

Dr. Genovese leaned over my file and began writing as if the world was coming to an end and she had thirty seconds to put down her final words.

"What are you doing?" I was incredulous. "All I said was 'it's alright'."

She sat up straight in her chair no longer jotting down notes.

"Nothing," she answered plainly. "I'm writing a few notes. They're notes for me. I like to review my cases before each session."

"I don't think you're getting this," I replied. This is not a session. I arrived yesterday. I'm here to wash out my medications; to *purify* myself, and then see what medications I actually need. Dr. Wohl and I think that I might be over medicated and that's all there is to this. I think of my stay here as a colonic."

"Um, hmmm," Genovese commented.

"I'm not here for psychotherapy. Been there. Done that. Don't misunderstand, I think you're all very nice and I don't mind speaking with you or meeting with you, whatever you want to call it. We can meet every day if you like, especially if that's what I'm supposed to do. But this is not supposed to be a psychotherapeutic experience for me. I have a therapist and don't even feel that the focus is pure therapy with him anymore. My doctor is Dr. Wohl."

I purposely continued to mention Wohl because of his lengthy affiliation with Columbia Presbyterian and his high level of regard within its community. I was placing him in the room beside me as if Dr. Genovese was in danger of accidentally interfering with Dr. Wohl's work.

"It's a monitored washout. That's it," I added. "Which reminds me. That nurse, Barbara, said my Depakote is increased to 2000mg a day instead of 1500. That's a mistake, right? This is supposed to be washout, not an experiment in maximum drug tolerance!"

She was just itching to put pen to paper. But fuck her, I thought. I felt a little bad for Dr. Klein, this being a first experience and everything. I turned to her.

"I know I sound a little hostile here. I don't mean to sound so hostile."

"We both understand," replied Dr. Genovese. I couldn't tell if she was being sincere or trying to placate me. "I'll look into the Depakote."

I felt like I'd won a small battle but still wondered what she'd tell her student at the end of our session, once they were alone.

"Do you know Dr. Wohl?" I asked pleasantly.

"Of course."

"Is he around here, today?" I asked as if he and I hung out together.

"I think he is in the hospital on Thursdays but I'm not sure when. I don't know if he's around right now."

"Of course not," I replied, hoping that he was around and would visit me. He said he could come by but never suggested when that might be. I felt like I was sort of hanging around I-6 waiting for Dr. Wohl to appear. I didn't know quite how to handle all these strangers.

"Tell me something, Mr. Golden. I've been noticing your tics."

"Oh, please," I replied waving her investigation away.

"I've noticed that you have a variety of tics including your sniffing and those high pitched vocalizations," Dr. Genovese continued.

"Well, I suppose that makes you pretty fucking observant," I replied. "Pardon me Joanne. Didn't mean to curse."

"You've no need to be defensive, Mr. Golden. You're not the first person we've interviewed with tics."

"Do you want me to do some for you?" I said snorting in and out angrily. My face scrunched up and I let out two shrill squeals. The snorts were on purpose. The others were not. "I appreciate your pointing these tics out to me."

"How long have you had them?" she asked.

"At least over an hour," I replied uncooperatively. "This is bullshit," I said sneaking in a few taps on my dick, circling my hands around my wrists and then tapping my shoulders several times with the tips of my fingers.

"Have you ever consulted a neurologist about these mannerisms," she asked.

I had never used the term mannerisms to describe my tics and I liked it. It had a British sound to it. I thought there was a period of art named after it. The Period of Mannerism. The Mannerism School. I thought about a school for tics, myself director.

"I've been in therapy since I'm twelve," I replied.

"That's not what I'm asking you. I have a good idea of your time in therapy." I wondered if Wohl had shared his notes with Genovese. That would piss me off. "My question is have you ever consulted with a neurologist."

I didn't want to answer. I loved my psychiatrists, most of all Dr. Wohl and I didn't want to think that they should have sent me elsewhere. "I am wondering if anyone has ever ruled out a neurological basis for your tics and mannerisms."

"I'd love that," I muttered. "Thirty years and God knows how many thousands of dollars spent and it'll turn out that I have some little fucking neurological problem."

"I'm not diagnosing you with some little neurological problem, nor would I ever even imply that your many years of therapy are without value." I didn't speak now. I only listened.

"We have a movement disorder clinic here at Columbia Presbyterian run by Dr. Milton Bregman. Would you have any objections to his coming over to I-6 to examine you. It's one of the wonderful things about Columbia; that we have all these great experts on hand for consultations. In your case, Barry, perhaps it's just to rule things out. I don't know what's making you tic." I laughed quietly at her pun.

"Funny," I replied. "I would be willing to see him. Should I check with Dr. Wohl first?"

"You certainly can if you'd like to but it isn't necessary. He'll understand and agree with me." I was starting to like Dr. Genovese in spite of myself.

"It'd be pretty funny if after all this, this Dr. Bergman…"

"Bregman," she said correcting me.

"Whatever. It would be pretty funny if there was really something wrong with me after all this. That's all I'm saying." My arms jerked and I tapped my dick three quick times not covering it up quite as much as before.

"Then why don't we call it quits for today and let me first follow up with Dr. Bregman. Let's see when I can get him to come in."

"O.K. with me," I replied. Dr. Genovese began closing up

her papers and I stood up to leave.

"Mr. Golden?" Dr. Klein said. Dr. Genovese and I looked her way and paused. "Mr. Golden?"

"What?"

"Can you, uh, could you possibly repeat those three words I gave you earlier?"

"What? Oh, yeah. Sure, sure." I had to close my eyes and think. "They were music, red, and sad."

THE SHOWER

The following morning after breakfast and another quick nap I decided on a shower. I threw on my bathrobe and slippers.

"Could I get into the showers?" I asked.

The nurse was flipping through Ebony magazine and didn't look up at me. She was seated close to the dining area at the end of my corridor.

"The showers are available between 8:00 and 10:00 in the morning and 7:00 and 9:00 at night," she said.

"It's 10:10," I complained.

"And suppose it was 10:15, and then 10:20," she said finally looking up. "I don't make the rules. I follow them."

"I understand that and, hey, I know that rules are rules. They're made to be followed," I continued. But it's not like you're so fucking busy, I thought. Bring the goddamn magazine with you. I noticed an ad in it for some kind of hair straightener and tried to put the brakes on my vicious, obsessive, racist mental commentary.

"I'm new here. You realize that. Look in my chart. I'm Barry Golden. I don't know all the rules yet and I'm trying to get them all down as quickly as I can. I didn't know the shower timing. Now I do. Please. Nobody's around. No one will know if you let me in.'

"'Cause you don't know has nothin' to do with the rules," she snapped back.

"Please," I went on. "I'm filthy. Or, at least I feel filthy." I looked for her name tag. It read Tabitha Johnson, P.N. "Nurse

Johnson," I continued. "I'm ten minutes late. I'm trying to remember all the rules. It's not easy," I said with a shrug and a look of innocence.

She studied me for a moment. "Just this one time. And I'm only doing this 'cause you're still learning. The rules are the rules! Don't be askin' me to do this again." She was emphatic as she lay out the pecking order in I-6.

"I'll bring your chair," I said in an effort to thank her.

"I can do fine without that chair," she replied getting up. "I'm tired of sittin' here anyway."

We walked over to the nearby shower room. Looking around, making certain that there were no witnesses we'd have to kill later that day, she unlocked the door for me and leaned against the opposite wall going back to her magazine.

"Now don't take all day," she said.

As I entered the shower room I grabbed one of the threadbare towels folded and stacked on a white wicker table just inside the door. The showers were on my right and I was standing on a long bright blue rubber mat that ran in front of all four stalls. It was a shower corridor which I could see led to a larger room with toilets and sinks. I kicked off my slippers making sure that they were side by side neatly against the wall. I hung up my bathrobe and towels and stepped into the second of the metal stalls. I looked down at the bottom of the clear plastic shower curtain and, as reported at the community meeting, it was all green and mildewed.

In spite of the ugliness of a thin metal shower stall, the hot water felt good as I closed my eyes and let the water hit directly on my face. I felt as though I could fall asleep as I stood there but remembered that Tabitha was waiting for me in the corridor, no doubt, stopwatch in hand.

I looked for soap in the small dish attached to the corner of the stall but all I saw was some white slime. No body wash dispenser either. It suddenly dawned on me that perhaps these were supplies we were supposed to have brought from home and I felt stupid standing in the shower with no soap.

I scrubbed down with the slime as best I could assuming anything with soap as an ingredient was immune from bacteria. When finished, I stepped out of the stall stubbing my toe on the metal flange and found the room now freezing cold on my warm wet body. I looked in the next stall and noticed a small half used hotel bar of ivory soap floating in its own cold cloudy slime. I thought of Tabitha still waiting in the hall and passed on a second shower with a real bar of soap.

I toweled off quickly because of the cold and then I saw it. It looked like a brownish tar on wall. I approached the wall apprehensively. It wasn't tar. Someone had smeared shit on the wall. What was worse was that it appeared moist and fresh. Were it not for the chill in the air, I'm sure I would have smelled it when I first walked in.

I threw on my robe and slippers. It was disgusting and I wanted Nurse Tabitha to call someone to clean it up. But I stopped. What exactly was I going to tell her?

"There's some fresh shit smeared on the walls. Someone has to clean it." Why wouldn't she blame it on me? I opened the door and saw her still leaning against the wall with her magazine.

"Are you finished in there?" She asked.

"Not quite, but almost."

"Well, please hurry up. Remember. I wasn't supposed to let you in in the first place."

"I know. Thank you."

"Listen. You wouldn't happen to know who used the shower just before I did, would you?"

"Do you think that I sit here and watch who goes in, who goes out all day long?"

"Of course I don't think that," I replied. "I just thought you might have noticed. You know. Maybe you were on shower duty all morning. Someone goes in and someone says, O.K., that's it. That's the last one in and you might remember who that was. Do you?"

"Enough questions," she replied.

"Give me one more second," I said, closing the door behind me. I walked back up to the shit on the wall praying that this was a bad dream. But there it was again. Who the fuck did this? I asked myself. And what was I going to say? If I ignored it it could easily be blamed on me and if I pointed it out they could still lay the blame on me. One of the nuts smeared shit on the walls and I was inadvertently framed. I would have to somehow explain it away.

Believe it or not, this wasn't my first exposure to unclaimed shit. I worked in a hotel upstate New York where a mad shitter was dropping his loads unpredictably all over the hotel. Once it was in a hallway. Then they found some under a table in the dining room and some more near the entrance to the night club. He was finally caught by the owner's wife squatting in front of the windmill on the miniature golf course. He never lost his job because it was tough finding help in the Catskills and at least he didn't hurt anyone. But they did move him from his job in the kitchen and had him work with the social director instead.

The shit on the wall smelled now, but I think that the smell might have been worse in my head. I had to think this out.

I walked into the room with the toilets and sinks. Maybe I'd just clean it up. We all had toilets and sinks in our rooms so why would someone do this? Then again, this was I-6 and I was asking myself a stupid question. And I was *not* going to clean it! I didn't do it and I'd be damned if I would clean someone else's shit off the wall.

That was it. I was going to tell Tabitha. If I told her, the odds of them thinking it was me would be less, I figured. So I stepped out of the bathroom.

"At last," she said. "Do you take that long to shower at home?"

"No," I replied. "But I want to tell you about something that slowed me down."

"You don't have to get personal with me. I'm not one of the doctors."

"It's not personal!" I said far too loudly.

"O.K.," she responded as she moved to lock the doors.

"Listen to me," I said.

"Did you forget something?" She asked.

"No!" I said, again overreacting.

She locked the door. "Now, what is so important for you to tell me?" she asked.

I rethought my situation. Hell. She never went inside and they didn't open the showers again until seven that evening. The shit would be dry and hard by then.

"It's really nothing," I said.

"That's good," she replied.

"Thanks for letting me take the shower," I said offering a final gesture of peace.

"I'm glad you're nice and clean," she replied.

I didn't feel very clean as I turned and walked back to my room to take another nap.

A PHONE CALL

Several days into my stay, I was sitting in the community lounge again in my sweats, which had become some secret personal statement about not caring. Jimmy, the fireman, approached tapping me on the shoulder.

"Hey, Barry. You got a phone call."

"Thanks," Not having spent much time with him I was flattered that he remembered my name.

I got up, turned into our corridor and walked to the telephone. When I got there I saw that Jimmy had put the receiver very neatly on top of the old fashioned phone. I picked up the receiver, sat down on the small bench in the booth and tried to make myself comfortable.

"Hello?" I said.

"Hi, sweetheart." It was my mother.

I always found great relief in the sound of my mother's voice, although her advice was invariably poor and most of our conversations vapid. I felt both needy and impatient whenever we spoke. She was closest with my sister but worried about me the most. Saying good-bye to my mother often left tears in my eyes.

I felt that way since I was four. That was the first year my parents sent me away for the summer, an eight-week sleep away program at Camp Swanee. Some cousins I barely knew owned the camp and my parents told me that I would like it. "They are cousins," I was told. "Family. So it will be almost like staying at home." Not quite.

My mother added "the eight-weeks will fly by and you're going to love it." My mother told me this in a way that allowed no room for dissent.

Going to camp was apparently in our blood and I didn't want to act like the first big baby in the family even though I felt that way so I shut up.

They took me to Green Acres Shopping Center in Valley Stream to catch the camp bus. Everyone going to camp was older than me and they all seemed to be good friends. I didn't know anyone except for my big brother David and he hopped right on the bus saying hello and sitting with his friends from the previous summer. My brother never seemed to even give me a thought. I think he hated me.

My father was there as well but my Mom was handling all the details. Dad just stood there waiting to go home. My mother surprised me with a big tin of Animal Crackers and then she tried to bet me that I had never seen a tin of Animal Crackers that big. I knew that my parents had a bunch of them in a closet at home but I didn't tell my mother that I'd seen them because I wasn't ever supposed to be in that closet.

She called one of the counselors over and had him lift me onto the bus because I was too little to climb up myself especially with the big tin of crackers in my hands. He put me in a seat by a gigantic window in the second row. They said that I was lucky to be near the front but I didn't feel that way. All I felt was that I already missed my parents and my home. I hugged the big tin on my lap and immediately opened it. I had never looked inside the tins at home and had never seen so many Animal Crackers in one container.

Looking out the window I could see my mother standing with all the other mothers and fathers. They were all waving good-bye. My father was looking all around the bus. I think he couldn't find me even though I was right at the window. I felt my tears but stopped them from falling down my cheeks. I wanted my mother instead of the crackers. I wanted to trade back.I missed her too much already to go to camp.

A counselor sat down beside me. "And we're off. You can call me Uncle Ted."

He wasn't my uncle.

"This summer's sure gonna' be fun," he told me but I knew that it wasn't true. I knew if I talked to him I'd start to cry so I kept looking out the window. My mother smiled and waved.

"That's a heck of a lot of crackers," he said and then he got up and stood in the aisle. No one was with me now and the seats were very big. I couldn't stop my tears from falling but I did manage to form a tight make-believe smile with my lips. I don't know if my mother knew I was crying. She just kept smiling and waving good-bye. The bus jerked forward and began to pull away.

Uncle Ted raised his voice.

"I want everyone in their seat. If you're not in your seat I'll put you in your seat and I don't think you want that," he said. He wasn't as friendly as before.

I strained to see my mother but she was way behind the bus with all the other mothers and fathers. I couldn't find my Dad and then all the parents were out of sight; all gone. I cried for real now and the counselor sat down.

"You'll be fine," he said. "What's your name?"

I couldn't speak as I gasped for air and tried to wipe my eyes.

"I hope you're not gonna' cry for the next two and a half-hours," he said. "Wow," he added quickly. "Your mother gave you all those cookies? Why don't you eat them? Then you'll feel better. You're going to have lots of fun this summer. Everyone does."

I didn't believe him. I looked in the tin for a hippo. I liked the hippos most. Then I ate a lion and a giraffe. By the time we got to camp all the cookies were gone and I still didn't have my mother. I cried all summer long, sometimes even crying without tears.

When I came home from camp that very first horrible summer, I immediately ran upstairs. I wanted my little red dog that I kept on my bed. But it was nowhere! My mother told me that it got lost but I knew that my parents had thrown it out. It was a stuffed dog on my bed. I knew it couldn't run away. I supposed that they wanted me to grow up more quickly and that's why they took away my dog. I was ashamed to tell my parents that it was too soon for me to grow up, that it was only when I held my dog against my cheek and smelled it that I really wasn't afraid.

"Hi, Mom," I said into the phone. "I'm glad you called."

"I think this is the best thing you're doing."

"The hospital? I think so too. It's a little weird here."

"What are they going to do?"

"I'm going off all my medications and then starting over to see what I really need and what I don't," I replied.

"That's a good thing. How about work?" she asked.

"It'll be fine. Deidre's there and I'm not missing much."

She paid no attention to that. "How are you feeling?"

I could tell that she didn't want a long answer.

"Good. Everything is fine, Mom."

"Ellen and I were thinking of visiting you on Saturday. Is that good for you?"

"Well I have no other plans if that's what you mean. I'm going to be here," I replied.

"That's not what I meant and you know it."

"I'm just kidding around, Mom. It would be great if you two came here on Saturday."

"Dad's coming too," she added. I tried to imagine him in I-6 and couldn't. "Do you need anything, sweetheart?"

"Yeah."

"What?"

"Animal Crackers," I said.

"You're such a nut," she replied. "We'll see you on Saturday. I love you."

"I love you too," I told her and then waited for her to be the first one to hang up the phone.

MY SISTER, ELLEN

I got another phone call later that day. Emilia appeared in my doorway to tell me that my sister was on the phone. She lifted her shirt and flashed me a quick peek at her tits. Ignoring the flash I walked into the corridor and saw Thomas, the skinny little deaf mute, leaning on the wall in front of me. I assumed that her flash was her way of trying to make Thomas jealous and chuckled. I knew that he lived on the other side of I-6 so he was evidently travelling with Emilia. It was probably his first opportunity to see tits up close that didn't belong to a family member.

My sister was calling from work. She traded treasury bonds.

I was already in my mid-thirties with no obvious direction in life. Ellen was a few years younger and married to Hal. My little sister was earning an astounding amount of money. She seemed content. Whatever problems she may or may not have had at home, she kept them there showing a self-control that I never had.

"Hey," I said into the receiver. I closed the door to the telephone booth for some privacy.

"So are they all nuts?" she immediately asked.

"I don't know. I've been afraid to leave my room."

"Get out," she said in disbelief but still unsure.

"I really don't know, Ellen. I mean I obviously haven't been afraid to leave my room, but I don't have much of a desire to either. I haven't actually been hanging out with the inmates. I'm sure that some of them are nuts, O.K.?"

"Mommy said you'll be in there for thirty days." She made it sound like thirty days was forever.

"It's like a vacation," I replied, squeaking into the telephone.

"Oh, good. I'll go home and ask Hal if instead of a house in the Hamptons this summer maybe we should check into a mental hospital for thirty days."

"It's not a mental hospital. Well, it really is. But I'm not here because I'm crazy, Ellen. This is just a washout. Dr. Wohl thinks it's safer for me to go off my medications in a hospital setting. Maybe I really don't need them anymore, or maybe I need less."

"That would be good. So we're all thinking of visiting you on Saturday next week. Is that all right?"

"Who's all of you?"

"Me, Mommy and Daddy."

"Daddy too?"

"In person."

"It should be fine. They allow visitors on weekends. Oh, shit. I forgot, Ellen. That's the day we play with our imaginary pets. I'm getting a llama."

She laughed. "C'mon, really."

"Wouldn't that be funny?"

"What?"

"If I were really nuts. I mean *really* nuts. Completely insane."

"Whoever told you that you weren't?" she joked.

"No, listen. Imagine this. You guys don't really come to visit but I think you're all here. I'm having some imaginary conversation with you. Like I babble and, who knows, maybe we're not even talking on the phone right now."

"Calm down. Maybe we should limit our conversations to Saturdays," she replied. "I can't stay on the phone anyway. I have to work for a living."

"Well, I'm sure that you can visit me. People get visitors here all the time."

"I think we're going to come early afternoon. Maybe 1:00, 1:30. Is that good?" she asked.

"Oh, my God! There are lizards running up and down the hall!"

"Shut up, Barry. I have to get back to work," she said. I realized that working went hand in hand with her earning all that money. Time was money but not for me. I always had time to talk.

"Maybe we can play Bingo when you visit," I suggested.

"I'm getting off the phone," she said.

"See you Saturday," I replied. "Wait, bring some food."

"What do you want?"

"I trust your judgment."

"O.K., I love you," she said.

"I love you too." I listened to Ellen hang up the phone and sat there for a moment, lonely again, holding on to the receiver as if it still connected me to one of the only people I felt genuinely loved me. I held the receiver in my lap and leaned my head back against the wall. "Maybe I am really nuts."

As I opened the door and squeezed out of the telephone booth, someone was waiting to make a call.

"Are you through?" She asked.

"No, I'm still on the phone," I replied, deciding to act a bit insane. They are crazy in here, I thought. We're all crazy in here. Maybe everyone here thinks that they're here for some innocuous reason just like I do. It could be exactly like I described it to Ellen. I stopped. My thoughts blurred. This joke wasn't funny any longer.

I felt a rush of anxiety and wondered if the world would eventually look as distorted to me as my reflection in my parents' old toaster; a big nose, my face shooting off at sharp angles and a tiny little body that could barely support my large head. I looked up and down the hall and walked toward the dining area. I snapped my head from side to side until it hurt.

A short-white-creature perhaps pretending to be a nurse approached me. I tried to avoid her.

"Is everything all right, Barry?" I smiled and looked toward her but didn't answer. "I'm not playing this game," I thought and walked to the small window in the corner of the community room. I began to worry.

I could feel it when the nurse stopped staring at my back and moved on down the hallway. She knew that nothing was wrong with me. I was joking with Ellen. It was only a joke and I was letting it get the best of me. This whole thing, my thoughts, what I was doing here by the window. It was based on one stupid joke, the ridiculous idea that my life was a hallucination.

I decided to remember things from my past. I felt that if I were out of my mind I probably wouldn't have clear memories. When I was little I went to the Sunrise Park Elementary School. That was real. But they eventually tore the school down. Perhaps it had never been there. But I could remember having asbestos fights in the basement of the school outside the art room and my kindergarten room was around the corner from the art room but one floor up. I loved the solid heavy dark wooden entrance doors to my school. My teacher was Mrs. Hash and we used to call her Mrs. Hash Brown Potatoes. That's a kindergarten joke. They were memories but they weren't working as I wanted them to. They weren't steady.

My hands were now shaking slightly and my larger tics were out of control. I swung my arms in huge circular movements and twisted my wrists. I kept tightening my thighs and my stomach and held them as tensed up as possible until they hurt and then I'd let them relax. But the relaxing part of this movement was always too short and then I would tense them up again. I pushed my chin down hard into my neck and chest and my squeaking sounded more like a bark to me. I sniffed in and out quickly like an animal and looked around to be certain no one was near me.

No one seemed to be around but I had to consider that they might actually be there, just invisible to me. They might be talking and laughing at my ridiculous motions and noises. But I didn't plan to cultivate friends here and I tried not to care what they said.

I closed my eyes and told myself not to worry; that this obsession would wear off like a bad acid trip.

But what if this feeling never did wear off, never completed its course. My world was turning upside down and I started feeling cold and damp. Maybe I was dead. I wiped away small beads of perspiration on my forehead and couldn't ever remember having droplets on my forehead before.

I no longer recognized anyone in I-6. I didn't know if the nurses were really nurses or maybe just actors if they were even there at all. I no longer believed that the patients in front of me were even actual patients but couldn't fathom who else they might be. Were they judging me? They weren't asking questions or even speaking to one another but did seem to be following my every move. I didn't know what to do but I certainly didn't want to stand there under observation anymore. Was there actually a place called I-6?

I was shivering now but couldn't stop sweating. I could get away now. I could either run for the door and try to escape I-6 altogether or try to make it to my room. I was frightened and my mouth completely dry. I couldn't feel my teeth reaching up to feel them to be sure that they were there. Never once in my entire life had I told anyone when I was afraid and I wasn't going to change that now even though fear was whipping around me quickly turning into terror. I remembered that my room was number 616.

I had to ground myself somehow, create a tangible reality that I could believe in. I turned and began to walk as quickly to my room as I could, still trying to seem normal to those who were watching me. It seemed impossible to judge if I was walking too slowly or running. I tried so hard to remember how fast a normal person walked and hoped that I could mimic that. I think that I was in a proper walk.

When I got to my room I slid inside quickly and closed the

door. I'd have locked it if I could but there were no locks for the rooms on I-6. I was searching for some way to reestablish myself in this antiseptic environment.

I wanted my little red dog back. Where was it right now? It was missing one eye, spilling foam rubber from a slightly torn seam, dirty and I'm sure that it still smelled unclean. But I knew that I would be safe with him. My little red dog was the only real thing I'd ever had and I could put its floppy ear in my mouth and it would comfort me.

I was freezing. There was a blanket on the bed and I could crawl underneath it even without my red dog. I couldn't have my dog but I could position myself as if I did.

I was drained as I climbed in. I pulled my knees up to my chest, hugged my pillow tightly and shut my eyes pretending that my dog was with me. My little red dog was real and nothing could ever change that.

I closed my eyes so I couldn't see the stark white walls that reflected my fear.

I awoke several hours later my mind back in place.

I decided to go to dinner a little early, so I spruced myself up and headed out. I was earlier than I had anticipated and no one was around so I sat in the community room once again in front of the omnipresent TV.

"Do you mind if I sit on your couch and watch the television with you."

I answered the voice behind me in my most practiced nonchalance, "It's not my T.V. and it's not my furniture, so why would I care?"

"You could still care even if it's not yours," she said as she walked around the couch and sat down at the other end. It was Grace. I couldn't believe my blunder. If I'd known it was her I would have been animated when I answered, not lethargic and bored.

I did, however, suddenly come alive. At least my tics did. My loud squeak sounded like a sheep's bleating and my shoulders pivoted each in turn followed by my arms seeming to unwind like a twisted telephone cord. My hands continued to make tight circles around my wrists as my thighs tensed and then relaxed repeatedly. I shifted in my seat uncomfortably, secretly tapping my dick twice and pressing my toes down as hard as I could inside my sneakers. Throughout all of these movements I pretended to be trying to get more comfortable on the couch. I only hoped I could mask my tics and have a normal conversation with Grace.

"Hey, I didn't mean to sound like that. I mean, if I thought that it was you, hell, it wouldn't matter who it was, I just didn't mean to sound so harsh, you know what I mean? It's not my stuff, I mean the T.V. and the couch. None of it. It's not mine. What right would I have to tell someone..."

"It might not be yours but you could still want to sit here alone," she answered cutting my monologue short.

"But I don't. You see. I mean I care if *some* people sit here. No, that's, that's not really true, it doesn't really matter who sits here."

"It would matter to me," she said smiling. It was the same smile that she beamed around I-6 all day. For me it was a crippling smile. It left me with a thick tongue and a dry mouth. Grace turned toward the television. This was bad. I should get her attention now. I licked my dry lips planning to speak.

"What brings you here?" I asked, forgetting for a moment that we were in a mental institution. She looked straight at me with her dark sincere eyes, their heavy lids, and her beautiful eyebrows. I'd never thought so much about eyebrows before. "That's not what I mean, I mean what I just said. I don't mean what brings you here," I waved my arms about trying to indicate all of I-6. "I mean here," I tried again indicating the small seating area in front of the television set.

She laughed gently. I envied how relaxed she seemed. "What brings you here?"

"I'm just waiting for dinner," I replied.

"No, that's not what I mean," she said. "I mean what brings

you here?" Grace mimicked the way I swung my arms all around trying to indicate all of I-6.

"Oh, here," I began to joke back mimicking myself, hands and arms twirling all over the place.

"I looked at you when I was with Emilia and you seem fine to us, really normal. You know Emilia really likes you."

What was she trying to say, speaking about Emilia that way? Did she think that I was interested in Emilia or was this her way of telling me that she had no interest in me herself?

"Well, I don't think that Emilia and I will be an item and in answer to your question about my being here in I-6, I don't really have to be here." I was glad she thought that I didn't really belong here. I hoped that I didn't belong here as well. "I'm in the process of changing medications and my doctor felt that I should make the change in a controlled environment. So I came here. I'm a voluntary admission. I just checked myself in for a few weeks to make the change. That's it."

"I remember when you checked in. I remember the community meeting when you introduced yourself. We were glad you checked in. We both wanted to meet you." I couldn't believe my ears.

"I was sent here from emergency downstairs," Grace continued.

I was surprised. I never considered what circumstances brought each of the inmates to I-6. I knew that I checked in for my washout and the rest of them, well, I didn't give their individual situations much thought.

"If you can believe it I was in emergency for over thirty hours before I finally got up here."

I was shocked. "And what was that like?"

"Really shitty. You never went to emergency?" Grace asked. She paused. I was drifting. "You never went to emergency?" She asked again.

"I'm sorry," I said. "I don't know where I was. I mean I know where I was, or I should say that I know where I am. My mind wandered for a second. I was thinking that I have to call my mother later," I lied. "She worries. My sister as well. I missed the last few things you said."

"It's not so important," she replied.

"No. It is. I just got caught up in not forgetting to call my mother. Really. I want to know. What was emergency like?" I asked her again.

"I can't describe it. I don't have the words. It was terrible," she said. "It took so long and I just waited and waited. I was alone most of the time. That was where I met Emilia. She was there to. If she wasn't there, I probably would have gone crazy. When we were in emergency she offered herself to some young doctor if he could speed things up."

"Good God! And?"

"And it took us about thirty hours to get up here so you could answer your own question," Grace laughed as she spoke.

Jimmy walked into the room. He was wearing the same shirt, untucked and wrinkled, ever since I'd arrived. Then again, this was one place where fashion didn't matter. His hair was wet and he looked like he'd just showered.

"What are you guys watching?" he asked.

"The news I think. I don't really know. I wasn't paying much attention."

"Oh," he replied eyeing the space on the couch between Grace and me. "You mind if I sit down."

"Not at all," I answered moving quickly toward Grace. A hard-on popped up in my sweats. She looked down and saw it. I was mortified and she flushed a beautiful reddish tan. "Here." I patted the seat of the couch on my other side, away from Grace.

"Sit down," I said to Jimmy. I moved even closer to Grace, our thighs and hips were touching. I wondered if Jimmy actually planned to make a play for Grace. I liked Jimmy. But maybe I would have to hate him.

As Jimmy sat down facing the television other inmates began to come in.

"It must be close to dinner time, huh." I said. I could smell her clean hair and finally managed to look her directly in the eyes.

"I think so," she replied, our sides felt glued together. It was an exciting diversion.

VISITING DAY

It was Saturday morning and my first thought as I opened my eyes was that my mother, father and sister would be visiting me today.

I got dressed and walked bleary eyed down the corridor to see if there were any scraps of food left in our dining area. The walk seemed longer than usual. I was in the middle of my drug transition between the conglomeration of psychotropic drugs that I was taking when I entered I-6 and a more recently discovered drug called Tegretol which they felt could do it all for me.

I found myself repeating the old Certs commercial in my head but changing the words to 'two, two, two drugs in one'. But the Tegretol was making me fart constantly and not normal farts. These were horrid, billowing farts that one would never associate with digestion. They didn't smell but were unimaginably loud and impossible to control.

I began to scout around for something to eat, anything, to hold me over until my family arrived. I knew they were bringing food with them. That was how my mother always visited her children, laden with gifts, gifts of food, just like her mother before her and my sister was following in their footsteps except with far superior taste. There would be none of Grandma's famous Butter Rum Lifesavers in *her* gift basket.

I found a mealy apple on a plate underneath the cabinets. I bit into it. It was inedible.

Saturday and Sunday were always busy days on I-6 and

this was no exception. The buzzer sounded constantly as family members and friends of the inmates paraded through the entrance door. I had imagined the visitors acting more uptight and was amazed at some of the inmates' happy mood transformations.

"Hey," was all Jimmy could muster as I passed by. His visiting girlfriend nodded to me but didn't make eye contact. I saw Grace walking toward her room with, I assumed, some members of her family. I wished I were included with her in some way. Thomas was seated in a corner of the family room all alone; more alone than even a deaf mute had to be.

I felt bad that my family was late. They were no doubt shopping at Saks for themselves before visiting me, my father bored to tears. They had little reason to rush. I had never given them any indication that I was unhappy. I mean, I wasn't. I found I-6 relaxing; no one to perform for, no one to impress, just me, my meds and my thoughts. I wasn't frightened here. It was a pleasant world with an odd combination of self-preoccupation and empathy.

However, I was bored waiting for my family and got sleepy quickly so I went back down to my room to rest a little more. I looked through tired eyes at the chipped paint on the walls and ceiling. It disturbed me and I couldn't understand why I felt paralyzed when alone for long periods of time. All I seemed able to do is watch television, sleep, eat, and shit.

Before checking into I-6 I envisioned myself accomplishing great things here. I would be alert and full of life. I would write every day and go through this drug transition in a snap. In actual fact I had accomplished nothing. I spent most of my time on top of my bed staring at the ceiling and there was nothing on this bedroom ceiling to keep me amused.

I lay there now, drifting toward sleep on a puny hospital bed with a blanket that I didn't like to touch. It had this crisp spongy quality that shouldn't be associated with a blanket. Any stiffer and it would have been Styrofoam.

I got up restlessly and walked to my window to see if I

could see my mother and sister walking toward the building. I could see quite far. I could see the Hudson River if I looked out on a sharp angle. I suddenly let out a squeak so hard and loud that even I was surprised. It felt good so I repeated it a few times. I twisted my wrists around, stiffened my biceps and jabbed my arms out in the air a few times, then a few times more, again and again. I tapped my dick with both index fingers playing it like a xylophone. I sniffed, grunted and snorted my way around the room, clenching and unclenching my teeth hoping that they wouldn't break. Finally I lay down, again exhausted.

I was tired of waiting for my family and felt inadequately medicated. My forehead weighed heavy above my eyes. I closed my eyes and raised my eyebrows simultaneously stretching my lids smooth until they hurt. It felt as though a tiny little creature, some pint-sized furious devil, had taken up residence behind my head and just above my neck. I finally relaxed.

My sister and mother awakened me some time later. Apparently, they 'made it past the guards'.

"So this is it, Barry? It's a gorgeous room," Ellen said nudging me. "Love your blanket."

"Oh, fuck you," I said slowly swinging my legs to the side of the bed and sitting up.

"You know I hate it when you talk like that," my mother said. I got up and kissed my mother and sister hello. They were pecks, not kisses. My mother's skin was pockmarked from her youthful bout with acne but all I ever considered was the softness of my family's skin. I loved to touch cheek to cheek.

My mother's cheek was important to me for as long as I could remember. I'd wait compulsively to give my mother the last kiss good-bye. Even if I'd already kissed her and someone inadvertently snuck in and gave her a kiss after me, I would go back for that last buss. It meant the world to me. She didn't have to love me the most but I wanted that last kiss, even if she didn't realize it. Chalk it up to whatever you want. I don't really care.

I was thrilled they had finally arrived. I suppressed my inclination for a big emotional display.

"Daddy couldn't walk down to my room?" I asked. "What's he waiting inside? He must be so uptight with this scene." I noticed their shopping bags from Saks and Zabar's.

"He couldn't come in with us. Besides that, we had our stops to make and he doesn't have that kind of patience. You know what happens. Plus Daddy got tied up with someone about one of his rentals."

"So he didn't come. He's not here, right? Well that's not such a big surprise. It's not the first visit with me he's ever missed."

"You know your Dad."

"Sadly true."

"You don't mean that," she replied wishfully.

I turned to Ellen. "What's in the bag?" I asked pointing to the shopping bag from Zabar's.

"As much as would fit," Ellen smiled but wasn't kidding. My sister was dressed all in black with a colorful knit scarf. She looked like she had her hair done today. So did my mother. My mother's hair was blonde, supported by hair spray three or four inches above her head and my sister's hair was auburn. Ellen's hair was closely cut and casual. They both looked so clean that I realized that at least part of this visiting day was spent at Georgette Klinger's.

My mother wore a camel colored skirt with a matching light sweater. She wore a huge marcasite pin shaped like a pyramid with her initials near the top. She was weighed down by her additional jewelry; necklaces, bracelets, and rings, all matching her outfit. That was how they shopped; never for a blouse, or a skirt, but for outfits; outfits with accessories.

Both my sister and mother were round and needed to lose some weight. I was also overweight, tipping the scales at one hundred ninety-eight pounds and still swelling fast. I would normally weigh around one eighty five, give or take a few pounds. That's why, at one hundred ninety eight, all I liked to wear were my sweats. I couldn't buy new clothes and allow myself comfort at this weight.

"I hope there's something else in there besides Rugelach," I said.

"Of course there is. I bought everything. Bread, a bunch of cheeses. I got some beluga. It was on sale for fifty dollars an ounce. Hal gets angry with me because the kids like it for breakfast."

"So what does that come to? Hundred dollar breakfasts? You're nuts."

"You're in a mental hospital telling me I'm nuts? Should we hide the bags somewhere in your room? Do the inmates swarm?" Ellen asked.

"Let's go to inside and eat. They don't like us eating a lot of food in our rooms."

"I think I saw the dining room when I came in. It's quite plush," Ellen said.

"Just go," I replied.

We sat at the corner of the table in the dining area; lots of people milling about.

"Give me some of the caviar." I said.

"You don't need caviar," my mother added.

"Crack it open," I said. My sister reached into the bag. "With some of the bread," I added.

"You shouldn't open it now. It will go bad," mother said. "Anyway, I brought you some hard candy."

"Oh, thank you," I said gratefully. "I'll save that for later, Mom. You haven't had to eat hospital food for weeks. I'm eating caviar." My sister opened the jar and we broke off some pieces of freshly baked bread.

"Wait until you taste this cheese I bought."

I looked at my mother as I took a plastic spoon and reached for the caviar. "And you can't have any," I told her.

"I'm older than you," Mom answered back. "And I'm your mother. As long as it's already open, I get the first taste."

"That's a pretty big jump from candy to caviar," I told her.

"Your father loves caviar too," mother added taking the first bite of our snack.

"And what? If he knew we were having caviar nothing would have kept him away," I said sarcastically.

"Be fair, Barry. He's so busy at the school."

"Bullshit. Do you think I still believe in the tooth fairy? Daddy's busy. Daddy wishes he could be here. Daddy sends his love."

"Stop that."

"Why? Did he ever miss a fucking episode of Gunsmoke?"

"It's on in the evening. He always watches television in the evening. And watch your language."

"Right."

"Come on. He's never made more than a pit stop for anything in my entire life. Why should this be an exception?"

"He does the best he can."

That was probably true but not good enough for me.

My life suddenly felt pathetic. It was sad seeing my mother and sister in this institutional dining area. "I'm sorry. I appreciate your being here; both of you." I tried to smile.

Ellen also wanted to get off the subject of Dad. And here came Roseanne; Roseanne, my new "best friend" in I-6, my gin rummy buddy. She was a relief, my respite; the most vulgar patient in the house. Everyone avoided her but me. I was drawn to her because her profanity made me laugh.

"Roseanne. Come meet my family," I suggested knowing from her history that she wouldn't be having any visitors. She was carrying her deck of cards.

"Gin?" She asked.

"No. Family," I replied. "This is my family, Roseanne." Roseanne was all skin and bones, skeletal with a wrinkled smile.

"Them?" She pointed at my mother and sister as if they were across the room. "I should say hello."

"I think so."

"He's good at rummy," she told my Mom, "but not that

good. I can always beat him. He knows it. I used to always beat my fucking husband too. He sucked at rummy. He's dead. He was a fucking queer. We fucked one time, that's all, and I got a son in Philadelphia. What's the odds a' that?" She asked.

My mother looked at me. This was not a conversation Mom could have. Even my sister was taken aback.

"The odds are not very good," I told them in a humorous tone trying to relieve some of their discomfort.

Roseanne turned to me. "Hey. I saw that cunt pussy Lorraine walking around with some asshole. I think he has taps on his shoes. If they walk by I'll point him out, or you'll hear him. The taps echo in here. They should throw him out."

"What the hell," I said. "It's visiting day."

"I say throw his fucking ass out. It's noisy, all that tapping."

"We'll play later," I told her.

"Good," she replied. Looking over my family one more time she said, "You should see some of the fucking people in here; makes me feel normal. Shit...makes me normal." I really liked Roseanne. I certainly didn't have to stand on ceremony with her.

As she walked away it was my turn to change the subject. "Hey, let's not let this feast go to waste."

"Have you ever had this?" Ellen asked pulling out some more small packages from Zabar's. "Farmer cheese with blueberries and farmer cheese with walnuts."

"Like I said, let's eat."

After some of the best tasting snack food I ever had I'd became more of a happy idiot.

"Hey, wanna' tour of a madhouse?" I asked.

"It's not a 'madhouse'," my mother replied. "You're in here because of your medications."

"That's true. But I-6 is a madhouse."

"I'll take a tour," Ellen interjected.

"Put the rest of the food away and come on," I said "Leave your bags outside the nurses' station. Just take this marker and put your name on them. No one'll touch them. So, come on."

We walked down the hall, my mother unhappy that I was in 'this place'. She understood why I was there but would have preferred it not be true. My sister was the only one who gave me unconditional love. And she seemed to love the tour of I-6! It fascinated her.

"Tell me what's wrong with each person," Ellen whispered, a smile glued to her face in case anyone saw us speaking.

"Look for missing shoelaces, or someone so doped up that their head's in their lap or chin to chest, or ... if they pissed on themselves," I answered.

"You're both not nice," mother said quietly to both of us.

"Well I'm certainly not nice," my sister answered.

"I'm not either. I know I'm not nice. In fact I'm evil," I said. My mother poked me in the back so the two of us would stop.

"I don't have to see the entire floor."

"Come on. There's not that much to it. See the exit doors. I think the knobs are electrified," I told her. Ellen laughed.

"I think I'll bring Hal and the kids here next year for vacation. It beats the Bronx Zoo," she smiled at me.

Grace turned the far corner with her own family and was leading them to the exit.

"That's the one I have the hots for," I told my sister.

"She's pretty," my sister replied. "Is she intelligent?"

"There's a thought that never even crossed my mind."

When Grace was alone, I introduced her to my mother and sister. Then she returned to her room. I was sorry Grace walked away. I missed her immediately. I'm really a sap.

I thought about my only trip to Tijuana, Mexico. I was in a bar, selected a hooker and went upstairs with her. I enjoyed both the talk and the sex. I asked her about her life. She showed me how hookers can cheat and make it seem like you're getting laid while you're really getting a mere handjob. When we returned to the bar, I sat down at a table for another tequila and she moved on with her work. She was smiling and chatting it up with some fat, sweaty guy who probably hadn't seen his dick in years. She took his hand and led him up the stairs.

I was angry. Jealous! I wanted to feel special and it didn't take much for me to feel disappointed.

I introduced my family to a few other inmates and staff as they passed by. At one point Ellen said, "You know, Barry. Being here doesn't really seem like fun." I shrugged, still unsure about how I felt about I-6.

We talked for a half-hour more and Ellen said that she had to get back because of her kids. I was glad they came. I helped them with their bags and slowly said good-by to them at the door. I accidentally kissed my mother good-by first and then I kissed Ellen. It disturbed me. So just as they were leaving, I called my mother back and gave her the last kiss. I felt like they were leaving me alone at camp.

KING BREGMAN

It was just two days later that I sat and watched this circle of human lab coats enter I-6. I was certain that Dr. Bregman was amongst them. It had to be Bregman and his entourage. I was sitting near the pool table in the patients' lounge. Dr. Bregman looked tiny surrounded by his students. They towered over him as if they had been chosen by size rather than intelligence specifically to protect him. The nurses on duty thought that I was in my room and directed the group down the corridor to find me. I got up immediately and joined them, walking slightly behind, so I could peer into the room with them as if trying to find myself.

The door was ajar when we reached my room. Dr. Bregman stepped forward, gave a quiet knock on the door and held the doorknob waiting to be invited in.

"Is he in there?" I asked them from behind.

"Yes," one of the students replied.

"OK, then," I said. We waited a moment more. "Knock again," I suggested, smothering a squeak and snapping my head to the side. It hurt my neck.

Dr. Bregman knocked again and then slowly opened the door. He looked inside the room. "He's not here."

"I'm here."

"Who are you?"

" Barry Golden," I replied as his students separated into

two polite lines with Dr. Bregman and me at either end as if in the middle of the Virginia Reel. "I'm Barry Golden."

"How do you do?" Bregman replied walking forward very seriously and extending his tiny little hand.

"Pretty good." We shook hands. "You want to do this in my room or in a quiet room? I mean my room is quiet but I don't know how an examination like this works."

"I think your room will be fine. We'll mostly be talking." He stepped aside and invited me to go in first. I quickly sat on my bed. Let them stand, I figured. I didn't want to be standing there tapping my dick and performing my monkey tricks for all these people. I knew I would be more comfortable on the bed and didn't care about being polite.

Everyone settled down quickly and Dr. Bregman spoke. His students looked on and listened reverentially.

He had each of his assistants introduce themselves one by one. "Now, the first thing, of course, we need the basics," he said. "Name, address, telephone, etc." He asked his tallest student to ask me the basics. Her name was Kaitlin and she seemed about six foot five. They were starting my file.

Even though Dr. Bregman was a small man he carried himself with the knowledge of his own importance. His hair was gray, thick and close cropped. He was broad and stocky, not fat at all. And mostly he was very neat. Not a hair was out of place. His tie was in a tight perfect knot close to his neck and his lab coat pure white and unwrinkled. It looked as if he had even stopped to have his shoes polished before coming to see me. His hands were small and manicured and, all in all, Dr. Bregman smacked of wisdom, politics, and wealth, perhaps not in that order. He was a consummate professional and didn't take his eyes off me as I answered all the *basics.*

"Good," he said as I answered the last question. "Now if you would be kind enough to stand up." He extended his hands to help me up from the bed. His hands were gentle, almost feminine to the touch. He had me touch my nose with my index fingers, eyes closed and hands extended out from my sides. He had me walk forward on my toes, turn and walk back to him on my heels. He checked my reflexes and gave me a few other minor tests during the short physical segment of my evaluation explaining every detail to his coterie. I had no idea what the results were as we continued on now with my interview.

"Tell me, Barry. How old were you when you had the onset of your symptoms?"

I had plenty of experience talking about my tics having been in therapy or analysis on and off since I was twelve. But I was never the only one obliged to confess in front of a group of virtual strangers. I sniffed out three times quietly and blinked tightly hoping that when I opened my eyes either Bregman's entourage or I would have disappeared.

"I was just starting the third grade," I answered. "I skipped the second grade, went from first right to third, and I think the tics began because of the anxiety I felt being in a new classroom with none of my old friends. Then I just couldn't stop them. Bad habits." I thought about my friends in the second grade and how hyperactive I had been. I remembered gobbling down an entire bowl of popcorn candy at someone's birthday party. It had been impulsive, provocative and embarrassing; a sad attempt to be funny.

"Approximately how old were you when you started the third grade."

"I don't know? Seven. Maybe eight?"

Some of the students took notes but not Bregman. He looked at me with a gentle intensity, his gaze never wavering from mine. "What was your first tic?" I wished he had called it a mannerism.

"I'm not sure. I wiggled my nose and blinked. Those were the first. I'm sure."

"Sort of grimaces? Facial grimaces," he replied.

"I guess so. I don't know. I never thought of them as grimaces."

"Can you show me what you used to do?"

"I still do it," I replied desperately trying not to tic, to display some control over my body. But I was not in control. My 'mannerisms' fired away. The least I could do was make believe I was doing them on purpose. I sniffed out and snapped my head down. As I thought about the third grade my nose wiggled, I blinked and rolled my eyes. I pinched my face together in Dr. Bregman's renamed tight little grimace, so tight that my upper lip touched the bottom of my nose. I sniffed again and this time snapped my head back and then side-to-side. My neck hurt from all the snapping. "How was that?" I asked annoyed with their triggers.

"Oh fine, just fine. It was very helpful." He smiled a little, acknowledging both my sarcasm and my discomfort. I squeaked, once at first, and then followed that up with a short musical scale. His students glanced at one another. I couldn't tell if they were surprised by my noises or delighted. My stomach muscles flexed and released under my T-shirt then my thighs did the same, each in succession. My tics were at full throttle. I even tapped my dick. I was a disgrace.

"Do you always have the same tics?" Dr. Bregman asked.

"Pretty much," I said not wanting him to know how easy it was for me to pick up new ones. "I'll tell you one thing I can't do."

"What is that?"

"If someone tells me not to make a fist, I have to. It becomes an overwhelming compulsion."

"Just making a fist?"

"No. Anything. For you it's like 'don't think of elephants'. For me it's way beyond that. The urges are so strong they lead to action. I mean, not like jumping off a bridge."

"Well that's good to hear."

"If I think about not making a fist, I can't resist the sudden urge. And how's this? I used to spin the steering wheel of my car." It was with some relief that I chattered on, after all, this is what they came to hear. "No. I would actually spin it. With one finger. Like this." I demonstrated the way I would hook my finger into a steering wheel and spin it fully around while driving. "It really sucked at fifty-five miles an hour."

"Did you ever have an accident?"

"Not really. Certainly not with another car. I scraped a side rail once. It was no big deal; just a scratch. Did a few three-sixties, seven-twenties. I would usually do it after a snowstorm when there weren't cars all around me. I'd just spin. I was pretty careful."

"Do you still do that?"

"Not really. Haven't thought about it for years. But watch. Now that I'm talking about it, I'll probably do it first thing when I leave here."

"I hope not. Tell me, Barry. Do your tics ever disappear completely?" he asked.

"No. Well, almost. Sometimes I just don't think about them for months. It seems like they're gone. But then I think about them and they come raging back even worse than before."

His entourage was busy taking notes; a great day for learning.

"And there's one thing more that I haven't mentioned. I don't like to talk about it. Enough people notice it on their own and it's embarrassing."

"Do you want to speak with me about it privately?"

"Fuck it," I said. "I'm in the middle of my confessions. Would a priest want me to stop? He'd be figuring out how many Hail Mary's I owed Him. I haven't even gotten to the good stuff. Isn't this how everyone learns?" I asked, indicating his students. "What's one more embarrassing thing? I'll just let it all hang out."

"Speaking for everyone, I can say we all appreciate your letting us come here and speak with you."

I squeaked and sniffed at his compliment.

"I tap my dick."

"Excuse me."

"I said I tap my dick. Like this." I tapped my dick a few times to make sure I was being very accurate in my depiction. "Cute, huh. I stopped wearing white pants in high school."

"Believe me," Dr. Bregman tried to reassure me. "I've seen far worse."

"I hope I'm not in some kind of bizarre behavior competition here at Columbia."

"Of course not. I was simply trying to make a point."

"I get your point."

" Barry, would you mind if we stopped things here for a little while. I'd like to talk with the other doctors and then come back and join you again in about ten or fifteen minutes."

"That's real nice," I replied. "I have to confess in front of all of you but you can go and talk behind my back. Real nice."

"It's not that, Barry," Bregman started to explain.

"I'm joking," I reassured them with a straight face, never smiling. "Go. Do whatever you have to do?" I chuckled at the thought of him referring to them all as doctors.

"We'll be right back."

I smiled a dumb broad grin as they left my room. What were they going to talk about, I wondered? That I was nuts, for sure. I reassured myself that the door was closed tightly and allowed my tics full freedom. They went wild. I squeaked a long one that traveled octaves for about ten seconds. I sniffed and snapped my head down hard chin into my chest and then back and forth until it was so painful. But the pain felt good. My hands twirled around my wrists and then I shook them one by one the way a baby waves bye, bye. I followed that cutting a huge Tegretol fart. Now that was not a tic.

I remembered being twenty and really stoned in our apartment on 21st Street. We were lighting farts and Fred was naked sitting on the edge of the bed. He grabbed his legs behind his knees and rocked back wanting to fart and gross me out. Instead he shit on the bed. It was one of my funniest memories. We were just friends, no holds barred friends. Fred died six months later from an overdose of Quaaludes. Dead Fred. We went through his clothes right after he died and split a lot of them up amongst ourselves. I still kept his belt and denim shirt even though they didn't fit me anymore: souvenirs from my youth. I'd always miss Fred.

I went into my bathroom and sat down on the toilet to take a shit. I never twitched when I took a shit and wondered why. I didn't twitch when I made love either. Those seemed the only two times I was tic free and they were certainly mutually exclusive, at least, thankfully, in *my* sex life. My sex life was pretty normal, I figured. No big history of fucking dwarves and amputees. I liked big tits but so did a lot of people. I laughed to myself. I should have told Dr. Bregman about some of this stuff. I felt like I left out a lot of information during my interview and it worried me.

It would be great if he could help me but I didn't believe he could. It was just more bullshit, more medical bullshit for me. I was a peculiar man, a twitchy little man, made even smaller by his tics. I squeaked twice, pursed my lips and sniffed twice as I shook my head. Guess I had to dismiss my "no twitching while shitting" concept. But I *was* spared my tics while getting laid. I thought about it many times before, even in the immediacy of the moment and still I barely ticced. I heard a knock on my door.

"Just a second," I shouted frantically wiping myself. "One second. I'm in the bathroom." At least by telling them the truth I knew that they wouldn't simply barge in. "I'll be right there." I flushed, pulled up my sweatpants and ran to the door. Dr. Bregman was leading them as usual.

"Mind if we come in?"

"You're already in." I wanted a big glass of scotch, something to make me woozy, dull my senses to this medical team of fresh clean faces and gleaming whites. They each had their stethoscopes deep in their side pocket and as I looked at them I figured stethoscopes were part of their uniform like name tags. They used them periodically but.....not on me. I felt for a moment like I was being examined by aliens.

"So Mr. Golden. Why don't you have a seat?"

As soon as he called me Mr. Golden I realized I was being charged separately for this examination and assumed he would be padding his bill. I was only Barry up until now. I thought this "examination" was included, mustard for my hotdog. I didn't even give a shit if my insurance would cover it. This should be included. It should be an automatic part of being in a nut house. It was a fucking interview for Christ's sake! Who told them to come in a group? Fuck them, I said to myself over and over again as I sat back down on my bed.

"What you have is a neurobiological disorder called Tourette Syndrome."

"Right," I replied. "What are you talking about?"

"Your condition has a name. It's called Tourette Syndrome."

I flashed on an episode of The Twilight Zone in which everyone at some hospital was hideously ugly except for the patients who were there for plastic surgery. It was a "beauty is in the eye of the beholder" tale. There was something odd going on here. I tried to focus.

"What is it called?"

"Tourette Syndrome."

I looked around at his students faces. They were gleaming as if they had given me some great news, as if they told me I had won the lottery.

"How do you know? I mean, how can you tell?" I asked.

"From our interview. Tourette Syndrome is not a condition that can be diagnosed through neurological testing. We rely on interviews, your history; the onset of symptoms, sequence, type, their waxing and waning…"

"Waxing and waning?"

"How your symptoms seem to improve only to come back again sometime later. That's all a part of the symptomatology of Tourette Syndrome. So is your touching yourself. That's a symptom. It's called copropraxia." I was stunned.

"There's a name for tapping a dick?"

"Not exclusively. It's a name for compulsions of an obscene nature like giving someone the finger or in your case tapping your genitalia.

"If it includes giving the finger then I know many

sufferers."

"Compulsively," he laughed. "You've seen people cursing out loud. That's coprolalia. Maybe five percent of Touretters have coprolalia."

"My squeaking? My tics and noises? My sniffing?"

"All symptoms of Tourette Syndrome. Here's what I'd like to do, Barry. I'll send some literature over about Tourette's for you to read. Start there and then I can answer your additional questions. The pamphlets should answer most of your questions. After that we'll meet again."

"Well is there a cure or something? Don't leave things here. Can you do something about this?"

"There's no cure for it, Barry. It isn't a disease. Frankly, we don't know that much about it. It's rare but in many cases it can be treated. There are medicines available that have helped control many of the symptoms."

"Like what?" I asked.

"Look over the pamphlets I'm going to send you and then we can make an appointment and talk about this further. The more you know about Tourette's the more intelligent our conversation and ultimately the better our plan of treatment will be. How does that sound?"

I had a condition, I thought. There was something specifically wrong with me.

"I've been in therapy all my life. How come you're the first to know?"

"I can't answer that one for you but I will tell you that most people being treated for Tourette Syndrome are also in some sort of psychotherapy. In most cases it's an integral part of its treatment."

"Yeah, I'm sure," I replied trying to hide my anger and my excitement at the news. And what of my years of embarrassment? What did this mean? Did I waste so many years in therapy? Did I waste my money?

"Here's my card," he continued. I was blinded by my rushing wave of questions. "Call my receptionist and tell her I want you to arrange for an appointment with me in about three or four weeks." I sat there trying to read his card. It seemed odd to me that he even carried one. "All right? You'll do that, Barry? Following up is very important."

"Sure," I replied.

"I'll see you then. Thanks again for letting us come here."

"Thank you," I answered politely hiding my excitement.

Each of his students thanked me as well.

As I watched and listened to them leave I considered what I would do if each one billed me separately. How I didn't plan to pay any of them? I sat staring at Dr. Bregman's card and waited. I was making sure that they had enough time to leave before I bolted down the hall to tell my family. I didn't want them to see my excitement.

I stopped short realizing I forgot money for the telephone. No change. I hustled back to my room and grabbed a five-dollar bill before running to the locked, carefully protected nurses' station. I rapped on the thick glass window to get their attention. Their room seemed sound proofed but I knew that couldn't be true. They would miss all the possible screams and howling. But they still never seemed to move quickly, always seeming to want to finish some pleasant gossipy conversation before acknowledging a patient interrupting their privacy.

"Come on," I muttered aloud rapping again impatiently. At least they looked my way this time. I squeaked, scrunched my face and snapped my head side to side. For the first time I was purposely making an exaggerated display of my tics for effect. It wasn't hard. I mean, after all, I did have Tourette Syndrome. One of them walked to the door to my left and I moved to meet her as she opened the door.

"Thank you," I said controlling my sarcasm. "I need some change to make a few phone calls." She looked at my money.

"I don't know if we have change of a five."

"Then pretend it's a one, or a three. Whatever works for you. I just need some change. I'll overpay for it."

"We're not allowed to do that."

"So you're telling me that if you don't have enough change that I can't have any at all."

"Hold your horses," she replied. "Let me see exactly what we have." I felt an impending confrontation. I watched her at the desk in their puny cash box. She was counting change. "I'm short about a dollar," she said.

"That's fine."

"I can't give you *all* our change," she added. "What if someone else needs change? You're not the only one on the floor, you know."

"If anyone else needs change you can tell them to see me. I don't need that much. Just give me two dollars in change and hold the additional three dollars I'm giving you as collateral."

"This isn't a bank, Mr. Golden."

"O.K, then," I said working hard to control my frustration. "You tell me how to work this out. I'll do whatever you want. I need change to make some phone calls. I have money here so you know that I'm not looking to cheat you or the telephone company. You tell me how to handle this."

"Barbara will be back in about a half hour and she probably..."

"No. This can't wait for Barbara to return. How about the other nurses?"

"Who do you mean?"

"Inside. In there. The other nurses in your room."

"They're not on duty."

"Oh, Come on! I need to make a few phone calls! Why are you making this so complicated?"

"All right," she said tersely. "I'll ask them."

Within a minute or so we worked out the complex negotiations and I had the change to make some calls. The phone booth was empty.

I sat down trying to get comfortable on the cold hard seat as I spread two dollars in dimes and nickels on the small gray metal shelf underneath the phone. My first call was to my mother and father.

"Hello, Oakdale."

"Janet?" It was the woman who ran the office. "Is my mother there?"

"Hi, Barry. I haven't seen you in such a long time. When are you coming to visit us?"

Janet had worked for my parents for some time. She had a dark complexion, was friendly and fun; a sexual fantasy for me since I could remember.

"Soon. Maybe very soon."

"I'd love to see you. I'm sure you're as handsome as ever."

"I'm trying to get a hold of my mother. Is she nearby?"

"Well, she's somewhere."

"Can you get her for me?"

"I expect her back anytime. Your Dad's in his office. Would you like to speak with him?"

"Uh…" I paused my conversation for too long. Could she read my indecision, my discomfort? "Nah. It's not that important. She can call me back."

"Are you at home?"

I realized my parents would never tell anyone our "family business", that I was in I-6. How stupid of me to forget that everything was publicly perfect in our world.

"She has the number."

"I'll give her your message and when you visit we'll catch up."

"Sure."

"Promise?"

"Yup."

"OK then. Bye bye." She hung up the phone. I sat in the phone booth reflecting on my news and the conversations I'd be having with friends and family. Maybe I should call Dr. Wohl and let him know the good news. I hoped that Bregman rushed out of I-6 and ran to the telephone to call him but knew that he didn't. Who would focus on my diagnosis? Who would pay attention? Who would really care? Even Dr. Wohl. I mean, what's a tic and what's plain crazy?

When I was ten and checked that our house was locked eight times a night, was that a tic? How about when I ate two pounds of chocolate in less than an hour? A tic? I don't think so. *Is obsession a tic? Is an eating disorder? Is a hair-trigger temper part of Tourette's?*

I needed more detail; the pamphlets Bregman mentioned. I'll ask my Mom to get some. No. She'll never do it. She'd be embarrassed. *They will know why she wants them*; that her kid is fucked up. It would be like asking her to pick up condoms for me at the local pharmacy.

I took out Bregman's card, waited impatiently for the telephone and dialed his office. Of course he wasn't in. Maybe they were just telling me that he wasn't in, although he only left I-6 a short time ago.

I told his receptionist that I needed whatever information they had about Tourette Syndrome. I needed the pamphlets. She told me the best place to go was to the National Association. Bregman had to have something there. *Tourette Syndrome was a real condition.* I couldn't imagine that Bregman did the diagnosing and then simply sent his patients out to do their own research? Just how lazy was he?

I asked her again and she gave me the same answer. This was all wrong. I wasn't going to call the National Association. First off I didn't want them to have my name. Plus it would take too long to receive their information. I wasn't going to have them send it to me at I-6. My particular case was nobody's business.

I had to check out of here and take care of this shit on my own. Who would I see? Who to talk to?

I went back to my room and planned to speak with Barbara when she returned. I paced and ticced much more than usual. After all, there was a reason to tic now. I had Tourette Syndrome. I squeaked over and over, even yelping a few times. I was enjoying it. I could enjoy it now if I chose too; privately, at any rate. I didn't think this pleasure would translate well to my public persona.

Barbara returned a few hours later. Where did she go?

"Barbara. Gotta' talk to you."

"They left a message for me. So it's Tourette Syndrome." She smiled.

"You know a lot about it?" I asked.

"Not really. Bits and pieces. I've seen some people who had Tourette's and I know it's neurological but that's about it."

"You know I gotta' check out now, right? I have a lot to do."

"You can't simply check out, Barry."

"Why not? I'm not having a problem changing meds and I have a diagnosis now which I didn't expect. No one did."

"This is not a hotel," she said as nicely as she could.

"Of course not. But there's nothing wrong with me. I mean nothing that would keep me here, not in I-6."

"But that isn't how this works. I understand what you're saying, your feelings about it, but patients don't check in and out as they choose. You don't even have points from the group participation activities. You know all this. You're not even permitted to step outside yet."

"The classes?"

"You already know these things. I'll look at your file but I think you still have twelve or thirteen days remaining to complete your stay and, even then, you have to be signed out by Dr. Genovese."

"She's not even my doctor. Dr. Wohl sent me here. He's my doctor."

"You can call him if you like but Dr. Genovese is the doctor who has to sign for your release."

This was some bullshit. I didn't belong in the regular program here. I was here for a washout, not picked up wandering the streets talking to imaginary creatures.

"This is wrong Barbara. There are always exceptions to the rules."

"But I don't make them; neither the rules nor any exceptions."

I was getting angry. "I don't have to stay here for thirty days. Maybe under normal circumstances but that's not what this is," I replied. "I'll call Dr. Wohl."

"You should. Give him a call."

So I did and that proved a waste of my fucking time as well. Apparently, once I checked in here nothing was up to him. Genovese was in charge. I felt like I'd been abandoned on the steps of an abbey. I had no one to turn to.

"Hi, sweetheart. Is everything all right?"

My mother returned my call.

"You won't believe this, Mommy. After all this time. You really won't believe this!"

"What is it? What won't I believe?"

"I've got a fucking condition!"

"Right away with those words. You know I don't like it when you use those words"

"I've got a condition."

"Oh no, Barry. Not something else," she said sadly.

"No, no. I have Tourette Syndrome. It's a condition."

"What kind of condition, honey?"

"It's some condition. It's a neurological problem. That's why I twitch. That's why I make noises. I have a condition called Tourette Syndrome. That's why I have had all these tics since I was little. My tics! It's Tourettes Syndrome. I am not nuts."

There was a pause in our conversation before my mother spoke.

"How did you learn about this?"

"Some Dr. Bregman examined me. He's a very good guy. It seems Columbia has this movement disorders clinic. He's pretty famous. He's in charge of it. It's all his research or something."

"And he discovered Tonette Syndrome."

"Tourette Syndrome. Tonette is the instrument I played in the fourth grade. He didn't discover it. Some guy named

Tourette must've discovered it. Dr. Bregman is head of the movement disorders clinic. There're lots of movement disorders. I only have one of them. Thank God. That's where I should have gone in the first place; a movement disorder clinic, not to some shrink."

"Wait until Daddy hears this."

"I'm just happy to know now. Things are different now."

"All those times we yelled at you."

"None of that matters. You didn't know. You thought I could stop."

"We should have been more understanding. Your poor father. He'll feel terrible about this. You know what Daddy's like. He hides his feelings but this is just terrible. He'll feel so guilty."

"Is he home? Put him on the phone. Let me talk to him."

"He's upstairs, sweetheart."

"So call him. I want to tell him. This is good news, Mom. You're acting like I'm giving you bad news. Call Daddy. I want to tell him myself."

"He's resting. I don't want to wake him up."

"Are you kidding me? This is the most important thing that's ever happened to me."

She paused for a moment before speaking again. "Maybe it would be better if I tell him, Barry."

"I want to tell him, Mom."

"Please let me. I know how terrible he'll feel."

"Mom. You're supposed to be happy for me. This is good news."

"I know it is, Barry. It's just hard to hear it, that's all. It's difficult news for us as parents. I'm glad. I'm glad for you sweetheart. I really am," she said.

"Go wake up Daddy."

"It's wonderful news, darling. It really is. We'll have to learn all about it. What's it called again?"

"Tourette Syndrome. How can you feel bad about this diagnosis, Mom? Be happy for me."

"I am." Another pause. "Can they cure it?"

I squeaked and sniffed in and out snapping my head down simultaneously.

"Not really. They can treat it. You know, everybody's different. I don't know how all that works yet. Dr. Bregman will eventually let me know, I'm sure. He probably has some stuff about it. I'm sure it's in books. I'll find out."

"You be certain to get a copy of all the information you get for Daddy and me. All right, honey?"

"Sure," I replied. There was no way my father was coming to the phone. I envisioned him sound asleep on his bed. He lay down caddy corner every afternoon one hand angled under his chest, the other folded under his head. I lay in the same position when I went to sleep. I swore I'd never sleep like that again. I was going to find a different position, my own.

"We love you, darling."

"I love you too." I thought for a moment before continuing. I want you to do me one favor, Mom."

"Anything darling. What can I do for you?"

"I want Dad to pick me up when I check out. I'll come stay at home for a couple of days. But I want him to pick me up; a little quality time, right?"

"Well. He may be busy that day. Do you know what day it will be?"

"Not yet. We're in the middle of talking about that now. But whatever day it is I'd like him to come in."

"I'll speak with him, sweetie. But I can't promise."

"Yes, you can. I love you Mom."

"I love you too." And then there was silence. "Bye, bye," she said hanging up the phone. This one telephone call abruptly ended my calls for the day. It ended with the same sad lump in the throat I'd grown used to. I gathered up the change I fought so hard for and left the phone booth for my room planning to leave I-6 as soon as possible.

A day later I received information from Dr. Bregman. Again he recommended my getting in touch with the National Tourette Syndrome Association in Queens.

I discovered that it was Dr. Wohl who suggested testing me for Tourette Syndrome to Genovese and I contacted Deidre who I assume told some of our friends.

Ellen was pleased with the news. I squeaked into the phone while we spoke and, then, acting surprised, asked her "who was that?" She suggested that I might be better off in the future asking "what was that?" when squeaking rather than giving it away with a "who."

My residence in I-6 continued and it seemed a losing battle. Their regulations wouldn't bend. I couldn't simply leave I-6, and I tried everything. When no one on the outside was able help I focused my efforts toward becoming a model inmate. I began to participate in every activity I could fit into my "busy schedule."

Interestingly there were a few other floors of patients institutionalized for other reasons. I-6 was for depression and suicide risks. Other floors in this facility had their own specialized psychological issues and the populations were mixed for group activities.

My first activity was gym class. We played basketball, where true to my athletic prowess, I was even worse than the guy with OCD who had to step out of bounds every few seconds.

In arts and crafts I sat next to a guy who got upset because I was putting my trivet together faster than he could build his Popsicle stick house. I carefully avoided arguments during board games and won my choice of candy bar at Bingo. I ate all my food with no complaints, even helped clear the garbage off the dining room table. I was the first to share the TV remote and always acted like I enjoyed the popular choice.

Interestingly, in spite of knowing that these classes were used for our individual evaluations, I felt more relaxed now than at the start of this adventure in I-6. I wasn't pleased, but at least I knew why I jerked and twitched and I found myself announcing it to everyone on our floor. I was explaining it to some people who were so heavily medicated that they stared straight ahead with their mouths hung open as if suffering from Bell's Palsey.

Dr. Bregman had returned for a personal visit to discuss several options for treatment and to deliver some pamphlets he must have received in the mail. And....I was trying to work everything out during my frequent sessions with Dr. Genovese. I was finally a Level Five patient and that was stratospheric; it was as high as one could go.

"So am I a Level Five yet?" I asked Dr. Genovese at my next session with her. Of course I knew the answer. I was.

"There's less than a week left until it's thirty days, Barry," she replied.

"I'm assuming you're going to give me the all clear for check out, right?" I paused. "Listen, Dr. Genovese. My medications are stable and I want to go home." I was working hard to pretend my Tourette's had been cured by diagnosis alone, but couldn't suppress the powerful urges to tic. I poked my dick a few times, squeaked, wiggled my nose and snapped my head from side to side. "See that," I said. "I don't even mind ticcing in front of people anymore. That's very good, right?" I asked.

She smiled. "You have to stay the thirty days."

"I'm not here for the same reasons as the others." I was growing angry.

"How do you feel about being here?" She asked.

"Christ." I replied and there was a moment of silence followed by a flood of tics. I snapped, twisted and squealed followed by a fairly useless attempt at self-control. "What do you want me to say? I'm out of ideas and wasting my time. I want to go home." She didn't respond. "Seriously, tell me what to say that will get me the fuck out of this place."

"Don't you think you could make good use of your

remaining days here?"

"I don't want to. Give me the unique honor of an early parole. There are people here like Frank. I understand why he has to stay."

"Don't you like Frank?"

"I like him! But Frank belongs here. He's fucking nuts!" I was angry and raising my voice. "He thinks he's one of the fucking staff physicians, for Christ's sake!!"

"He doesn't raise his voice. I don't think he ever acts out. Have you ever seen him angry?"

"This is bullshit!" I got up from my seat and moved to the window. It was a beautiful day outside. "I'm not angry."

"You sound very angry."

"I'm not angry! I'm frustrated with this whole fucking thing. I'm working so hard to be agreeable. I help out all the time now. Whoever needs assistance; if I see it, I'm there."

"Hmmm," she said. "A bit like Frank tries to do."

"Stop it! Don't fucking play with me. I'm not one of your regular patients."

She didn t respond and I felt boxed in.

"You've been diagnosed with Tourette Syndrome. You should take some time to think about that; to reevaluate your life. That doesn't happen overnight. Isn't it wonderful to have a few days to indulge yourself without the whole world watching? What changes now that you've learned this information about yourself? How will your relationships change? You have a great deal to think about. Try to take advantage of one more private week to consider the implications of all that you've discovered.

"You must have given the valedictorian address at one of the schools you attended."

"There're people who would fight for this opportunity."

"Well I'm in their room. Let's give them a chance to get in. I want to go home."

"But you can't. I don't get any snow days and you can't have an early dismissal."

Thirty seconds ticked by and it felt like an hour. My

session was over.

CHECK OUT

"Hey, what's happening?" I asked people as they were running past me. I was relaxing in the large family room. People were flying by and I didn't like the fact that it was in the direction of my room.

"Hey, what's up?" I asked Jimmy, the only one strolling.

"I don't know," he replied. "I'm going to see like everyone else." Jimmy continued as he passed. "Come on, man."

I saw Mary pass, then Leonardo. It seemed as though everyone on I-6 was headed in the direction of my room. I joined the mob. My things were packed and ready to go and I didn't want anyone near my room getting into my stuff. I wanted to protect my room.

I raced down the hall and reached the outer edge of the throng. Big Dave was behind me.

"I'm trying to get to my room," I told him.

"I'm comin' through. Lookout now!" Big Dave said raising his voice. A small aisle opened up as he touched people's shoulders with his powerful hands. I followed him like a car swerving lanes trying to follow an ambulance to save a little time.

I found myself next to Dr. Genovese.

"Dr. Genovese," I said tapping her on the shoulder. "What's going on? I'm checking out today."

"We have a situation here," she replied, never looking me in the eyes.

"I have one quick question," I said, but Genovese apparently didn't hear me. She was moving people out of her way as well.

"Is anyone in my room?" I asked no one in particular.

"Let's go now," Big Dave continued. I could see a bunch of I-6's staff in the family room with Mr. Martin. Mr. Martin was seated on one of the plastic orange chairs in the family room with a white paper plate tied around his head. There were two eyeholes torn haphazardly out of the plate so that Mr. Martin could peer out.

"The phantom of the op-er-a ...," he sang out to his audience. His voice was stronger and more melodic than I ever would have imagined. One of the nurses told him to get up.

"The phantom of the op-er-a!" Mr. Martin continued.

I pushed through the crowd toward my room and could see Mr. Martin clearly now. He was dressed only in an undershirt and sat in a pile of his own shit on one of the plastic orange chairs. Jimmy was next to me.

"Is this something?" he said poking me. "He's having some kind of fit."

I remembered my first shower and the shit smeared all over the walls in the bathroom. Maybe it had been Mr. Martin.

"The phantom of the ..."

"Let's get him up," one of the nurses said.

"Did you see anyone in my room?" I asked Jimmy. Jimmy was picking his nose and watching what was going on intently. I made it to my doorway and was glad that no one was inside my room. The smell of shit was everywhere. I was relieved that Mr. Martin chose a community gathering spot for his histrionics and not my room.

"Great Jesus. What is wrong with you, Mr. Martin? You can't be actin' like this." Nurse Bridget scolded him.

"The phantom of the op-er-a ..."

"You ain't the phantom a' nuthin'," I heard another nurse say. "Could we get a cleanup in here?" Someone else called for maintenance; janitorial maintenance.

I could hear Big Dave telling Mr. Martin to get up. Big Dave wasn't fucking around. This was one of the times they relied on Big Dave. "Up! That's your only choice. You can sing all you want but git' up now."

"You're not a member of my family," Mr. Martin said.

"Damn right." I'd never even heard Big Dave raise his voice until now.

"That's my mask," Mr. Martin shouted out. "Don't touch my mask! Give it back to me. I can't be seen."

"Here's your mask. Now let's go."

Most of the residents stood outside of the small TV room and watched this odd parade. Mr. Martin was frightened and it struck a chord with everyone. The corridor was thick with empathy; not a smile or a wisecrack.

"Close your eyes, Mr. Martin," Dr. Genovese said gently. "That way no one can see you." It reminded me of The Emperor's New Clothes. "You have to go to your room now."

"Do you have my mask?" he asked sounding like a child.

"Yes, I do," Genovese replied.

"Could we have a path here?" Big Dave spoke to the onlookers. Everyone backed up to the walls to give them a clear path. Mr. Martin held his mask over his face. Big Dave didn't sound tough at all. He sounded gentle and kind as he helped Mr. Martin. Leonardo and Mary were squeezed into my room.

"This is my room," I told them.

"We have to let them pass," Mary replied. I didn't like Mary. She looked too clean, too blonde, too wealthy. I could see Dr. Genovese and Big Dave on either side of Mr. Martin. Mr. Martin's undershirt wasn't long enough to cover him up. You could see his old dick and low hanging balls swinging as he walked. His droopy shit-covered ass hung low behind him. I believed that Mr. Martin was glad to be rescued.

As Mr. Martin passed I said to Mary, "You have to get out of my room."

"We are," Mary replied. She didn't like me either.

Leonardo didn't speak very much English and I didn't feel like speaking Spanish so I just watched them in silence as they left. My head jerked from side to side and I tapped my dick with abandon knowing that no one was watching me and even if they were I had a scientifically approved reason to be doing this stuff now. I squeaked loudly a few times, waited a few moments longer and then left my room after the commotion died down. I wanted to complete my check out.

What I didn't realize was that my father had arrived during all the commotion. He was buzzed in by the lone nurse in the nurses' station and was standing in our dining area as the parade marched by and Mr. Martin whisked away to be cleaned up and medicated.

"Hey, Dad." My father was speechless. "Did you see Mr. Martin?"

"I, I don't know."

"The phantom of the opera."

"I saw a man singing," he said.

"Yeah. He's very good," I replied, "but I prefer the Broadway version."

My father was horrified by what he'd just seen. It was quite a change from the safety of the Oakdale School.

"Excuse me, Mr. Golden." Both my father and I turned. It was a weird feeling for me as I thought of my father as Mr. Golden and myself as Barry. But there we were, not certain who the nurse was referring to. Like magic, Nurse Barbara suddenly appeared.

"I'm sorry Barry, I'd have thought we'd have had everything together by now but with all the commotion…"

"Not much more than usual."

"Please, a few minutes more can't hurt. I need to confirm the new meds with Dr. Genovese and get your envelope from security."

"I don't have anything with security."

"That's right. I forgot." She smiled as a friend. "Are you all packed?"

"I've been packed for three days."

"We can wait a few minutes, Barry. It's not such a big deal," my father interjected.

"You haven't lived here for weeks. Minutes can be like hours, days like weeks and weeks like years."

I considered my anger issues. This might not be the best time even to pretend to lose it. Maybe they'd cancel my release. "It's no problem. We'll wait. C'mon down to my room Dad. We'll wait in there."

"What's there?"

"I made a trivet in arts and crafts. It's not finished but maybe they'll let me take it home anyway. Come with me. Let's go sit in my room, or the TV room if it's been cleaned up."

"Your room would be better," he suggested.

"That's fine." We walked silently to my room and I closed the door behind us minimizing the smell of Lestoil and shit.

"Here. Have a seat," I said indicating the only chair in the room. "I hope you're not hungry because there's nothing here to eat."

"I had a bite at home before leaving for the city."

"Let me guess; one scoop of cottage cheese, a half a' tomato, one stalk of celery, coffee with evaporated skimmed milk and two Vienna Fingers."

"Correct." He cracked a smile.

"I couldn't do it," I said. "Same thing every day."

"It couldn't hurt you to lose a little weight. I've lost approximately ten pounds," he said tugging on the waistband of his trousers.

I tapped my dick and adjusted it in my jeans. He looked away. I sniffed twice and snapped my head down hard, chin into my chest. I squeaked three times, then three times again, that time purposely, resentfully. I made a new sound crossing a hiccough with a yelp and tensed my arms and legs.

"What are you looking at?"

"Just looking out the window," he replied.

"How is it? Nice view?" I said squeaking again. "I mean you seem to be very hung up on that view."

"I was simply looking out."

"No you weren't, Dad."

"Of course I was."

"No you weren't! You weren't looking out the window. You just weren't looking at me. You never do. You never did."

"Don't say ridiculous things, Barry. I'm here to pick you up, aren't I?"

"You can't stand to look at me. Well, too bad. I'm your son." I was more upset than I wanted to be. I swallowed and went on. "And there's a bunch of shit wrong with me, Dad. I can't help this stuff. I have tics. I make noises. There's nothing I can do about it. But I'm smart! And I'm funny. And I'm a nice person. No thanks to anyone."

"Is that so? We've done plenty to help you over the years. When I wanted to go to college you know what my father said to me?"

"Stop right there. Get some new material. Get real. What the fuck do you think college ever did for me? I couldn't even go to classes. You don't know a goddamn thing about me and my college experiences; my humiliations, my tics, my noises. I never got a word of support from you. You're embarrassed by me!"

"No I'm not."

"And I grew up just like you. I'm your wild, crazy twin. Here's a secret, Dad. I'm embarrassed by me too."

"Let's continue this at home. OK? Isn't it time for us to go?" he asked in an effort to escape.

"You know why I insisted that you pick me up? So you could see where I live. This was my vacation. I'm here with my friends."

"You have a condition. You can't help it. You're not the same as the others."

"Oh Daddy. I think now that I'm exactly the same and that's the point. They can't help their shit either."

"You don't have to talk like that."

"But that's the deal, you know? Everyone has their own personal shit. And I have mine. I've got news. You've got yours too."

He really couldn't stand being in this place. It was all very much for him. I wished I could stop picking on him. I felt guilty for insisting that he come alone.

We were called from my room and I signed some papers completing my check out from I-6. I said good-by to all my favorite nuts knowing that I'd never see them again but would nonetheless miss so many of them.

THE RIDE HOME

We were having very little conversation as we drove home. I wondered what my Dad was thinking.

"You know why I take the 59th Street Bridge?" He asked me.

"No toll," I replied for the two hundredth time in my life.

"That's right. The tolls in and out of Manhattan have gone up and up and up. It used to cost next to nothing to travel in and out of the city. I wouldn't pay a nickel. I'd take the train before paying any tolls."

I didn't want to hear about the tolls or have any innocuous conversation. I wanted him to bring up the diagnosis, the fact that I had Tourette Syndrome; that I wasn't crazy after all. I purposely squeaked but that set off a real twitching jag. My eyes closed tight and my features scrunched tighter than ever before. My squeaks seemed louder than usual.

"Don't you think it's a little ironic?" I asked.

"What is that, Barry"

"That I'm really not crazy; that it's not unbearable stress causing my tics. That's what we've been told all along, right? He's anxious, stressed out."

"You don't feel stress."

"Of course I do. But how much of that stress is causing my tics and how much is caused by them and other peoples's reactions to them?" I asked with a yelp then sniffed in and out and blinked tightly. My father said nothing. "Not that it ultimately makes a lot of difference. I watched my father purse his lips." I tapped my stomach, wiggled my fingers and squeaked loudly. "So now that's my Tourette Syndrome. Maybe I'll wear a sign."

"I read up on your condition before I came in the pick you up. It's fairly obscure, Tourette Syndrome. It's rare. No one could have known you had it," he suggested.

"Yeah. Isn't that true? It's a little like winning the Irish Sweepstakes except it's fucked up my life instead of making me rich."

My father didn't answer. I was feeling angrier than I should have and wondered if I shouldn't get off it but I went on.

"Right? It's pretty fucked up."

"Please stop talking like that," he replied.

"How should I talk? I'm in my thirties and have Tourette Syndrome. How would you feel?"

"I still wouldn't talk like that."

"That's not an answer. How would you feel if you were me? Forget that. How do you feel that I am me? That I have it?"

"Your life hasn't been that bad, Barry. You had a lot of advantages that others didn't."

"Were you one of them?"

"I was there for you. I was always your father. I never punished you."

"I wish you had," I muttered.

"Every decision we made, your mother and I made together. She'd ask me all the time, what should we do? What should we do? I was there for everything important; every important moment of your life. We took you on vacations with us. I went to every graduation, everything, everywhere."

"Everywhere you *had* to go. You were only with me in crowds, where your eyes could wander. You could ignore me, not have to touch me, your own son. Places where you didn't have to claim me as your own. You left me all alone."

My father hesitated before speaking. "Well, things are different now," he offered.

"They've been different for years. I don't live at home. I'm not *your* pariah anymore."

"Don't you think you're being a little dramatic?" He asked trying to be gentle. "I'm the one who just picked you up."

"Because I insisted you come. I wanted you to pick me up. I wanted you to be the first to see who I am."

"I'm not saying I'm perfect, Barry; that I've never made mistakes," he said.

"Maybe you just never had the patience to be a father. Maybe you shouldn't have had kids." There was silence in the car.

"That's a very nice thing to say."

"What if I'd been retarded or autistic?"

"That's ridiculous. You weren't." He answered.

"And if I were."

"Then we'd have known about it. You'd have been diagnosed."

"You'd have treated me the same way."

We sat again in silence. The silence was awkward.

"You know," I finally continued. "That 'nut house', I-6, it really felt like a vacation for me. It was a place where no one gave a shit how other people acted. The people, my *inmate* friends all know that nobody's perfect and everyone there admits it. People don't sit around passing judgment. Everyone up there is flawed, some of them crippled by their issues. But we were very special to each other. It's different from outside. Everyone was kind. They had kind hearts."

"But you weren't really a patient. You seem to have forgotten that. You were there because of overmedication."

"I belonged there, Dad. You just don't want to look at that. You ignore things to keep yourself together or something. You ignore me. You ignore who I am."

"Now that's simply not true. I'm the first to admit that I've had some problems dealing with your issues over the years but it wasn't as bad as all that."

"You never talked to me; not to *me*! You talked at me. You

never listened to me. You didn't want to pay attention. I had too many flaws." I wiggled in my seat, tapping, blinking, and squeaking quietly.

"I did the very best I could." I felt our silence again, the awkwardness we'd shared our entire lives. My father continued. "Maybe I'm not so good at that. I don't know, Barry. Everyone has their strengths and weaknesses. *My* father never talked to me. He gave instructions. I think that's all he knew how to do." He paused, took a breath and continued.

"All this makes me think of Walter Lipkin. He was a little boy in our school. It was Lipkin, maybe Lipton, I don't remember. He used to be impossible, cursing and twitching. He would throw his arms everywhere. No one could handle him. They used to send him to my office. Everyone assumes that the owner of the school will know what to do."

My father choked up. Neither my father nor I could tell emotional stories without some tears. I saw the tears in his eyes. He swallowed, choking his feelings back again.

"Well I didn't know what to do with him either. I made him sit under my desk, near my feet. I told him he had to stop. I tried to make him stop. I told him that if he wouldn't stop he could stay there all day. He was there so often." A tear rolled down his cheek that he wiped quickly away with his hand and pretended to yawn. "I think he had Tourette Syndrome. I didn't know. I couldn't have. I have never forgotten that poor little boy and what I did to him."

"You're crying for *him*?" I asked.

"I'm not crying," my father replied. But he was.

I've always hoped he was shedding those tears for me.

THE END